TARAN

Books by Kee Briggs

The Third Removed
The Painted War
Finders-Keepers
Losers-Weepers
The Painted Lady
A Few Good Old Men

The Usher Orlop Mysteries

The Golden Janus
The Pewter Masks
The Nickel Trophy
The Bronze Bones
The Brass Portraits
The Zinc Ormolu
The Silver Scepter
The Rhodium Dragon
The Copper Shakes
The Stainless Steel Sign

The Asti Fantasies

Charm Catcher
Dream Weaver

The Sage Grayling Mysteries

The Yellow Ochre Stain
The Lamp Black Pit
The Cad Red Dot

Ebooks

Write to Live Longer
The Oregon Vortex
The Painted War

TARAN

Kee Briggs

First of the TARAN Trilogy

Keescapes Publishing

Satellite Beach, Florida

TARAN

Copyright © 2012 by Kee Briggs

Keescape Publishing books may be ordered through booksellers or by contacting:

Keescape Publishing

90 Flamingo Dr.

Satellite Beach, Florida 32937

www.keescapes.com

KeescapesPublishing@gmail.com

This is a work of fiction. All characters, names, incidents, organizations are all figments of the author's imagination and are used fictionally.

ISBN 978-0-9847524-1-6

Published in the United States of America

TARAN

Kee Briggs

Chapter 1

Andrew Dawson, you're a genius, Andy thought as he bounded up the steps of Straud Hall, the men's dorm, which had served as his home for the last four years. He shouldn't have had that much energy, even though it was just the end of the first day of finals week, but he had beaten the system. During registration, he had arranged his schedule to include two classes with term papers instead of final exams. Two more courses were taught by professors who did not require a final if a student maintained a straight A on all the dailies. The final two classes he selected because their finals fell on the opening Monday. So, after one day of finals week, Andy was finished.

The rest of the week was his. Saturday was graduation day. Then Sunday he would have to move out of his room. He had two weeks to get his stuff back to his mother's house for temporary storage and clear away all personal business before reporting to Houston for work at Galaxy Enterprises.

The dorm was almost vacant. Most of the other inhabitants were probably either still in a test, or at the library studying for the next round of misery. Andy banged into his room. Dan, his roommate, wasn't there. The only thing to greet him was a blinking red light on his voice mail. Andy thought about ignoring the light. He had planned to celebrate by having dinner out instead of eating institutional food.

Curiosity got the better of him. He played the message. He shouldn't have. It was from Walter Hale, his proctor with Gal X, who started out by saying, "Congratulations on completing your finals."

"Something important has come up." Hale continued, "We need you to come to the office tomorrow at 10:00 AM. Since you've finished your exams, we won't need to reschedule anything. See you tomorrow. Don't be late."

"*Damn.*" Andy thumped his notebook down on the desk and spun his chair to the wall before dropping into it. He leaned back precariously on two chair legs, putting the heel of his shoe on a little black spot on the wall. He crossed his ankles and knitted his fingers behind his head. This was his common studying and thinking position. He was angry, momentarily, but that emotion faded to disappointment. As he concentrated on the nail hole just above his toes, everything leveled out. Really, he hadn't planned anything in particular. He just wanted to be shed of the routine of the last four years. He'd had the course. Now he was ready for something else.

Actually, he had been very fortunate. With the cost of education being what it was these days, a kid had to come from a very wealthy family to afford any advanced schooling. Businesses had found that to get quality employees they had to train their own people. The private sector stepped in. Corporations began combing the high schools for prospects to fill their future needs. Once a candidate was found, he or she was interviewed and rigorously tested. Depending on the needs of the company and the quality of the applicant, scholarships were offered to the students at schools that taught the required subjects.

In return for this financial sponsorship, the student had to sign a contract with the company promising so much time at a certain salary. The contracts varied widely depending on the job specs and the quality of the candidate.

Andy had been apprehensive about being able to get any education beyond high school. He lived with his working mother, who could just barely provide the necessities for the two of them. He had never known his father. He had no idea if his dad was still living, nor did he really care.

To get any further education, Andy had to land a corporate sponsorship. However, he held little hopes there. Andy had been a very good student in a small high school. He had never really been tested, so he didn't know where he stood in relation to his peers. He was short. He was only 5'6" and wiry. Most of the better companies liked brains who were jocks and could enhance the company image through prowess on the playing field. Andy was a superb soccer player, but only major sports counted in the hiring game.

It had come as a complete shock when he walked into the house after school to find his mother talking to a recruiting representative of Galaxy Enterprises, one of the leading companies in space exploration. With provisions, Gal X might be interested in him. He was asked if he would, at company expense, of course, come to Houston for testing during spring break.

Both Andy and his mother could hardly contain their excitement. This had been the only company to respond to Andy's applications, and it was the top one on his wish list.

On the appointed date, Andy made the trip to Houston, where he was interviewed by a host of people. He was given batteries of strange tests. He was told someone would call him when all the material had been evaluated. It took weeks for the company to come to any conclusion. The Dawsons were wrecks from anticipation.

Finally, a call came from a man named Walter Hale. He set up an appointment to come to the Dawson house. He came directly to the point. "The company has decided to sponsor your college education, provided you take a field of study which will benefit the company's programs and do sufficiently well to maintain an overall B+ average and an A- in your professional field, which will be astrophysics. With your record, that shouldn't provide you with too much of a challenge."

Andy's mother was ecstatic. Her son would get an opportunity she had not been able to provide for him. Andy held his emotions in check waiting for the rest of the story. Where? Would it be a decent school with a degree that would help him down through the years? How long would his repayment period be? Would he be paid enough to do more than subsist during that period? He knew he would take whatever was offered, but he could hope for the best.

Andy was grateful that Hale did not prolong the suspense. He gave short answers to the obvious questions. "International Technical Institute, seven years repayment, which may be cut to four with the right projects....standard starting salary with annual performance evaluation and increases. There are also other ways to enhance that."

Now it was time for Andy to be ecstatic. They had offered him the best science school in the country, perhaps the world, a very generous repayment plan and a fair salary. He couldn't believe his good fortune. There must be a clinker in there somewhere.

Hale continued, "This may seem like a very generous offer. It is. However, the company is embarking on a project that will take some time to complete. We're looking to prepare personnel simultaneously. We won't know until you graduate if you'll be suited to participate in the project or whether you'd even care to work on it. Each cadet—that is what the company calls people in your position—has a proctor to follow you through school. I'll be yours. It's my business to watch over you and your education. I'll be your contact with the company. Everything between the two of you flows through me. I may become your best friend or your worst enemy, depending on your progress and willingness to do what has to be done."

The company man stood up. He handed Andy a card with a phone number and address on it. "I know the two of you have a lot do discuss. Should these terms and conditions be acceptable, please come to my room tomorrow at 10:00 am to sign a contract. If they aren't to your liking, please call so I won't have to wait all day." With that, Hale left. It was a take-it-or-leave-it deal.

There really wasn't much to discuss. Andy and his mother reveled in their good luck. Andy was at the appointed spot promptly at 10:00 am. In the fall, he started his program of astrophysics at ITI. His four years had been fruitful, but uneventful. During the summers he worked for the company in varying capacities that permitted him to familiarize himself with the organization and its goals.

During his stay at ITI, he had availed himself of all the educational opportunities open to him. Since he did not have any money outside of the small monthly stipend the company provided, he didn't pursue much of a social life. That meant he had time to advance his studies. He took more courses than he was required to take. He successfully competed at the highest level easily maintaining his required grade levels.

Now Andy was on the verge of entering the rough, tough world outside of academia. Could he cut it? His original disappointment at having his plans interrupted was replaced by curiosity about why they would require his presence a week and a half early. Maybe it was the project.

The door banged open. In stomped Dan Pugh, his roommate. "I thought you'd be long gone, having completed your final week." There was sarcasm in his tone. Dan was nowhere near the student that Andy was. Furthermore, he had a horrendous finals schedule. Dan's advance planning was never more than a week ahead.

"No, I got a call from the company. They want me to go to the local office tomorrow," said Andy.

"Really? What could be so important to have you come in during finals week?"

Andy had been repeatedly warned not to discuss any company

business with anyone. He passed the question off. "Who knows?" Besides Dan had been asking too many questions lately. Andy didn't figure it was any of his business anyway.

The next morning, Andy was at the company reception desk at the appointed time. Mr. Hale met him there. Instead of going upstairs as usual, they took the elevator to the basement. They entered a large, bare room where a young man and woman were waiting for them. Andy gave the room a quick look as Hale greeted the pair. There were new sinks along the back wall and what looked like a shower stall in a corner. There were stacks of buckets and some sacks lined up beside two tables. In the center of the room was a wooden stand about eighteen inches high and a couple of feet square. The floor was bare concrete. Overhead flood lights were pointed at the stand.

Mr. Hale introduced them by their first names saying, "I'd like you to meet Mike and Judy. They're sculptors, but for the moment they're functioning as mold makers."

The pair smiled, shook hands with Andy, and turned to some sort of preparation.

Hale led Andy off to the side. "We need a full, nude body cast of you. From the cast we'll make a positive to be used to design a new type of pressure suit. If we're successful, you'll help test the suit when you join the company. That's all I can tell you about the project at this time."

"Nude?" asked Andy as he eyed Judy drawing water into a bucket at the sink.

"Making a body cast is a hands-on type of project. We didn't know your choice of hands so we brought in a set of each. It won't hurt for long. Once they've seen it, they've seen it. Don't forget, these people are pros. They spend a good part of their time around naked bodies. I'll be back when you're finished." Hale headed for the door.

Mike nodded his head toward a chair and a bunch of hooks on the wall. "Strip down to your shorts."

As Andy sat on the chair taking off his shoes and socks, he was glad he had properly attended to his personal hygiene and underwear that morning. As Andy hung his pants on a hook, Mike motioned him to a position in the center of the paraphernalia. He was instructed to stand with his feet ten inches apart, look straight ahead, and hold his arms slightly away from his body.

"Boy," Judy said, "Look at those legs. Cyclist?"

"No, soccer." He was pleased she had been impressed. His well developed legs were a source of pride.

Judy started stretching a rubber cap, like a swimming cap, over his head, except this was fashioned tightly around his ears.

Mike had what looked like a felt tip pen. He started a line on the top of Andy's left shoulder, continued down his arm, between each of his five fingers, and up the under side of his arm. He was dividing the body into front and back halves. When he came to Andy's shorts, Mike pulled them down to the floor and got rid of them. The line continued to the floor on the outside of the leg and back up the inside to the crotch. The line on the right side mirrored the one on the left, finally meeting at the starting point.

Because Judy had been working on his head Andy hadn't been able to look down, but he was aware he was reacting to the situation and the handling. Neither sculptor seemed to pay any attention. Judy started working petroleum jelly into his eyebrows.

Using a pair of electric shears, Mike began clipping his chest hair. When Andy started to object Mike cut him off by suggesting it would be better to cut it off than to pull it out.

Judy continued working petroleum jelly into his eyebrows. After the eyebrows Judy dropped down to start the same procedure on the pubic hair. Andy lost his struggle. He began blushing furiously. No one paid any attention.

The next step was to spray him all over with a liquid Mike called "mold release." It was chilly. Then they had him step onto the model stand. His feet were again moved about ten inches apart. His hands hung a foot or so from his sides. Plugs were put into his nose. They were connected to a tube through which a gentle current of air was flowing.

Using another spray gun, Mike started spraying some sort of white goop on his left foot. As Mike continued over his body, Judy began wrapping the surface with something that looked like gauze with a slight stretch. The stuff seemed to just melt into the goop and become a single entity. It began to get warmer.

The two sculptors worked their way up his body. As they approached the head Judy had him close his eyes. She put patches over his eyes to seal them from the spray and Mike installed a brace at his waist so he wouldn't fall.

It was a strange sensation. He was completely cut off from the world. The only contact was with the air in his nose. The mold material was hardening quickly. He tried to take a deeper breath. He couldn't. He was completely entombed. Panic began to well up. He was having difficulty even swallowing.

Suddenly there was a release of pressure on the left side of his head. The mold was being severed along the pen line Mike had made on him. As the mold opened, Judy pulled it away from his face. She removed the nose plugs and eye patches. The panic that had begun to mount faded as soon as Andy could see and breathe naturally again. Mike used an electric wand and as he passed it down the edge of his body, Andy could feel a slight tingling along the marker line. The mold separated smoothly. Andy speculated that an energy field was set up between the line drawn on his body and the wand being passed over it, which sliced through the mold.

It didn't take long until he was standing naked on the model stand again. The two halves of the mold were laid out on the table. They looked like something he'd seen in the dinosaur museum workshop.

Judy took off his skull cap and wiped the grease out of his eyebrows and pubic hair. He remembered he was standing there naked.

"Go take a shower," Mike said. "The stuff in the squeeze bottle will get all that gunk off you. Congratulations, we have a perfect mold. We don't have to do it again."

Andy was finishing dressing when Mr. Hale came into the room, all smiles. "Great. I see we've a successful effort."

As the two returned to ground level, Mr. Hale informed him that the taking of the mold was company business and not to be discussed with anyone.

"Yeah," said Andy. "That'll be a lot of fun. My roommate's been getting very nosey lately. When he sees me shorn of body hair he'll die of curiosity."

"Really. Well, we'll just have to see he has a nice funeral." Hale chuckled.

Since Andy didn't have a building pass, Hale escorted him to the main entry. As they parted, Hale told Andy to enjoy his contrived time, but not to be late to work in twenty days.

Chapter   2

As she crossed the porch, Andie checked her mail. It was of the junk variety. While she had the mailbox open, she stripped out the tag to the postman with her name on it, Andrea Carson. She had qualms every time she closed the door a little more on this portion of her life. At the end of the week, she would be graduating from International Technical Institute. The four years had been good ones. Now, she would be stepping into the unknown. She had a job, which was better than a lot of the grads would have, but she had no idea of what was going to be expected of her.

In high school, she had been at the top of her class in math, chemistry, and physics, but there had been no further education in her immediate future. She didn't have the money to go on to college. Her best prospect was to try for professional sports. She had been good in basketball, softball, and track. The only moneymaking area for a girl was in running. Her last year in school had been divided between the classroom and the gym, excluding everything else.

She had a physique most boys would die for. She had sacrificed curves for muscles. She kept her blonde hair very short. To compensate, she wore long, dangly earrings.

After graduation, she was considered for a computer related job with a branch office of Galaxy Enterprises, located near her hometown. A few days later, she received a call from personnel to report for testing and an interview. Andie thought she had done well on both phases. She was told that there were many more applicants. To be fair, everyone would be seen. A final decision would be made in a couple of weeks. Andie would be advised one way or the other.

The following Monday, Andie got a phone call from personnel asking if she would, at the company's expense, travel to the home office in Houston for another interview. They said that, after looking at her resume, the company felt it might have something more interesting for her to consider.

So on Wednesday, Andie flew to Texas. She was met at the airport by a driver who took her directly to the impressive office complex of Gal X, as everyone called the company. A woman, who identified herself as Sharon Chasti, took over. She said the company would like to administer some tests before going any further. Andie was assured the tests were not the kind for which she could prepare. They were personality and thinking tests, four hours of them.

Following the testing Ms. Chasti took Andie out to eat. Andie confined herself to a baked potato, salad, and bottled water. Trying to maintain a training diet was difficult when eating at restaurants. After dinner Andie was dropped off at her hotel. A driver would pick her up at 9:00 in the morning. Andie put in a few laps in the hotel swimming pool before retiring. It had been a long, tiring day.

Precisely at 9:00, the driver appeared. At the headquarters complex, she was turned over to Ms. Chasti, who ushered her to the office of Wayne Percy.

Mr. Percy began the interview by saying, "Miss Carson, the company has been impressed by you and your background. We're looking to make people of your calibre a part of our team. We have a project in mind, that is currently under development.

We're recruiting individuals who might be able to work with us on it. You might fit into the scheme of things, but you'll need some specialized training. The company is prepared to make the following offer: We'll give you a full, four year scholarship to International Technical Institute to pursue a degree in astral navigation. At this time, it is a theoretical discipline, but it appears that before long there'll be a call for people trained in this area. To retain your scholarship, you'll have to maintain a B+ overall grade point with an A- average in your professional field. Upon graduation you'll work for us for seven years, starting at the standard salary for entry at your level of education. There are other salary benefits that'll probably come your way as well, if you are chosen to work on this project."

Never in her wildest flights of fancy had she ever thought that this could happen. Not trusting her voice, Andie simply said, "Agreed."

Thus started a wild four years. Everything seemed to be going her way. When Andie got to school she knew she would have to live in the dorms because the scholarship was insufficient for anything more luxurious. Life in the dorms turned out to be a problem. She was used to working out during her off hours. She particularly enjoyed early morning runs. But she couldn't get out of the dorm without special permission and permission didn't carry over from one day to the next. Eating was a real challenge. Dorm food in no way corresponded with her idea of a training diet. She was prohibited from cooking in her room and she could not afford to eat out, even if she could find an eatery that would cater to her whims.

Frustration was beginning to set in when one of the girls on her floor mentioned that a woman who lived nearby was looking for a companion to live with. She was willing to be very reasonable with the household expenses. Andie followed up on the information. The house was only a couple of blocks from campus in a very good neighborhood. It was a huge house with spacious grounds.

The owner, Sally Morris, was an attractive woman in her mid-thirties who seemed to take a shine to Andie from the start. Ms. Morris explained that she had recently purchased the house and found out that it was just too big and lonely for a single person to handle. Money did not seem to present any particular problem, so Sally decided to find some young, energetic woman who would share the house to make it more livable. She was quite impressed to learn that Andie was on scholarship from one of the largest and most prestigious companies in the country. She was intrigued that a woman would major in astral navigation.

The deal was for Andie to pay for half of the utilities and provide her own food. She would have complete kitchen privileges, if she cleaned up her own mess. The master bedroom was separated from the rest of the house. Andie could use one of the other bedrooms for sleeping and another for studying or exercise. There were still guest rooms for visitors.

Andie immediately accepted the offer, figuring all her problems were solved. She could come and go at will, have a workout room, a quiet study area and a whole, well equipped kitchen at her disposal. All of this at less than the cost of the dorm.

The arrangement worked beautifully. Sally seemed to feel better about the house and to enjoy Andie's company. She never made any particular demands on Andie's time or energies once a routine had developed. The two women occasionally jogged together and soon became good friends.

Andie was bright enough to handle her schooling with no more problems than ITI could give any qualified student. It wasn't easy, but that didn't bother her. Since, in this field of study she was the only girl, it gave her plenty of opportunity to compete with the guys. This made life worth living.

Now, this phase of her life was closing. She didn't like losing so much that was familiar. On the other hand, there were new challenges out there. Finals week was not too much of a nail-biting event. Since Andie had maintained an almost perfect average, the test grades didn't mean that much. It was just a case of perseverance to get through the week.

When Andie entered the house, she could hear Sally bumping around in the kitchen. She dumped the junk mail on the entry table on the way to the kitchen. "What are you up to?"

"Oh, I thought that since you were in finals week, I'd make up some of your veggie stuff for dinner so you wouldn't have to take the time."

"How thoughtful. Thanks. Tomorrow's my worst exam. Then I have Wednesday off before the final sprint to the finish."

Sally pointed a paring knife at the note pad by the telephone. "Your Mr. Percy wants you to phone him as soon as you get in."

Andie knew the number after four years of calling the company. She was put through to Percy. Her proctor was his normal, cheery self. "I know this is finals week, but according to the schedule I have, Wednesday is an off day for you. The company needs half a day of your time. We want to take advantage of the skills of a couple of people who are in town. Could you be at the office at one?"

"Sure. Do I need bring or prepare for anything?"

"No, not at all. This is informal, so come in casual attire. See you Wednesday. Good luck tomorrow with the terror of the department."

Andie shrugged as she hung up the phone.

Sally was watching her. "What was that all about? You look perplexed."

The company wants me to come to the office on Wednesday. Mr. Percy didn't say why. I guess I just figured there wasn't much need for me until I begin work in a few days."

Andie shook off the thought. She grabbed a paring knife to attack the kohlrabi.

"Casual" to Andie was jeans, sneakers and a sweat shirt. Since she was going to the company she put on a more formal pair of clean, white sneakers and a sweat shirt with the company logo.

She was glad she was punctual. Mr. Percy was coming down the hall as she approached the reception desk.

 Mr. Percy led her in a different direction from the way to his office. He explained as they went. "We have a couple of professional sculptors in town at the moment who're excellent mold makers. We need a full body mold of you so we can get an exact positive figure to fit a new prototype pressure suit we're working on for a project."

They took the elevator to the basement. Mr. Percy stopped before an unmarked door. He became serious. "From here on out, whatever you see or hear or just plain know about the company is company business. It shouldn't be discussed in any way with anyone outside of the company, and within the company discussed only with your supervisors and other employees on-a-need-to-know basis. An example of that policy is the mold-making for a pressure suit. It's company business. Industrial espionage has risen to a high art form, so we must always be wary."

"Understood," she said.

They entered a large room where Mr. Percy introduced her to the other two occupants, Mike and Judy. They were going to make the mold.

A couple of hours later, Andie was back in her jeans and sweat shirt feeling a bit itchy where the chemicals had irritated her skin or her hair had been pulled out. It had been an interesting experience. Mike and Judy had gone about their task professionally.

Mr. Percy showed up to escort her back to the surface. He wished her well on the remaining exams and reminded her that she was to report for duty in Houston two weeks later.

Time was getting short. There were so many things to do. She had to close out the last four years of her life. All accounts had to be settled, all library books returned, her dry cleaning retrieved. Then there were the goodbyes to friends and professors.

Sally was the closest friend she had made while in college. That farewell would be the most difficult. Sally had offered to store her personal items until she got settled, but since Andie was relocating to Houston it would be easier to dump the stuff on her mother.

The company said to bring a minimum of personal items for the initial reporting. At first, she would be put up in a company housing unit until an assignment was made. It sounded a little strange, but these days business practice had taken a weird turn.

Chapter 3

Galaxy Enterprises World Headquarters was an impressive compound situated on the edge of Houston. It was a walled city. The administration building, a six-story glass covered structure facing one of the main arteries of the city, was the company's facility for direct contact with the public. The front half of the structure sat among magnificent garden tiers, which led into a forest of tall trees. Behind the sight barrier of trees, a ten-foot high, solid wall encompassed ten acres, the rest of the World Headquarters complex. That portion of the company was well beyond the view of outsiders.

Anyone having dealings with the company had to come through the administration building. That included new employees reporting for the first time. Andy was wearing his best suit, shirt, and tie. What was correct fashion at school looked a little out of place, even to him, in the Gal X environment. His old car was even more noticeable than his attire. He parked at the far side of the vast parking lot. The morning was already hot and humid. He didn't want to be late for the first day on the job, but he did not want to show up drenched with sweat either.

As he approached the entry, an attractive blonde with big, dangly earrings bounded to trigger the sensor that opened the sliding doors. The girl stepped aside to let him pass into the entry first. With his trajectory and velocity, it would have been awkward and probably clumsy to have tried to be an old fashioned gentleman. As he shot past, he caught a quick smile, suggesting some sort of victory had been won. All he could offer was a lame "Thanks."

In an attempt to salvage some dignity, he purposefully strode on to the reception desk as if he were on a mission of the utmost importance. A door off to the side opened. Walter Hale motioned him inside. Andy was surprised to find Hale there. It hadn't occurred to him that his proctor at school would show up in Houston. There was another man in the room. As Hale ushered Andy into a corridor behind the office, he said to the other man, "See you soon."

Hale talked as he and Andy walked down what seemed like an endless corridor. "We're now going to an orientation meeting with one of the company officers. This is unusual. Normally such things are left to lower level functionaries. Remember that project we mentioned when you were originally recruited?"

"Yes."

"The project has progressed right on schedule. We now have to make final personnel selections to move on to the next stage. There are a number of considerations to make. All this will be explained shortly."

They stopped at an elevator marked "Execution Floor." Hale punched in a number on a key pad and the doors slid open. "We go up to the mountain. The mountain doesn't come down to us."

They ended up in a large conference room. There were several other people already present. Two men sat on the far side of a long table. At the foot, an older woman was talking softly with a young woman. Near the head of the table, a bookkeeper type man fussed over a stack of papers. Andy didn't have time to more than glance at the others when the door opened again. In walked the man from the reception room and the girl with the dangly earrings. When she saw Andy she smiled sweetly.

There wasn't time for anything else because the door at the other end of the room snapped open. In walked Artis Malvane, the CEO of Galaxy Enterprises. The company men jumped to their feet, and the new people followed suit. Mr. Malvane inspected the group before seating himself in the high-backed chair at the head of the table. He waved the rest to their seats. Turning to the bookkeeper, he said, "Proceed Mr. Lombard." He turned to the group again. "Mr. Lombard is our personnel manager."

Lombard picked up a stack of papers and started distributing them down the far side of the table from Andy. His first stop was alongside a man who was maybe 35. The guy appeared out of place in these surroundings. His dress was too casual for the occasion and he was fidgeted nervously. Mr. Lombard placed a paper in front of him. "Corky Smith," he said, "You aren't a new employee, but since you're changing job assignments and responsibilities we're entering into a new employment contract with you."

The personnel manager moved on to the next man. "Mr. Thomas Rolland, you've been employed by one of our subsidiaries, so now the parent company will issue its own agreement. Please read this."

He placed a sheet in front of the young woman at the end of the table. Apparently, the other woman was a proctor. "Beatrice Bell, you are a new employee. Here's your initial employment agreement laying out the various duties and obligations. Please read it well."

Next came the girl with the dangly earrings. "Andrea Carson, you are likewise a new employee. Here are the terms and conditions of your employment. They are pretty much the same as your original education contract, but brought up to date factoring in the inflation index."

Ah, thought Andy, another student. Before he had time to speculate any further, Lombard was beside him. "Andrew Dawson, this is your initial employment contract with Gal X.

Please read it well before signing."

Mr. Lombard returned to his seat. The CEO made no move to take control of the meeting. Each employee went back to the contract and read it carefully. Andy noted that his education had cost the company over half a million dollars. He was lucky to be shed of that big of a debt in only seven years, if things went right.

After all employees finished reading the contracts, Mr. Lombard asked if there were any questions. There didn't seemed to be any, so he continued. "Will everybody please sign your name as listed at the bottom of the sheet." Once everyone had signed, Mr. Malvane stood up.

"There's one other item to transact before we'll be contractually bound. Please turn your contracts over. On the back is a security oath. It is full of legalese, but what it says is that you're bound to secrecy concerning any and all activities of the company. There are provisions spelled out for penalties and punishment for violations of this agreement. The company views this agreement as vital to the well-being of the company and all of its employees. Breaches won't be tolerated. Read it word by word and if you won't sign the document, please leave the room."

Everyone read and signed the document. Mr. Malvane asked Lombard to pick up the papers before returning to his office. He then dismissed the three proctors, leaving the five new employees wondering what was happening. Nothing was going the way Andy expected the first day on the job to go.

Mr. Malvane looked sternly at the few faces scattered around the table. He let a strained silence hang over their heads. Corky Smith started fidgeting, making tiny mouse sounds as his rubber heels squeaked on the marble floor. Andy would have like to sneak a peek at the others, but he was facing the CEO, and they were behind him.

"First," Malvane began. "I wish to remind you of the security oath you all have just signed because what I'm going to tell you is known by only a handful of people in the world. This information is the most closely guarded secret of Gal X. Our biggest competitor, Centurion, would kill for the data I'm about to give to you. I can tell this is baffling all of you, but remember back to the original contacts with the company, or when a representative asked you to transfer. References were made to a project that was being developed. This information concerns that project and your relationship to it. Let me say here, that the company has full faith that each of you is the right person for the job. Now it remains for each of you to come to a firm decision on whether you wish to participate in it. Should you elect not to take the job offered, then you will be transferred to another job. However, you'll be closely watched until the information I'm about to give you is no longer of value."

By this time the CEO had the undivided attention of the five.

Malvane seated himself and swung a console out from under the edge of the table. As he manipulated buttons he directed their attention to the other end of the room where panels in the wall were sliding back to reveal a gigantic screen. "There's an official name for the project, but employees have dubbed it 'Taran'. We'll use it for the sake of brevity."

A slide of an artist's concept came up on the screen. It looked like half a tennis ball with knees sticking up into the air, standing on eight huge legs. The tennis ball portion appeared to be crew or cargo area. In the center was a large, tube-like structure extending downward. It looked like part of a propulsion system. It wasn't hard to see why the craft had been nicknamed Taran, short for Tarantula.

Another slide came on the screen. It appeared to be a small mockup, until a figure was noted standing beside one of the legs. The thing was enormous. Judging from the size of the man, Andy guessed it would have straddled about half of a football field.

"Taran is a prototype for an entirely new concept in space travel. It has always been considered that the great weights involved meant that any space craft, other than those like the old space shuttles, would have to be assembled in space. Such a project would be so expensive that even the largest enterprises or governments tremble at the mere thought.

"However, Gal X has made a breakthrough in basic propulsion research. This brought out some interesting notions concerning the fourth force, gravity. We know gravity is a long range force that glues the universe together. One of our people came up with a method of nullifying the force of gravity, thus causing objects to lose weight. As an object loses its weight, it can be moved by lesser and lesser forces. Taran has been equipped with 'nulls,' which block gravity. As air above a nulled object loses its weight, gases from outside the system force their way in and up, causing weightless objects to rise, albeit slowly and with a terrible windstorm."

Malvane's description was accompanied by sweeping gestures and hand motions. He was excited and he was passing that feeling on to his audience.

He continued, "We discovered that when we applied more power to the nulls, they began to repulse gravity like positive poles on two magnets. Briefly, that's how we plan to get Taran off the ground. Normally, Taran will stay in space once she gets there. She's equipped with two smaller shuttles. One's designed to carry cargo, and the second is primarily a personnel carrier. The shuttles are fitted with smaller null devices as well as more conventional propulsion systems.

"Taran is a prototype for another type of spaceship. Going anywhere except to our local planets has been pretty much out of the question because of the enormous time involved. We're just too slow. We still haven't perfected a successful system for human hibernation or inanimate suspension so the crews can sleep through the trips. It's difficult on the ground, too, if the scientists die of old age before they can see the results of their projects. Companies don't like to carry a project on the books that long, before finding out if there is a possibility of profit.

"For decades we've known of the solar winds. Through new

electronics, we are now aware of what we are calling 'solar jets,' like the jet stream on Earth. We can now trace the solar jets which continually snake through the galaxy. Gal X has developed new technology that we think will permit us to ride these jets, thus enhancing our space speeds enormously. Taran will be the test vehicle for this new science.

"You're thinking this is all well and good, but why am I being given all this highly classified information? And how do I fit into the scheme of things?" Malvane looked at each of the five before him. He still had their undivided attention. "You five have been selected, and to some extent trained, to be the troubleshooters for the prelaunch sequence. The construction of Taran is now complete, but we need to know of any bugs, glitches, anomalies and idiosyncrasies. You five are going to be locked up in Taran for six months, during which time there'll be constant simulations of routine procedures, emergencies and day-to-day operations. Taran will be seated on the ground, but as far as you can tell you'll be flying. At the end of the six months an evaluation will be made to determine if she's truly ready to fly. A real crew of test pilots is being assembled, who'll take the risks of outer space. To give them the best chance of success, you're going to put the ship and its systems through a rigorous shakedown.

"When I say locked in, that's exactly what I mean. Taran won't be opened in less than six months unless it's a truly a life and death circumstance. Before you go in, there'll be complete medical examinations and dental checks. Anything that looks like it might go wrong will be corrected."

The CEO paused while he selected a folder from a stack at the edge of the table. He opened it and started down a list. "Andrew Dawson, you're the pilot of the craft. Andrea Carson, you're the navigator. Thomas Rolland, you're the engineer. Corky Smith, you're supply. Beatrice Bell, you're the librarian. Each of you have been chosen for these positions due to either specialized training or certain unique skills."

Now everyone was squirming. Malvane held up his hand. "I can see a million questions forming already. For the moment, I can only give you some short answers." He looked around the table. He pointed at Rolland, who was the oldest and probably the most secure person of the five. "You start it off."

"Sir, you have assigned everyone a job. I'm sure no one knows how to perform it."

The CEO smiled. "Don't be concerned about that. We've devised an exceptional on-the-job training program which will give each of you the competence to handle the job as it comes along. There is even a high degree of cross-training in case something were to happen requiring one of you to wear someone else's hat. That's the least of our fears." Malvane pointed to Beatrice Bell.

"Why me?" she said in a small voice.

"Miss Bell, you have one of those unique talents I mentioned. With your useable total recall, you'll be able to sort out information that would take others much longer to access. In a real situation, such time may not be available to the crew. Your computer will have access to a good portion of the knowledge of mankind. This will be an opportunity which may never come your way again. The more you can assimilate and process, the more valuable a person you become. You'll have to mountains of data to sort and file into useable form."

Andrea raised her hand. "What happens if something goes wrong?"

"Your activities will be monitored around the clock. Should something life threatening occur, then the mission would be aborted. If it is something fixable you'll be expected to fix it. If it can't be repaired, the procedure would be stopped and repairs effected. Then we'll plug in another quarter and start again. Safeguards are built into all the systems."

Corky Smith was squirming again. The CEO looked at him and smiled. Corky became immobile.

"All right, Corky. What is it?"

"Well, err, why do ya need a supply guy? You can carry all

you'll need for six months."

Malvane was serious again. "This ship is designed to be on missions covering months and maybe years. In addition to replacement parts and various necessary supplies, it'll also carry a load of raw materials. It'll be up to you to synthesize whatever is needed from a patch in the outer skin to a food supplement to feed the crew. You're noted as one of those peculiar talents that can make something out of nothing."

Since Andy was the only one that had not spoken, all eyes turned toward him. He swiveled around to face Malvane and asked, "When do we leave?"'

There were some strained snickers. The CEO glanced around the table silencing everyone. "There's one more consideration at this time. You know basically what's involved. If you don't wish to participate in this venture, now's the time to so indicate. No blemish will appear on your record. You'll remain a member of the Gal X family. The only thing that will happen is that you'll be assigned to a station where you can be monitored to make sure none of the information you received today finds its way into the hands of others. Does anyone wish to leave?"

Andy had already stated his position. He turned around to see if there were any dropouts. The only one to indicate any uncertainty was Beatrice Bell. She was wring her hands. Apparently she came to a decision, because she settled down staring straight ahead.

"Fine. I'm happy to have you aboard. We have high expectations for this project. You people are in on the early stages, which should be very beneficial to your careers. Now I'm going to turn you over to the proctors, who'll take you through the next steps. Good luck." Mr. Malvane had apparently touch a button on the console because the door opened admitting the proctors. The CEO strode out of the room.

Andy's proctor, Walter Hale, was the senior, for he took the head chair. He introduced himself and the other proctors, then launched into the immediate considerations. "For the duration of this phase of the mission you five will be known as 'TC,' short for Taran Crew. This designation is for internal use only among those who are in the know. For outside consumption, each of you'll have a title and job description, which will give you believable reasons to cover what you actually will be doing.

"The next two weeks will be very busy ones," he continued. "We know from your annual exams that you're all in good physical condition, but everyone will go through both physical and dental exams to look for anything that might cause you problems in the next six months. For instance, if you have the start of a cavity, it'll be fixed before it develops.

"One of the main things that has to be done, you'll have to do for yourselves. You must tie up all loose ends in your personal lives so that there'll be no problems developing in the six months you'll be out of touch. We don't want any relatives, or girl or boyfriends complaining to missing persons that you've disappeared. Nor do we want creditors dunning us for delinquent bills. All such items will be taken care of before you leave. If you have any contractual obligations make advance payments or pay the debt off. Get your insurance premiums paid in advance or have someone you can trust handle them for you. Should you need more money to settle accounts, we will advance the necessary funds. Each of you has a different agenda, so please accompany your proctors. We have much to do in a very short time. The future is almost here."

Chapter 4

Walter Hale took Andy from one division to another for the remainder of the morning. The main hazard associated with the first day on the job seemed to be writer's cramp. There were so many forms to be filled out and signed.

At noon, Hale and Andy took a break at one of the several cafeterias scattered about the World Headquarters complex. Hale guided meal conversation away from shop talk.

Andy inquired about Hale's family. In the four years at school he'd been to the Hale household many times. He was like an extra uncle to five-year-old, Shellee.

Hale chuckled. "Shellee has memorized that poem you wrote for her, 'Rimlick, the Cat.' She thinks all that nonsense is perfectly logical. You may have ruined her thought process for life. I didn't know you had so much illogic in you."

"It can be quite logical to juxtapose things into deliciously illogical relationships. It's quite a study. You ought to indulge in it some time."

Hale shook his head. "I'll be perfectly content to return home, so I can play around my old fashioned ham radio equipment. That is all the diversion I need to keep me happy."

After lunch, Hale guided Andy into an elevator. "Now we're going to have the first fitting of the pressure suit that is being made from your body cast."

When they stepped out of the elevator they nearly ran into Wayne Percy and Andrea. The two older men fell into step as they headed down a long corridor. The new employees followed behind.

Andrew took the initiative. "How can we spend four years in the same small school, taking similar courses, and not run into one another?"

Andrea grinned. "I remember you. We were in a few lecture classes together. You always sat near the front of the room and I always sat as far back as I could get. I get up early to run, so I took most of my classes as early as possible. You probably took yours later in the day. And I used to watch you at soccer practice."

Suddenly, Andrew looked at the dangly earrings. "You're the one running laps in the gaudy sweats and the big earrings. Do you always wear those things?" He indicated the ear jewelry.

At that moment the proctors opened a door and the employees followed them in. Standing in the center of the room were the two flesh colored mannequins taken from their body molds. Andrea was just saying, "Oh, I like dangly things.....," Her voice trailed off as she saw the figures. The strange intonation caused the three men to glance at her and follow her gaze to the crotch on the male figure. As Andrea recalled what she had just said, the men nearly choked trying not to laugh.

Andrea stood with her feet apart and her hands on her hips. She rolled her eyes to the ceiling and walked over to Andy's figure giving it a close scrutiny from all sides. "The rest of it isn't too bad either." That brought the laughter.

Andy knew he was going to have to be on his toes at all times or he would always be on the defensive with this gal.

If it hadn't been for the "dangly thing" and the faces of the two mannequins, they could have been made using the same mold. They were practically peas out of the same pod.

Hale got the situation back under control. "Okay, you guys. You'd better get used to this because there will be very little privacy on Taran. Furthermore, these suits are skin tight. It's easier to get in and out with someone to help. The technicians here will start training you in how to suit up and then make whatever fitting adjustments are necessary. You'll have several fittings in the next couple of weeks. The rest of TC will be doing the same thing, but your suits are further along since we got your molds first."

One of the techs called, "Andy, will you step over here?" Both Andrew and Andrea started in his direction. They stopped to look at each other. Another round of laughter broke out.

The rest of the afternoon was spent with technicians swarming over them poking, patting, and marking. They had to bend and twist in every direction. Others brought gloves or boots or helmets. It was a tedious few hours, but by the end of the session they were no longer self-conscious.

They were relieved when the proctors arrived to rescue them. The workday was ending. The TC ended up in a guest residential complex. Each had a small bedroom and bath off a common sitting room. They were shown a 24-hour cafeteria and they were issued ID cards so they could get in and out of an employee entrance. This would be their home for the next two weeks.

Chapter 4

The two weeks at World Headquarters had been hectic for everyone. All day long they were poked, prodded, questioned, lectured, and hustled about. Then they were given some free time to close out their personal business.

In the evenings, the two older men, Corky and Tom, played gin in the sitting room. For the most part, Beatrice stayed to herself. She always seemed to have her nose in a book, or she was at a computer terminal. The name problem for Andy and Andie was resolved by Corky, who started using the first letter of their last names as the prefix to Andy, thus Dandy and Candie. To the chagrin of the holders, the names stuck.

Andy didn't like the compromise. He'd had that name all his life, and he didn't want to give it up or share it with a girl. Dandy was only tolerable when Andie became Candie. That didn't fit her self-image at all.

After dinner the Andies would sit in the lounge chatting. They were getting to know each other better, but competition wasn't far beneath the surface. Candie was usually the instigator of the verbal sparring matches. Dandy was learning to see them coming. He didn't care for that kind of confrontation. He had always been the arbitrator type. He would bow out by excusing himself to watch a ball game or boxing match. That was his kind of competition.

The other Gal X employees were becoming more curious about TC. It was obvious to everyone that the five new people were special. No one else had ever had their own personal proctors. New employees were never housed in the HQ building. Speculation around the water cooler was taking on absurd proportions. Their every move was surreptitiously watched.

Suddenly, the two weeks were over. They packed up their few belongings and some newly issued uniforms. Monday morning, after a hasty breakfast, they were ushered into a minibus for transportation to a Gal X airport.

An executive jet was waiting for them. When the plane took off, there were nine passengers and the flight crew aboard, the Taran Crew and their individual proctors, and the project director, Calvin Harder. From what TC had learned Harder was a pragmatic, no-frills type of guy.

When the aircraft reached its cruising altitude, Mr. Harder called them to attention. After introducing himself, he launched into a background report on the project. "It started about six years ago," he began. "The company's always involved in research and development. In the course of this R & D, many machines and instruments are constructed in hopes that they do certain things. Sometimes they don't perform the desired tasks. Sometimes a better way comes along and the equipment is abandoned. All this stuff is put into storage. If anyone wants to try to apply the equipment to some other use or he has a new wrinkle on how to get it to work, he could check it out of storage.

"About six years ago, the company had a high school kid on a summer training program working in the storage facility cataloging equipment. He'd landed the job by being a prize winner in a science fair. The job wasn't too demanding and the kid had time to poke around. He started investigating the various pieces of equipment and what they were supposed to do. His high school project had been to devise a containment field of some sort. His research led him to hook a couple of the machines together to form a new wave pattern. He hooked wires to a steel chair which he'd hung upside down on the edge of a work bench. He was hoping to build a field within the steel legs of the chair. He made two mistakes. First he reversed the polarity in one of his wiring sequences, and second he had no power modulation device. When he was ready, he just threw a switch.

"The chair slammed into the ceiling hard enough to poke the legs through the concrete into the room above. Pow," Harder shouted as he thrust his hands straight over his head, The crew jumped. With a smile Harder continued. "Fortunately, the lead wires were too short to get to the ceiling. They snapped off, breaking the circuit. Even at that, a whirlwind developed in the room. No one was hurt and not much was damaged but the kid was really shaken up. As it turned out he had developed the first anti-gravitational wave generator. The wave pushes away from gravity like two magnets repelling each other. It also shields whatever is above the object from the force of gravity. Pressure from the sides causes a vortex to develop if the wave is applied too quickly and in too great a strength. This atmospheric pressure also helps propel the object upward.

"With this new technology, Gal X made the decision to proceed with construction of a new type of space vehicle on the surface with the expectations of being able to fly it up.

"However, there's a another element to this project. Along with the development of the A/G generator, other research was paying off at the same time. We've known about the solar winds for decades. These are particle emissions radiating outward from stars. It was thought that these winds extended outward about 100 astronomical units before they were stopped by interstellar gas. This isn't the case. Due to various forces, they coalesce into what we call solar jets, which plot variable courses through the universe. They're constantly in motion, much like ocean currents. They follow general courses but constantly vary in subtle ways.

"Our research found a way to see these jets. Once we knew of their existence, then work began on finding a way to use them. In recent years there've been several experiments to increase the speed of space travel. Various propellants have been tested, but none have proven feasible because the human body can't withstand the various forces that are experienced, or their force to weight or volume ratio is not sufficient.

"Gal X believes we may have come across a method of riding those solar jets, thus increasing our speed sufficiently that it may now be feasible to travel into the further reaches of our solar system and perhaps into the galaxy. You'll learn all about this in the coming weeks.

"The company has invested a good portion of its financial being into building what everybody calls Taran. It's staking its future on positive results from these new systems. Time is becoming critical. Our biggest competitor, Centurion, has gotten wind of this project. They'll stop at nothing to acquire it, including taking it by force of arms, which has become an acceptable business practice in recent years. By the time the courts rule on the act, the aggressor can milk all the info or benefits out of the project so that it's a hollow shell when they are forced to return it to the legal owners years down the line.

"We think security's been good enough that Centurion still doesn't know enough to become too aggressive. At the moment, there's a hostile takeover being repulsed in the board rooms. We believe Centurion is behind this financial maneuver. Gal X is in a weakened position because of the enormous construction cost of Taran, but we think we can hold. We're dragging this gambit out as long as possible to give us time to get Taran operational. Our time table gives you six months of simulated operation to find all the bugs, both in hardware and software. The actual flight crew will be getting much the same type of training as you, but they'll also be working out the bugs you locate. We hope to launch in six months." Harder paused to take a drink of water. As he surveyed his tense audience Dandy developed some sort of itch.

Harder noticed. "Andrew, do you have a question?"

"Whatever happened to the kid and his flying chair?"

The question caught everyone by surprise. They all laughed. The tension was broken.

Mr. Harder smiled, too. "That young man is presently finishing his education. He's deeply involved in this project when he's not in school. If everything goes right, he'll be a very well-known and wealthy young scientist. Gal X takes care of its own."

His last comment was not lost on anyone.

"Now to the immediate situation." Harder continued. "We are heading for Taran's base right now. We'd been constructing it closer to home, but we found security too hard to maintain so we changed locations. It's at an old salt mine that the government once developed to test nuclear weapons. It's in the middle of nowhere in New Mexico. There's a small armed force guarding it and a limited scientific detail stationed there to provide you with the necessary backup. We've kept the personnel to a minimum. It's easier to obscure the real mission of the place. In this case, secrecy is a better plan than force. We can be outgunned by our closest competitors."

Harder got up to get a cup of coffee. "Enjoy the view. It will be some time before you will see the real thing again."

Chapter 5

The sun was overhead as the jet approached their destination. They'd started their descent some time back, but Harder had kept their attention focused elsewhere until he said, "There it is."

The pilot had to compensate as weight shifted when they all looked out the port windows. The sight was remarkably uninteresting. There were a few scattered buildings that looked as if they could use some repair. Dusty, utility vehicles were parked about. An old Army duce-and-a-half sat at the end of a dirt air strip. The main feature of the landscape was what appeared to be a building covering a mine shaft. A long conveyer belt shoved its nose up over the edge of a huge pile of tailings. This little enclave was surrounded by vast emptiness that only jack rabbits and tarantulas could love.

The plane landed in a swirl of dust. It came to rest at the end of the strip, but no one made any move to leave. In a moment, the dust cloud caught up with the craft and it took a few minutes for the dust storm to dissipate in the desert breeze.

The passengers disembarked into the scorching dry heat of the desert. After the air-conditioned cabin of the aircraft, the sudden blast made everyone gasp. The old army truck headed in their direction.

Tom Rolland slowly turned in a 360 degree circle. His only comment was, "Wow. This is a lot of nothing."

Dandy nodded his agreement as did the rest of TC. The truck pulled up on the downwind side to keep from covering them with dust.

"This is your chariot," said Mr. Harder . "All aboard."

There was a canvas cover over the bed so they couldn't see where they were heading. Andy watched Beatrice who was looking like she was sorry for making the decision to come along. She had the air of being a city girl. All this nothingness seemed to be getting to her. However, she was probably not alone in wondering how far they were going to have to travel in the miserable truck before they got to Taran's base.

The truck slowed and it suddenly became quite dark. They had entered something. Corky was the first to figure it out. "That tailing pile is really a camouflage net. I thought the angle of repose was a little steep."

Mr. Harder thumped on the cab. The driver pulled up. "Everybody out," Harder said. "This your home for the next few months."

The hair on the back of Dandy's neck twitched. He was thunderstruck by the enormity of the ship that loomed over his head. He wasn't alone. The whole crew and their proctors slowly rotated trying to take in the view of the ship that loomed over them. They had been told the dimensions of the vehicle, but the raw figures didn't register until that moment. From one leg across to the opposing leg was at least the width of a football field. Because Taran was painted black it seemed to disappear into the netting. The underside looked like the scaled belly of a snake. The rest of the ship was smooth. Each of its eight feet was approximately 40 feet across and between the legs graceful parabolas arched upward like great cathedral windows. The random pattern of the camouflage net emphasized the resemblance.

Harder and Walter Hale were the only ones who had been been there before. The rest resembled tourists in New York viewing at the skyline for the first time.

"You'll see it all later," Harder said, finally. "But now let's go into the control center."

After they all had retrieved their gear from the truck, Harder led the way toward a little, concrete building squatting near one of the legs. He punched a code into a pad by the door and it swung open, revealing a desk with a guard behind bullet proof glass, with his hands hovering above a battery of switches. TC found out later that he controlled an assortment of weapons that covered them.

The room was an entry to an elevator that took them to a lower level of one of the old salt mines, an immense complex far below ground. Its primary function was to house a state of the art communications system, which would direct the operations of Taran. This was the brains of the whole project.

At the time, it looked like a deserted city. It was designed to handle hundreds of people when actual flight began, but now there was just a skeleton crew. Due to security constraints, only a few people were on hand for this phase of the operation.

Harder led them into the control room. With a hint of pride, he swept his hand in a circle encompassing the large room full of high tech apparatus. "Welcome to my office. For the next six months this'll be your only direct contact with anything outside of Taran. This is command central."

He led the way to a large, freestanding console on the far side of the room. "This is my control unit. From here I can monitor anything that goes on and if necessary I can take control in case of any emergency."

Harder stepped up to the console. He threw five switches. In front of the station was a wall of monitors. Five came to life, showing separate work areas. On-screen labels indicated pilot, navigator, engineer, librarian, and supply. "This is just a preview of your new work places. You'll get to know them very well starting tomorrow morning. Then this place will become a beehive of activity. For now we'll get something to eat. Then you'll be shown around the ground facility."

Chapter 6

The wake-up call came at 6:00 AM. TC had to take the time on faith or trust their watches because that far underground there was no way to check. Each had a small, spartan cubical with minimal facilities. Their human alarm clocks gave them fifteen minutes to get cleaned up and into their uniform coveralls.

At the appointed time, TC ushered to a cafeteria for breakfast. Everyone's day must begin at the same time or the word was out that big things were about to happen because the eating facility was getting a good play. There was a tension in the air. Today was day one of the big experiment, and TC was the center of attention. They had been seated at a long table with their backs to the wall, facing the rest of the room. Midway through the meal Calvin Harder made his appearance. He walked to a small lectern at the end of the table and picked up a microphone.

"May I have your attention, please. Today's an important milestone for Gal X. I'd like to introduce the shakedown crew for Taran who'll spend the next six months getting all the bugs out of the various systems so that when the flight crew arrives we'll be ready to fly. Pilot....Andrew Dawson." One by one Harder presented each of the crew so the support personnel could more closely identify with the various people to be locked away for half a year.

Following breakfast TC was joined by their proctors. Then Harder led the group up out of the subterranean complex to the underside of Taran. The warm, early morning sun made dappled designs on everything. Members of the support group for Taran started filtering to the surface to watch the first actual step in getting the vehicle operational. Until now it had been a pile of technology. A human element was being added with the hope that the animate and inanimate could become a viable unit.

No program was planned. That would wait until the actual crew stepped aboard when Gal X could announce its achievement to the world. No competitor could intervene at that late date and there would be international news coverage. The whole scientific community would be represented. Taran would be proclaimed one of the true wonders of the world.

Until then, everyone was skulking around as if this was some unlawful undertaking. Secrecy had to be maintained. Centurion was getting too close as it was. Elaborate schemes were being concocted to keep the competition off balance for another six months.

Harder led the way to Taran's closest leg. A hatch in the side stood open. It was an elevator. The group entered and turned to face the crowd. As the door slid shut, a cheer went up.

The elevator moved upward. As the door on the reverse side, opened revealing their new home for the next half of a year, each crew member was wrapped up in his or her personal feelings. Dandy had butterflies just as if he were taking the field to start an important match. He noticed Candie was so excited that she was almost hyperventilating.

Beatrice was practically paralyzed with fear. Each day had gotten her further and further from her comfort zone. Her only real considerations had always been cerebral. Physical surroundings were of no particular interest. Now she was in the intestines of some mechanical insect. The physical was so dominant that the mental side of her was beginning to slip.

Ms. Bean, Beatrice's proctor, spotted the problem before anyone else became aware of it. She gave Harder a sign, stepped up beside Beatrice and firmly moved her off in the opposite direction saying, "Come along, dear. Let me show you to your library."

Harder instantly lost both Tom and Corky. They were so curious about everything in sight, they were in worlds of their own. The Project Director had to drag them back to the guided tour.

The group entered directly onto the round bridge of the ship located at the very top of the structure. Facing outward around the perimeter of the hull were a series of work stations. Each unit was huge and each counter top was loaded with instrumentation twenty feet long. Above the working surface were batteries of monitors at eye level. The commanding item in each area was a moveable, articulated chair. There were five chairs along a curved corridor, one for each crew member at their stations.

The inner side of the corridor was formed by a wall. Behind each chair was a door and between the stations was a passageway leading toward the center.

The doors entered into the private quarters for each crewman. The rooms were each laid out in a similar manner with a built-in bunk on one end, flanked by closets and drawers for clothing and personal items. On the other side of the room was a desk with a computer terminal and a strange-looking apparatus, which proved to be a hygiene booth. Everybody located their room by the personal luggage on each bed. They assumed Beatrice was in the room with the closed door.

Opposite each door to the work station was another door which led into a central commons with a lounging area and an eating arrangement. There was a table for Corky and Tom to play their incessant game of gin. Against the far wall was another elevator, access to the three other levels below. Along the elevator and the perimeter corridor were utility areas for garbage, laundry and other housekeeping chores.

They were ushered into the elevator off the commons. The second level down was devoted to an engineering repair shop in a donut-shaped area around the propulsion hardware in the center. Harder lost Tom who seemed awestricken with the facilities, an engineer's sweetest dream come true.

Harder moved them back into the elevator. On the third level, the center was still occupied by the propulsion system. The outer ring was larger due to the greater diameter of the sphere. It was filled with storage bins for all manner of parts and raw materials. The functional section really brought Corky to life. It was a work shop filled with equipment needed to reproduce any mechanical item aboard. The group watched as Corky moved around the area cooing like a dove as he touched various pieces of equipment. They had trouble prying him loose and back into the elevator.

Besides the propulsion system, the final level was devoted to two shuttle launching bays and storage areas around the perimeter. One shuttle was sleek looking and primarily a personnel carrier. The other was the pickup truck of the fleet designed to handle cargo. Both were equipped to move either in atmosphere or space. They were also the emergency escape pods.

There was too much to take in. After the brief tour, the crew was in a state of shock. Much of their information was directed toward preparing them for the nature of the project, but nothing could have adequately prepared them for such a monumental machine. TC was getting jittery thinking about their parts in this experiment. The proportions were completely out of their realm of consciousness. Dandy likened it to dealing with the national budget deficit out of his own checkbook.

Harder had sense not to push anyone but directed them back to the commons area. He went to a dispenser in the corner and asked for beverage orders. Corky jokingly asked for scotch, which of course was not in the machine. Everyone eventually settled for coffee, which proved to be about as appealing as synthetic, fat-free butter.

After everyone was seated with their coffee, Mr. Harder began a pep talk. "I have been on this project for years, but every time I walk through Taran I get goose bumps. There's a great deal of difference seeing this thing on a computer screen or on a piece of paper and then seeing it on its full scale. We knew this would seem overwhelming. That's why we're taking things a step at a time.

"Here is the plan," he went on. "For the moment picture this. You're just moving into a new apartment. Everything's strange. It'll take a little time to find everything and get the layout in mind. You'll need to know how to feed yourself and tend to your personal needs. You have to be able to find your way to your work place as you start a new job. You have to learn the ropes. You have to figure out how you fit into the scheme of things. As time goes on many things will become so commonplace they'll no longer cause any concern. Just think of it as moving to a new town and starting a new job.

"To help you get oriented, we've devised a comprehensive computer system of instruction that'll carry you step-by-step through every conceivable problem. It'll start with the basics of survival and operation of the various systems on board. It'll give you practical and theoretical information. Each station's instruction will be somewhat different, but there's enough-cross training as time goes along that everyone will be capable of handling everyone else's job.

"As you probably have already noticed, each of you has a complete work station, which contains all the equipment you'll need to carry out your specialty. In addition, the pilot's station has emergency backup systems for all functions on the ship. The internal communication system is such that from your work station you can see and talk to any other station or all at once. There are terminals all over the ship so you can maintain constant contact with everyone else, audibly or visually. Only the viewers in your quarters are not automatically activated on call.

"The next item on the agenda is that your proctors will walk each of you through living arrangements on board. You have two sets of items to learn. One is for normal gravity, which we experience now and would experience when the gravity generator is operating if you were in actual flight. You must also know how to function in case you were to fall into a null gravity state—weightless. A whole different set of rules apply, such as using a toilet or drinking coffee. Your proctors will provide you with enough information to survive the night. In the morning, at 0800, I want each of you sitting at your own work station. I'll come on one of the screens and begin giving instructions for the day's activities. Are there any questions?"

Dandy nodded toward the closed door assuming was Beatrice's room.

Mr. Harder dropped his voice somewhat to say. "We knew we'd have a special problem here, but we're prepared to handle it. Beatrice will be somewhat difficult in several areas. However, the critical importance to everyone is her mind. We have computers jammed full of information, but limited methods of accessing it. Beatrice has an amazing organizational pattern in her head that we hope she can input into the computer so that you and I can find what we need. We think that once she becomes involved in the work process she'll become so engrossed that she'll cease being a problem. Those same computers hold information she can't get elsewhere. Her self-image involves knowing all things. This is the one chance she may have to achieve that goal. We hope that it'll all come out mutually beneficial."

Harder turned on his heels heading for the exterior elevator. He tossed the parting shot over his shoulder. "Be at your work stations on time."

Chapter 7

The elevator door hissed shut. Harder was gone. They could hear the faint hum of the lift motors. Then there was silence. It was amazing how devoid of sound the craft was. There was no nearby machinery functioning. They were completely insulated from all exterior sound. Dandy thought he could hear his heartbeat.

Everyone jumped when Walter Hale scraped a shoe on the floor as he prepared to stand. He gave a nervous laugh before he launched into his phase of the indoctrination. "There are only two things that we're going to master today....how to feed yourself and personal sanitation. In the morning we'll begin your formal instruction covering all phases of life and operations aboard Taran. For the moment, please join me at the food dispenser."

TC grouped around Hale in front of a bank of machines that looked like soft drink and junk food dispensers. One was designated for beverages. Beer was not included. In fact, no alcoholic beverages were listed. The next machine was for hot foods. The third in line was cold foods.

"This will not be exactly like dining at the Ritz. The majority of what you'll be eating will be coming from stored earth foods. There's enough to last you the six months you'll be aboard, unless everyone likes one particular entrée. Then you may run out of that popular item. There's also a supply of foods especially prepared to be used during any weightless period. We can't have peas floating around getting into the works. Then there's another category of foods which are synthetic. They can be compounded on board in case of emergency. Occasionally, during a few of the exercises you'll find those are the only selections available. I'll tell you here and now, they won't be included in the list of your most favorite dishes, but they'll keep you alive and healthy. If that emergency were to arise for any prolonged period of time, Corky would become the chef in his little kitchen down below.

"You have columns A, B, and C—meat, starch, and vegetables. The vertical numbers are for the specific items. Let's punch in A-6, B-6 and C-6. That'll be hamburger, mashed potatoes with gravy, and steamed carrots."

In a few seconds, three fat packages slid onto a tray behind a clear window in the lower part of the machine. Hale raised the window to pull out the tray. Plastic utensils came with the food packets. "Your dinner is served. Be very careful. When those packages are shaped like this, they contain steam. Either wait for a bit or puncture the sack to relieve the pressure. You'll learn how to handle them so that the gravy arrives on the top of the potatoes instead of underneath. The other machines work in much the same manner.

"Now, this is a very important housekeeping function. Everything aboard is recycled in one form or another. As soon as you're finished, uneaten food and the packages it came in go down that chute, and the utensils go there. The trays go in that bin. Don't leave anything lying around, because if you lose gravity, you'll find food smeared all over everything. The solid objects can also become lethal projectiles in case of sudden acceleration. You'll be constantly reminded not to leave anything loose. You may not be leaving the ground, but the flight crew will need to learn that lesson. If you don't learn it, then we have to modify our program so they will.

"Candie, Mr. Percy will acquaint you with your quarters. This'll be our last contact because when we leave, you'll be locked in for the next six months."

Hale motioned the three men toward Dandy's room. Candie smirked at the men, waving goodbye with her fingers as she followed Wayne Percy into her quarters.

Hale was finding something quite funny. After he closed the door, he said, "Wayne's going to have to tell Candie how to use the female version of that." Hale pointed to the strange-looking apparatus that Dandy took to be the toilet. As instruction proceeded, the men found more humor in Mr. Percy's predicament.

After all the mandatory instruction had been given, Corky and Tom went to investigate their quarters. Hale and Dandy both sat down. They looked at one another for a period of time.

"What happens to you now?" said Dandy.

"Tonight I have a flight back home. It'll be good to see the family again and sleep in my own bed. I'm too much of a stick-in-the-mud type for high adventure. One side of me envies you for what you're about to do, but the other side is content to be a facilitator. I want to play with Shellee again and after she goes to bed, talk with people I've never met over my ham radio. My sense of adventure can be satisfied vicariously through you. Do well and I'll do well."

A tone sounded in the ship, the hour mark. Walter Hale stood up. He gave Dandy a handshake. "For some reason I feel like a proud parent," he said. "Clear sailing." He turned on his heel and opened the door.

As Dandy followed him into the common area, he silently vowed to do Walter proud.

Ms. Bean let herself out of Beatrice's door and closed it. Everyone was looking at her expectantly. She smiled. "Everything is all right. Beatrice is working. She will be out when she's ready."

Hale had called the elevator. He held the door open while the other proctors filed in. They turned to face forward. They waved as the door slid shut.

Chapter 8

The four members of TC stood silently for some time, lost in their own thoughts. Corky broke the mood. "I'm hungry. Who wants to see what kind of grub we've got for the next six months?"

"I'm game." Tom moved to join Corky before the dining machines.

Dandy looked questioningly at Candie.

"I think I would rather just have something to drink for the moment until I settle down," she said.

"How about trying the cappuccino?" Dandy asked. "I see it on the menu."

"Fine. I hope it's better than the regular coffee."

Dandy drew two plastic cups from the dispenser. He handed one to Candie. They tasted the brew and gave each other indifferent shrugs. Instead of sitting down, they wandered through the passageway between their quarters toward the work areas.

The pilot's station was more elaborate than the other stations They had been told that the backup to all systems was at that location. The navigator's position was about equal in size, but it had a vastly different array of equipment. The notable differences were some very large screens and what looked like a oversized printer to one side.

Dandy interrupted their contemplation. "I think the first order of business should be to get some music, anything to break this deadly silence. You're the communications officer. Do you think you can find some elevator music? Did Percy tell you how to get in touch with the outside just in case some emergency were to arise?"

"No. All he told me was to be sitting in my chair at 0800. I'd hate to screw things up before the starter's gun goes off."

Both jumped as a voice came to them from the consoles. "Don't worry. You're covered. If you want music, check the wall units in the rooms."

The only life from on the console was a little red light in the middle of the array. A closer look revealed a video lens just above the center screen. It tracked their movement as they traversed the navigator's station. They moved out of its range to the pilot area. Their movements were picked up by another camera.

"Big brother is watching," said Candie with a hint of displeasure.

Dandy led the way into his quarters. On the wall by the bed was a selector that looked like hardware right off the shelf. There were nine channels listed by letter and an off-and-on volume knob. He flipped it on and found elevator music. He didn't bother to check the other channels but began an inspection of the room, looking for a camera. The only one he found was on the face of the terminal screen. It had its own off-and-on switch. He was still a little suspicious because he didn't know whether the mike was on the same switch.

When he turned around, he found Candie grinning broadly as she inspected his toilet facility. "When we adjourned to our rooms," Dandy said. "Walter was laughing so hard he could hardly talk at the thought of Percy having to explain that thing to you. What happened?"

Candie laughed. "It was delicious. He tried to give me the tech manual, but I played dumb and made him explain the whole thing to me. I kept asking, 'Why?' He figured I was pulling his leg, but wasn't sure enough to tell me to shove it. We both had a good laugh."

Dandy checked his watch against the clock on the terminal. His said 2:00 o'clock and the other said 1400 hours. He looked at Candy. "I'm hungry now. How about you?"

"It isn't a case of not being hungry. It is a question of getting up enough courage. I've always kept on a very strict diet. I can just imagine how that's going to suffer here. Let's go see just how bad it'll be."

In the lounge, Tom and Corky were playing cards. As Dandy walked by he nodded toward the empty eating containers that had been stashed on an adjacent table.

"Oh, yeah," said Corky as he jumped up to dispose of the items in their proper containers. "Can't have any deadly missiles loose on board."

Candie faced off with the menu as if it was a mortal enemy. Finally, she punched two selections in the center column and one in the third. Three fat, hot bags dropped into a tray: beans, rice, and broccoli.

"I may survive if they haven't mixed in some horrible sauce."

Dandy selected a pork chop, potatoes and gravy, and green peas. Candie wrinkled her nose at his choices.

The food was irradiated, not frozen. That was why the machine could spit out hot meals so quickly. Even though the various dishes would win no culinary awards, the food was not all that bad. Dandy had just come out of college where the food was not anything to shout about.

The two Andies ate without much conversation. When they finished, they disposed of the debris. Dandy got a cup of coffee and Candy a cup of tea. They moved to the game table to see who was winning the gin game.

A door opened and Beatrice came out of her room. The other four watched as she made her way to a table. She had a loose-leaf notebook into which she was making notations. Without looking up she said, "I'm hungry."

The other team members looked at one another. Finally, Dandy put down his coffee. He walked over to the machines. "What do you want?"

"I don't care."

Dandy glanced at the others. "I had the pork chop, potatoes, and peas. It wasn't too bad."

"Okay," she said, without looking up from her notebook.

"Tea or coffee?"

"Tea."

Dandy punched in the order. The requested items plopped onto a tray along with the necessary implements. He carried the tray and beverage over to Beatrice's table. She moved her notebook enough to accommodate the tray. She didn't say anything.

Dandy stood there for a moment, shrugged and went back to the others. They all watched as the fat little bags lost their steam. Finally, they assumed the shape of their contents. Beatrice continued to work on the notebook. Eventually, she ripped open the bags and absently poked a little of the food into her mouth. It could have been sawdust and she wouldn't have known. She was completely unaware that she was the center of interest of the rest to the crew.

Candie excused herself, saying she wanted to arrange her nest. Dandy watched the card game resume. Before long he went to his room. His bags had been left beside his built-in bunk. He turned on the radio. The channels were tuned into a variety of commercial radio stations. He chose the lesser of the available evils.

He started putting his clothes into drawers and toiletries in the appropriate cabinets. His possessions seemed meager. He began to think of all sorts of things that would be nice to have. He hadn't brought any reading material. That was going to be a problem.

It hadn't taken him long to do all that there was to do. Now he could only sit and look at bare walls and listen to insipid music. He sat down in front of the computer on his desk. He could see his reflection in the dark screen before him and he made faces at himself in the glass. In exasperation he punched the power source. His action was rewarded with a full menu of items in alphabetical order. As he read down the list he found most of it was work oriented, but there were two items that caught his attention. The first was "communications" and the second "entertainment."

At the moment, Dandy was looking for diversion, so he punched up "entertainment." There was an extensive menu of items: TV, movies, books, games, puzzles. Under movies there were other subdivisions: classic, love stories, action, historical, biographical, humor. The listings for books were even longer. The only problem was that one had to snuggle up with a computer to read them instead of carrying a volume to the bathroom each morning.

Under "communications" he found he could call up any station on board as well as others on the ground. He moved the cursor to the title "Carson" and hit "enter" After a short pause, the screen came alive showing Candie's hand moving away from the "on" switch. She was looking at the keyboard trying to figure out what to do.

"Activate your computer and look under entertainment. The company certainly seems concerned that we don't get bored. You might even find some aerobics tapes."

Candie stuck out her tongue at him and killed the screen.

Dandy switched over to TV, where he came up with a baseball game to watch until dinner time.

Chapter 9

Dandy set his alarm beside the bed for 6:30, allowing himself enough time to figure out the new hygiene facilities, get cleaned up, eat and be at his work station at the prescribed time. What he hadn't counted on was the miserable night he had spent and how stiff he was in the morning. He could hardly walk. Plans were revised. First he needed a cup of coffee. He pulled on a pair of pants and padded out into the commons. Tom and Corky were already there. They didn't look any better than he felt. Corky took one look at him. "I think we now have a majority vote. Those beds have to go."

He repeated his story for Dandy. "I woke up in middle of the night with a whale of a backache. It was bad enough to get me out of bed to investigate. Some idiot engineer put a cross brace in the middle of the cot. Anyone heavy enough to compress the mattress enough teeter-totters all night on his hip or tail bone, depending on his sleeping habits."

Dandy arched his back trying to stretch out some of the stiffness. "Can you fix it?"

"Sure. Give me a little time and I can take care of it."

At 8:00 o'clock Dandy was at his work station. Because of the outer curve of the hull, he could look to his left to see Candie next to him and Beatrice's half-back further around the bend before the private rooms blocked his view. Tom was next door, to his right. Corky was further down the line. He could talk with either Candie or Tom, but it would be shouting distance to communicate with Beatrice or Corky directly. Of course, there were the electronics that tied everything together.

Precisely to the second the screen came on. There was Calvin Harder's smiling face. "Good morning, crew. I hope everyone slept well. We have a busy day ahead of us." Harder's gaze swung from side to side as he glanced at each monitor. The smile turned to a frown as he noted the men's expressions.

"Fire the guy who designed those beds." growled Tom.

Dandy broke in. "Corky says he can fix them. Let's get on with it."

Harder got down to business. "Please note the small green keypad to the upper right of your regular keyboard. For the moment, this is the only control you need to know about. It's your training program. When you hit the power button the program will begin. Hit it again to turn it off. You can rewind if you wish to see something again. There's also fast forward so you can return to the where you left off. You should know that the fast forward will not zip you through new material to shorten your time at the screen. The program will give you breaks and let you know when the day's work is done. There's a certain amount you'll be expected to cover each day.

"Generally, the training program gives you an overview of the major functions of the project. There are certain things everyone needs to know about operations. These duties aren't specific to any one particular job title. As time goes along, the programs begin introducing material specific to your station. When the various introductions are concluded, everyone is gradually introduced to the functions of the four other team members, so that in case of emergency, everyone'll have at least rudimentary knowledge of all the jobs aboard.

"These video training manuals will always be available at the primary work stations to refresh memories, or if necessary, to train another team member in the specific functions of the station.

"In conjunction with these training programs, you'll be expected to take care of any problem that arises. You've already come up with one such example, the beds. Fix the problem if you want to get any sleep. If at any time you find a design flaw or have a suggestion for an improvement, please enter that idea into the computer suggestion box.

"As you progress through your training programs, there'll be quizzes. They'll take the form of various simulations, which may involve anything from interplanetary flights to emergencies in the life-support systems. As time goes along and your proficiencies increase, the games'll become more sophisticated. They're designed to test both our training programs and your learning skills, initiative, and fortitude. Let me warn you here and now. Take these exercises seriously. If things get tough and you sit down, fold your arms, and say 'I don't want to play anymore,' while the ship is losing oxygen because of a simulated hull breach, you might suffocate, because the program will continue drawing off the air until the phantom hole is patched.

"By the end of the six month period, you'll have gone through simulations of all the possible scenarios that we can envision for the first interplanetary flight of Taran. Your experiences will pave the way for the first flight crew. We must get all the bugs out. There's a substantial difference between encountering problems while sitting in the middle of the New Mexico desert and being on the back side of Mars.

"Your voyage into the future is to begin now. Please power up your computers and snuggle in for the next six months. Good luck. Miss Carson, Big Brother will be watching, but not interfering."

Dandy leaned back in his flight chair to point a finger at Candie, who responded by sticking out her tongue. He then touched the power button. The screen came to life, showing him an overall shot of the control panel before him. A pleasant female voice started introducing him to the names and functions of the various pieces of equipment at his work station. Dandy could see this was going to take a long time.

By noon, he had made his way through a brief description of the instruments staring back at him. He had been at it continually. At the start, the computer voice had introduced herself as Holly. At 12:00 a bell sounded that triggered Holly, who informed him it was lunch time. He would be allowed a half hour break. The screen went black.

Dandy stood up to stretch. Candie was likewise pulling away from her console. On the other side, Tom and Corky were beginning to move about. Beatrice was still at her station with her nose in a notebook.

Dandy went into his quarters to make a relief stop and wash up. When he came out through the door into the commons, the two guys were already at the food dispenser. Candie was hanging back giving them time to make their decisions. Dandy picked up a couple of cappuccinos. He motioned Candie to the large circular table. As Tom and Corky came away from the machine, Dandy invited them to join him.

"Boy, does my computer have a sexy voice," Tom said.

"Holly?" asked Dandy.

"No, mine's named Helen."

"Mine's Heidi," said Corky.

"I've got a male. He sounds like a real hunk. I'd like to see Harold." Candie rolled her eyes skyward. She got a laugh out of everyone.

Dandy watched as the other two guys tore open their packets. "Have you found anything worth eating?"

"If I did, I sure wouldn't brag about it," said Corky. "Then everyone would work on a finite supply."

Candie and Dandy got their meals. They had just seated themselves when Beatrice came in. She sat down at one of the small tables and continued with her paper work. The others watched for a bit but shortly went back to their conversations.

Without looking up, Beatrice announced to the world in general that she was hungry. No one responded this time. A couple of minutes later she said again, "I'm hungry." When she got no service she finally looked at the other four eating at the adjoining table.

"Where is my meal?" she asked.

Dandy took in a long breath of air as he started to respond. Candie put a hand on his arm as she got to her feet. "I think this calls for a little girl talk."

Candie placed her hands on the edge of the table and leaned over toward Beatrice. In a voice that gave the impression that she was having a private conversation, but which in fact carried everywhere in the room, she said, "There is no personal service aboard this boat. You'll have to fend for yourself."

"But I don't do things like that."

"If you expect to eat, you'll do things like that. You'll also clean up after yourself. Furthermore, you'll do your own laundry, or you'll move your work station into the cargo bay."

Candie returned to her table. Beatrice's eyes followed her across the room. Her expression showed her confusion. Without even looking in the direction of the food machines, she returned to her work station and stuck her nose back into her notebooks.

The other four members of TC just looked at one another. There didn't seem to be much to say so they dumped their trash returned to their work stations.

Chapter   10

Over four months had gone by since the crew had been locked in Taran. Other than occasional bouts of loneliness or senses of social privation, the time slipped by rapidly. They were kept so busy that they had little time for any other considerations. The extraordinary computer programs took them step-by-step through all the phases of their training. What had originally been so scary become commonplace. At no time did the programs talk down to the crew. They were challenging enough to keep interest level high. The programs integrated all members into the project mission so even though they found themselves working in their various specialties, they still were aiding each other to achieve the common goal.

As each become more proficient in his task, the simulations that were presented became more complex. They were designed to tax the limits of everyone's knowledge and creative abilities. The crew was truly becoming a team. This harmony began when the individual members changed their daily routines. From the outset a watch schedule was established so someone was at his station all the time. Before long, the crew became so comfortable at their work stations, they preferred to sit there even when not on duty. With the communication links they could socialize as well as if they were sitting across the table from each other.

At meal times, they would go to the machines for the food and return to their own chairs. That way, whoever was on duty wasn't isolated from the group. This sense of community made extensive critiques of each problem a natural thing because "talking shop" became the main diversion. They would rehash the exercise or problem from a critical viewpoint. Usually they came up with viable alternatives that saved time and energy. Once a consensus was reached, the crew member closest to the problem would write a memo for the electronic suggestion box. In most cases, they found their work procedures altered to incorporate the proposed changes, which made everyone try harder to come up with better methods. It became the main game during free time.

It took some time before Beatrice got the idea that she had to tend herself. But eventually she learned to wait on herself and even do her own laundry. Finally, Dandy had to demand in a loud, authoritative voice, "Beatrice, clean up your room and work area. All of that stuff lying about are potentially lethal projectiles."

She wilted into a sobbing lump but complied. Thereafter, she did a fair job of maintaining her personal areas. She even turned on her viewing screen so she could at least follow the group discussions. When something came up that was in her direct area of expertise she could expound at length.

At first, Corky and Tom socialized together when they were off duty. Candie and Dandy sat together, and Beatrice stayed to herself. After the electronic connection was established the card games gave way to video games. When Tom would win, he might be challenged by Candie. No one could beat Beatrice at any of the cerebral games. The crew had an inexhaustible supply of electronic diversions.

The competition between Dandy and Candie had dropped off to an occasional good-natured skirmish. In their work, there was enough of a difference that they didn't have to challenge each other.

Tom was in his element. He had set about redesigning everything in sight. His first project had been the work station chairs, which also functioned as launch couches. He modified each to fit its occupant like a glove. It was no wonder everyone preferred sitting there. They even slept on them occasionally.

Then Tom turned his attention to the various operating systems aboard. He got into the theories involved in the drives and power-producing systems, which were new technologies. Next, he started a systematic exploration of the hardware with the help of the instructional tapes.

Corky spent much of his time on the lower levels in his bins of materials. Nearly everything aboard was backed up with spare parts. Then there were base elements from which most anything could be made. He had supplied Tom with all the various parts that had been needed. There was no way to keep track of all the inventory without computer logging.

One of the training exercises that ranked very low on everyone's list was when the food machines shut down. Using one of the computer recipes, Corky concocted a paste-like goop from the raw material bins. It served as food for three days, keeping body and soul together, but it unraveled dispositions. The milk-like fluid that served as a drink wasn't much better. It tasted vaguely like citrus.

Corky's popularity took a substantial beating until he devised a coffee machine independent of the normal food processors. It came close enough to what they had become used to that routines reverted back to almost normal.

No one really understood what Beatrice was doing. They knew she was trying to memorize all the accumulated knowledge of mankind, but in addition to that she was working on the computer. She was taking more and more of the memory capacity. Occasionally, Calvin Harder would try to get her to download her work into the ground computers, but she would say that it was not ready and no one would be able to use it until she had completed a directory.

She helped Corky locate parts in his inventory. Everyone occasionally needed to review previous instructional tapes for specific information. Dandy would get exasperated trying to find what he needed. Then he learned Beatrice had reviewed everyone's tapes. With a brief description of the material, she could direct him to the proper tape.

Candie's head was getting so full of mathematical formulas and navigational aides she thought it was going to split open. To ease the stress, she had gotten Corky to build some exercise equipment for her on deck two. He laughingly warned her that it would only work under a gravity situation. She got lots of use out of the equipment.

It became evident to Dandy that there was a considerable difference between driving his old car around campus and driving a spaceship. None of the rules were interchangeable. It seemed as if he was going to be called upon to pat his head and rub his tummy at the same time, while somehow scratching his left ear.

Since they still had their eight legs firmly planted on the ground, everything had to be done through simulation. On the first flight program where everyone was involved, he drove like a kid out for his first driving lesson with a clutch and stick shift. He really got a razzing over that. As time went on, the flights smoothed out considerably. He relaxed enough to enjoy the games. After all he wasn't really responsible for anyone's well being, nor was he risking a horrendously expensive piece of equipment.

The crew fell into a routine just like doing a familiar job. They were involved in simulation of going to an asteroid belt to gather information for a possible mining venture. Dandy was at the controls while the rest of the crew went about their daily routines. The calm was pierced by a shrill alarm everyone recognized at a breech warning. Simultaneously, a red light came on the board indicating depressurization of the shuttle level. Dandy glanced both ways noting Corky was the only member missing from the flight deck. Dandy flipped off the alarm so he could be heard over the intercom. "Corky. If you're on deck four, get into the elevator or a shuttle." The video cameras showed nothing. Reading off a meter he passed the message along. "You've thirteen seconds before complete vacuum."

All the decks had independent air pressure systems, so the breech would not affect other areas. There was nothing anyone could do until Corky checked in. If he had been on either of the other decks, they should have heard something. The seconds marched by. At ten there was no signal. Thirteen passed. Dandy was holding his breath. Fifteen. At twenty Corky announced he was safely in the pickup. A cheer went up.

"Stay put. Tom and I will be down to get you," said Dandy. "Candy. Take over up here. We'll get Corky and the three of us will have to patch the hole."

The operation sounded simple, but it took a lot of time. The space suits were on the second level. Dandy and Tom suited up. They collected Corky's equipment, which was too bulky for one person to carry. The two lugged it down to the pickup. Dandy went through the airlock with the suit so he could help Corky. Tom inspected the hole that the computer said was a baseball sized blue spot on the wall. Under real conditions there would have been no problem in finding the leak. Debris would have been piled around it.

It took another two hours to get Corky suited and complete the repair simulation to the inner hull. It had to be done in pressure suits because the ships pumps had created a partial vacuum.

Following the exercise the crew met for a meal and a discussion of the operation.

"It was pure luck I'm still here," reported Corky. "If I'd been on the other side of the propulsion system I'd never have been able to move against the air flow to get to safety. At that particular moment I was too far from the elevator, but in line with the shuttles. If an actual meteor had pierced the hull, there probably would have been considerable interior damage producing loads of shrapnel."

"The shuttle deck is the most vulnerable to meteor damage, said Tom. "The flight deck and the next one below have triple wall construction. The third is double, but the lowest is only single wall with exterior A/G tiles which also help insulate that area. The meteor hit was in a weak band between the legs. I think that region should be redesigned to offer better protection to the shuttle deck and the A/G tiles."

"Write up your recommendations for the suggestion box," said Dandy. "Did anyone see any other problems?"

Candie was nodding her head. "There was a long wait before we knew what to do because we couldn't account for Corky. How about flipping on an intercom whenever you enter one of the lower decks. Flip it off when you leave. That might accomplish a number of things. We'd be able to tell where others were located. We'd also have an emergency system activated. If someone got a hand caught in a piece of machinery and couldn't get to a console, a shout could be heard. He might otherwise spend hours down there before he was missed. Then too we'd immediately be able to see if something went wrong on that deck. We'd be able to see things flying so we'd know where the breech was located."

The simulation was discussed from all possible angles. Beatrice observed, but she did not participate. Physical things like that weren't in her realm. Dandy noted a subtle change move through the group. This was the first exercise that had the possibility of being fatal. It was a sobering realization. The crew was trying to cope with all the possibilities. Due to physical constraints no further consideration had been give to what the meteor might have done to the outside of the ship. The simulations had been too much like video games. They were loaded with death and destruction, but they were games, so they didn't really matter. Now Dandy expected a little more serious consideration would be given future exercises.

Chapter 11

Raucous klaxon vibrations ricocheted off the steel bulkhead and beat against the inside of the TC's skulls. It was the middle of the night. Tom was at his duty station working on a crossword puzzle on the computer. The other four were asleep in their rooms. In about three seconds, the alarm had smashed the sleep from everyone. Calvin Harder's voice came crashing through the ship. "This is not a drill. Everyone to his stations."

The crew came tumbling out of bed. Their viewing screens in their rooms showed a disheveled Harder in an undershirt and boxer shorts stooping over his desk to get to the control panel. In the background, they could hear screams and popping sounds like gunfire.

He glanced over his shoulder and then back to the camera. "We are under attack." Behind him a door flew inward. One of the company guards stumbled through. He tried to raise a gun toward the hallway. A spray of bullets lifted him up before he slumped into a heap on the floor. Harder reached for the control panel and threw some switches. On Taran, screens came alive showing various views of the control center. Harder grabbed his coffee mug that was always at hand. He smashed a control unit. The screens on the console showing the Taran crew went blank.

The technician that had been on duty in the control center started to go for the dead guard's gun, but three uniformed soldiers burst into the room. Their guns covered Harder and the tech. Harder was motioned away from the control panels. The tech raised his hands above his head, but Harder just stood there trying to look authoritative in his bare feet and underwear.

Dandy took time to look around. He activated the internal viewing system so everyone could see everyone else. Each crew member was at his station. Tom was the only one dressed. Dandy was naked, Candie was wearing a pair of panties, Beatrice wore a long T-Shirt, and Corky was in briefs. All eyes were glued to the screens. Dandy glanced at his. It looked as if someone had punched the pause button. The three soldiers pointed their guns at the tech, who still had his hands over his head, and Harder, who was still standing motionless. Silence fell on the scene.

Everyone jumped, as a hulk of a man strode into the control room. He towered over the troops. There was no question who was in charge. He dominated everything by walking into the room, with the air of arrogant superiority.

Dandy glanced at his navigator. She was practically snarling. This was the type of male who could pull all of Candie's strings in the wrong directions.

Ignoring the two captives, the commanding figure walked to the center control console. His uniform was a midnight blue, contrasting severely with the warm tan of his skin and the sunbleached hair.

The officer scanned the controls. He made note of the smashed switches. "I want an open channel to the ship," he said, without looking at the prisoners."

Neither Harder nor the tech moved. The three soldiers raised their weapons. The officer intervened. "Maybe this is being recorded. When this gets into the courts, I don't want to have to explain any murders. Get the professor."

One of the soldiers ran out the door. The officer continued to inspect the facility as he waited for the professor.

"Can you sever any connections ground control would have with us?" Dandy asked Tom.

"Sure. All I have to do is pull one tray out of the console. We're plugged into some ground lines, but they don't control anything. Most of that's for communications so we don't radiate interceptable energy. Since we started this project we've been running on internal power as part of the experiment."

Nothing was happening in the control center. "Tom," Dandy said. "You watch what is going on and warn us if anything starts to happen. The rest of you get into your coveralls and secure your areas. You have three minutes. Move!"

There was a mad scramble, but in three minutes everyone was back. "We don't know what's going to happen, so everyone strap into your couches," said Dandy. He activated his station. He threw the security switches, locking all hull openings from the inside. He turned on the cameras showing the areas under and around Taran. There was nothing to see. Light was poor. The camouflage net obscured everything outside. The only source was from a single bulb over the door to the guard house. Nothing was moving. Taran had floodlights, but Dandy chose not to use them. There was a possibility that the invaders thought TC was still asleep.

The initial shock was beginning to wear off. Corky kept repeating under his breath, "What the hell is going on?"

"We have been invaded," said Candie. "Those guys aren't military, they are company troops. Does anyone recognize the uniform?" She didn't get an answer.

Then on the monitors, the crew saw a man in civilian clothes being ushered into the control center. "That must be the professor," said Tom.

"Get me a channel to the ship's crew," the officer commanded,

The professor stepped to the communication panel. He made a brief examination. "I think they're watching us now. See the red indicator lights? There are three activated cameras on us. This one above the master control panel is the principal one. At the moment, there's no definite way of telling if they're watching because those smashed switches control our view of the inside of the craft."

The officer stared at the camera lens. He walked up to the console and leaned forward until his face filled the screens in Taran. His face was a mass of keloid scars. His whole face had been reconstructed. He said, "My name is Colonel Tokla, Commander of Centurion Security Forces," he said. "We've taken control of this installation to regain our stolen technology."

Then he sneered into the screen. "Okay, kids, it is time to quit playing house and come out. I'll give you five minutes to vacate the ship or I'll call room service for a can opener and come in to get you." His remarks were terminated with a sinister laugh. The screens showing the control center went black.

"Tom, get that tray out," shouted Dandy.

Tom dove for the panel. He ripped the cover off, pulling the tray out of its housing. "Now they have to say 'please'," he said with a smile.

Does anybody have any idea what's going on?" Corky said.

"It's the industrial warfare game," said Candie. "That big bastard is the muscle that takes what they can't do on their own. The dispute will go to court, but that can be dragged out for years. Give them Taran for a few weeks and they'll have all the technology. Then they could care less what happens in court. As long as they don't pull any heinous crime nothing'll happen to them."

Dandy concentrated on his board. "Tom, I think we'd better

power up to the line. Corky, will you go over the check-list with him?"

"What are you doing? He said to come out." Beatrice was standing next to her station.

"Bea, sit down and buckle up. We don't know what we're going to be doing, but we want to be prepared for anything."

Beatrice stood there.

"What are we going to do?" asked Tom.

Dandy stopped running checks on his control panel and looked up. "As far as I see it, we have three options. We can walk out like he demands. However, I have problems with that plan. I signed on to be a loyal employee of Gal X. I don't like the idea of handing over millions and millions of dollars worth of my employer's assets to the enemy. The second alternative is to do nothing, and let them take Taran away from us. We can't fight them. That would soothe my conscience a little, but not much. The third alternative is to move Taran to a safe location. Centurion would gain a small installation in the desert with a certain amount of technology in the computers, but they wouldn't have the prize. That alternative suits me better."

"But we don't know for sure this thing'll get off the ground," Tom chimed in.

"Maybe it's time to see whether or not we've been wasting our time here. Besides, I really wouldn't relish the idea of coming under the control of our Colonel Tokla," said Candie.

Their five minutes weren't up yet when the screen from control center came on again. Tokla's image filled the monitor. He was a study of barely contained fury. "Your time is almost up. Power down and open up or we'll blow our way in," he snarled. The screen went black again.

"Interesting," said Corky. "He apparently knows we're self-sufficient, with our own power. It also seems he's aware he can't control us from the ground."

"The whole board is green," Tom reported. "ready for anything."

"What're you doing?" screamed Beatrice. "We have to get out of here. We can't risk this." She ran for the elevator. The door wouldn't open. Candie had beaten her by throwing a switch to shut down the system. Beatrice sank to the floor, sobbing over and over that she had to protect her intellect.

Candie was getting exasperated. "If you let that Tokla get his hands on you he'll be dissecting your brain by sundown trying to figure out what makes it work. Since you can't get out, you have two choices. If we leap with you sitting there, we'll have to mop that precious brain of yours off the floor. Your only other alternative is to strap yourself in. Now."

The tone of Candie's voice made an impression. Beatrice dragged herself back to her station. Her self-preservation instinct was very high. Out of view of the camera, Dandy gave his navigator a thumbs-up.

"Are we sure we want to do this?" asked Tom. "There is no reason for them to do anything to us."

"Don't forget we're witnesses to murder and grand larceny," Corky reminded them.

Dandy activated the external lights and viewer. There were troops all over the place. An equipment vehicle of some sort was being backed up to the elevator door. The bright lights blinded everyone momentarily, causing a brief suspension of activity.

The control center screen came alive again. Now the professor was seated at the control panel. Colonel Tokla was standing a few feet behind him with his feet apart and his thumbs hooked in his belt. Off to one side and behind him was Calvin Harder slumped in a swivel chair. His head was rolled to one side. His face was a vast smear of blood, obviously positioned so the crew could see him.

Beatrice screamed.

"Bastard," growled Corky.

Tokla leered at the camera. "Now do as I say before I get --."

Harder rolled his head up. He utter just one fuzzy word. "Leap." Leap was the slang word for a quick takeoff. A tarantula was one of the leaping spiders.

Tokla whirled around. His hand streaked for the gun holster on his hip.

"Go," screamed Candie.

Dandy was already reacting. His hand had been resting on the slide control that activated the anti-gravity generators. Gradual force was supposed to be applied until the desired reactive field is formed to raise the ship gently. But Dandy jammed the control forward. Instant chaos was unleashed. Suddenly, there was no gravitational force over Taran to hold anything down, including the air. Lateral air pressure came roaring in from the side, creating a horrendous vortex that sucked in everything that wasn't firmly attached.

The energy produced by the generators rammed the crew from positive gravitational weight through neutral into negative. The repulse field jammed against gravity, hurtling Taran into the air. The crew was slammed against their couches.

In the control center, a loud roar rolled in through the hall. Suddenly papers were snatched off desks heading for the door like a flight of white doves. Office equipment and chairs started for the door. The armed guard by the door disappeared into the hall. Harder, Tokla, and the professor were trying to grab something substantial. Fortunately for them, the steel door swung inward. The sucking motion caught the door, slamming it shut. This all happened in the instant before the ground cable was ripped loose by the rising vessel. The control center screens went black.

The external cameras showed men and equipment being snatched off the ground and hurled into the air until the view faded into a dust storm. The sounds of objects striking the underbelly of Taran rattled like automatic weapons fire.

For a moment Dandy couldn't move against the force. He struggled to push the control back. An image flashed through his mind of his first attempt to drive an old standard shift car. He mustered his resolve sufficiently to push the control back to a neutral position. The pressure eased as the rate of acceleration slacked off.

"Damn, you're a lousy driver," yelled Candie when she could get enough breath.

The altimeter rushed past the 5000-foot reading. The ship was still rising at an awesome rate. Dandy eased back still more until the rate of increase brought the pressure down to one and a half Gs. The crew could move again.

With the A/G generators on, natural gravity was blocked, leaving the crew weightless, as if they were in space. They were subject only to G forces. Dandy activated the artificial gravity, which was about 70% of earth force. It would be a little strange, but sufficient to keep one's coffee in the cup. The force field applied only to the areas above the hull bottom. It did not extend into the legs of Taran, which were located under the A/G pads.

Tom was reviewing his panel. "Do you realize we hit 5.26 Gs from a standing start? I don't think the designers had a leap like that in mind. All systems seem to be working,, though."

Dandy called up Corky. "Can you tell if we damaged anything?"

"No damage shows up here. However, there may be something where the land line came into the leg. I don't show any pressure leak, but that may be because of the A/G. We may be trailing a lot of umbilical cord. We may have camo netting drapped all over us. If you want to turn on the exterior lights, we can see if we have some jeep stuck in the undercarriage."

"I don't think it'd be wise to advertise our position," Dandy replied. "Can you go down into the lower decks and the legs to see if there's any visible problem? Take an oxygen mask just in case. Don't forget you'll be weightless in the legs."

A whimper came over the sound system. Dandy glanced up to

see Beatrice dabbing a bloody nose. She was still cringing on her couch. He decided to leave her alone for the time being. There were other more important things crying for attention.

*****

The control center was plunged into darkness. Five seconds later, emergency lighting came on providing a faint glow to facilitate movement. As quickly as it had come, the noise faded into silence. Tokla disentangled himself from a heap of furniture that had been sucked along with him toward the door.

Tokla came up in a towering rage. "Professor! What the hell happened?"

"I don't know, sir," came a tremulous reply from off in the shadows.

From somewhere further back in the room Harder laughed, "Hee, hee, they launched."

As Tokla tried to brush the dirt off his uniform, he demanded, "Professor. Can you download anything from the computer?"

"No. With the power failure everything will have to be rebooted. We don't have time."

Tokla knew when to fold. It was damage control time. "Let's get out of here."

*****

"We're coming up on 10,000 feet. I think I'll park her there until we decide on a few things. We should be out of range of whatever Tokla has left after we sucked everything up into the sky." Dandy grimaced at that last thought.

Candie glanced his way. "There were a lot of Tokla's men out there."

Now that the immediate emergency was over, Dandy began plotting some action. "Candie, see if you can get Gal X headquarters on the radio. We need some instructions. Tom, get on the radar. We don't want to find ourselves in the middle of some airline flight path."

Dandy keyed the shipwide intercom. "Corky, have you found any problems?"

"No, everything looks in good shape. There aren't any leaks. I can't tell if we are towing any wire or not. This weightlessness stuff is weird."

"Okay," said Dandy, "check the underside to see if any of that debris we sucked up caused any obvious problems. We'll scan outside later. Get back up here as soon as possible. We might get busy again."

When Dandy turned off the intercom, he could hear Candie talking slowly in a voice dripping with venom. "Now get this straight. Call Artis Malvane. Tell him two words. 'Taran airborne.' Do it now."

"Wait one," came the flippant reply.

Candie threw her arms in the air. "I told that smart-ass duty operator that we had an emergency with Taran. He suggested I stomp on it like he does with cockroaches. He doesn't know who we are. He knows nothing about New Mexico base. They haven't any idea about Centurion's attack."

"Yipes," shouted Tom. "We're going to have company. It looks like an Air Force flight coming our way in a big hurry. White Sands scrambled three fighters."

"How much time have we got?"

"It's just a guess, but I'd say 7 minutes."

Dandy flipped on the intercom. "Corky, get strapped in down there. We're moving again." Even as he talked, he began easing the power to the A/Gs.

Candie was scanning radio frequencies. She found the one being used by the Air Force. "They think we're a UFO. When they get into visual range, there's no telling how they're going to react."

Dandy turned up the volume on his mike. "Beatrice, Beatrice." He wasn't getting any reaction. If she wasn't strapped in, she would have been in the fetal position. "Beatrice," Dandy barked. "How high can the best jet fighter in the US Air Force fly? Open up that library of yours and give me an answer. Now."

She stirred a little, but didn't respond.

"If that brain of yours can't come up with an answer to a simple question, is it worth trying to save? Give me an answer or we run the risk of being shot out of the sky."

Corky came over the intercom. "All strapped in. Let's go."

This time Dandy moved the slide in a gentler motion. No one was slammed into their couches. The pressure grew steadily greater.

"80,000 feet," a small voice answered." It was Beatrice. She wasn't consulting the computer, but drawing the information from her memory.

"How much higher can their rockets reach?"

There was no answer.

Corky's voice came over the system. "I bet they can shoot another couple miles higher."

Beatrice said something, but it was so frail a voice Dandy couldn't make it out. "Say again?"

"Five to six miles."

Tom jumped in. "We better get a move on. At this rate we'll still be in firing range when they arrive."

"Candie, get on the radio to those jet jocks. Tell them anything to keep them from firing at us," said Dandy as he put more power to the A/Gs.

Candie punched in the frequency. "Good morning, Owl Squadron. Are you coming all this way just to see me?"

Dandy glanced at Candie's monitor. She had a distinctly impish grin as she used her most seductive voice. The extra G-force made it even sexier.

A voice came over the radio. "Jeez, Major, did you hear that?"

"Unidentified aircraft, please identify yourself," a more authoritative voice said.

"What do you mean, 'unidentified'? I know exactly who I am," She brightened. "But, who could resist such a commanding presence? I'm just a civilian, experimental craft out on a tune-up flight."

Ground control broke in. "Major, this is the OD. Escort that ship back to base."

"Yes, sir."

"Experimental aircraft, we'll escort you to the landing field at White Sands."

Candie stuck out her lower lip. "Oh, gee. I'm sorry. I can't do that. I can't go horizontally. I can only go up and down. I go up until the computer says stop, and then I go down, kind of like riding an elevator."

Tom came on. "It's working. They're easing off. Another 30 seconds and they can't touch us."

Candie continued. "Hey, guys. Don't get caught underneath me. I hate to see anyone get sucked in. If you want to see me, you'll have to come home with me. But, come to think of it, there's no room for you guys to land those things unless they can land vertically."

The fighters started executing a large circle well away from the path of Taran.

"They can't reach us now," announced Tom.

Dandy eased back on the throttle making it more comfortable for everyone. "Corky, you can come back up now."

Everyone drew a sigh of relief. Beatrice even levered her couch into sitting position. Only a few minutes ago they had been asleep.

Dandy exhaled sharply. "I'm going to park this thing in synchronous orbit until we figure out what to do. Candie, give me a plot to put us right over the home office."

Chapter 12

Candie produced the coordinates for a stationary orbit over Houston. Dandy laid in the course. To conserve fuel they would move into space using the A/Gs. Then they would try out the new hydrogen engines to propel them into the desired position. Now that they were out of reach of the military aircraft, they were in no hurry. They didn't have anywhere to go until they got orders from headquarters.

Now that Candie had some time, she turned her attention back to trying to get some intelligent response out of Houston. All she could get was, "Wait one."

Finally a message came back. "Houston to TC. Please go to channel one-four."

Candie switched to the designated channel, a secure one. An unfamiliar face come on the screen.

"My name is Byron Charn. I'm a member of the board of directors. Artis Malvane is not available at this time. For the moment, I'm the only one around here who has any specific knowledge of this mission. I was told you were airborne. What's happened?"

Candie looked at Dandy, who nodded. "Tell him."

Candie launched into a brief description. "At one o'clock we were awakened by the emergency alarm. When we got to our stations, there was a battle going on in the control center. Centurion took over the center and demanded we open up or they'd blast their way in. Calvin Harder instructed us to leap, and we did. We were standing at about 10,000 feet when the Air Force took an interest in us. We've moved to orbit altitude to keep from being shot down. We need instructions."

The face on the monitor stared at Candie. "You did well to protect the craft. I'll give you instructions as soon as a plan can be formulated. Stand by."

The screen went dark. Candie frowned. "Am I mistaken, or was that a weird response for a member of the board? The company has everything riding on this project. He didn't seem concerned. Also I got the distinct impression I wasn't telling him anything new."

Dandy could see Beatrice sitting like a lump in front of her station. "Beatrice, are you with us?"

"Yes."

"Pull up anything the computer has on Byron Charn. Tom, keep an eye on that radar. We don't want any more surprises. Monitor the military, too, so we know what they're doing. Corky, since we are no longer a deep, dark secret, use the external lights to see if there is any damage. I bet there are going to be a lot of UFO reports from the Southwest tonight."

Beatrice broke in. "There is nothing in our computer about Byron Charn except that he's listed as on the board, but I think I can still access the main computer in Houston. I've been using the ground link to download our experimental information. However, our instructional material was for doing the same thing while in flight. I have the pathways."

"Great. Dig around to see what you can find out. Keep it as quiet as possible. We don't know what's going on down there."

Dandy watched as Beatrice got back to work, looking more like herself, hunched over the keyboard.

"Hey, gang. Switch on monitor 6. Take a look at our belly," said Corky.

The camera was doing a slow pan of the underside of the ship. Great gobs of debris clung to it. Some things were recognizable, like chunks of camouflage netting, boulders, and vegetation. As the view changed, a jeep with a mounted recoilless rifle was smashed flat against the hull. All sorts of other unrecognizable shapes were tangled in the mess.

"We have had the A/Gs activated ever since the leap," Tom speculated. The air pressure sucked all that junk up. As long as we're in the atmosphere it'll stay there. But when we get into the rarefied air, this stuff'll start to drop off. However, I think we should drop it right now over the desert so we don't start giving people headaches."

"We'll have to wait until we get a little higher," said Dandy. "If we just turn off the A/Gs, we'll drop too. What we'll have to do is get almost to orbit altitude, shut off the A-G, and fire the engines. That'll push us away from the debris. A lot of it will burn up re-entering the atmosphere."

Dandy was doing his homework. "Okay, here's the routine. In a little over two minutes I'm shutting down the A/Gs. I'm going to give a five-second delay to clear the debris. Then I'll fire the engines for only eight seconds. That'll nudge us in the right direction. We don't have far to go. Since we're in no hurry, we can endure the five and a half minutes it'll take us to get there. That way we don't have to negotiate a panic stop to put us in position over Houston. Everyone secure your stations and buckle up."

The whole procedure went just as they had practiced so many times in simulation. All of Candie's figures were plugged into the computer. Dandy decided how he wanted it to happen. That information was also fed into the computer. Everything proceeded as it was programmed. Before long, they were over Houston.

Candie was waiting for some communication from the home office, but the screen remained blank. "It looks like this is going to take a while. Who wants something to drink?"

Everyone, including Candie, opted for coffee. She got five sealed cups, just in case they lost their internal gravity. No one wanted droplets of coffee drifting around the place.

Once everyone had their coffee, the atmosphere relaxed somewhat. "It looks like our vacation is over," Corky said. "Now we're going to have to go to a real job, battle traffic, bosses, girlfriends, boyfriends. The Andies can get their own names back."

Everyone laughed.

Chapter 13

Colonel Tokla was in a thunderous mood. Everything had gone wrong on the raid. He had lost most of his men and equipment. That did not particularly bother him. It was not achieving his objective that hurt. Now he was waiting in the office of the head of Centurion to explain that failure. He was intentionally being kept waiting. Hacker wanted it that way.

Hacker was Centurion's dictator. No one was sure what his real name was. He had been known as "Hacker" since he appeared out of nowhere as a fourteen-year-old computer genius. No one could keep him out of the mainframe computer at International Technical Institute. Before long he could worm his way into any computer. Eventually, he lost interest in leaving messages or viruses or just disrupting transactions. He needed to conquer.

He turned his attention to Centurion. Before long he was on the payroll. He hired himself with his own computer. Quickly, he became a department head. Anyone who objected found himself in a world of trouble from unexpected sources. Hacker started climbing the corporate ladder. His first real opponent suddenly found himself in prison on massive tax evasion charges. Another was found to be embezzling from the company. It finally got so bad that people would quit when they found themselves in Hacker's way.

The other side of the coin was that as Hacker advanced, so did the profits of the company. He could manipulate anything to get the results he wanted. Every decision made was based on logic derived from the best computer analyses. No human considerations were applied to a situation. Hacker enhanced the profits of the company like no one had ever done before. The board of directors and the stockholders were ecstatic.

Centurion had never been a benevolent organization, but with the rise of Hacker it became a malevolent, money-making machine. He moved into the top office and he seldom left it. When he slept, it was on a cot he had moved in. He still wore a T-shirt and jeans. He was usually unwashed. It really didn't matter much. No one wanted to confront him face to face. He was in contact with everyone through his computer. He didn't seek consensus, he just ordered.

To be summoned into Hacker's presence was a bad omen, as Tokla was well aware. The outer office was vacant except for a very nervous secretary. Few people passed through. Most cowered in one of the chairs that lined the walls. But Tokla stood in front of the inner door with his feet apart and his fists on his hips. He was determined not to be intimidated.

Suddenly, the doors slid into the walls on either side, startling Tokla. They were electronically controlled. The back of his neck tingled as the hair stood on end

Hacker was seated behind his terminal. He didn't look up. "Come on in, Colonel. Sit down."

Tokla moved to a position in front of the desk, but remained standing.

When Tokla didn't take a seat, Hacker turned a palm upward for a moment in a brief gesture. Then he cleared the screen of what he had been doing so he could call up something else. He scanned the screen for a moment. "You have a son, Atill, at the Citadel. Sit."

Tokla sat. He hadn't shown any reaction, but Hacker had surprised him. Atill was an illegitimate child that no one was supposed to know about.

Hacker swung around to look at him through dead, watery eyes. "You lost Taran."

"You didn't tell me it was operational."

"You should've been prepared for that possibility."

"Your computer readout didn't suggest such a scenario. It gave a 93% chance those kids would fold without resistance. The other seven percent said we'd have to blow our way in."

Tokla knew he was on thin ice. His only hope was to stalemate the computer. "You didn't have correct information. Therefore, your computer couldn't give me a true analysis. My plan followed the guidelines as laid out on the printout."

"You'll have one more chance. We have Gal X's CEO, Artis Malvane, out of communication. One of our people is supposedly talking for Malvane. He's in contact with Taran. The ship will be directed to home in on a beacon in Nebraska where it'll be ordered to land. We have a complete underground facility which used to be an ICBM silo. Now it looks like a wheat farm. You'll be waiting. If you have to, disable the craft without destroying any of the technology."

Hacker swung around to his keyboard. From where Tokla was sitting he could see his personnel file appear on the screen. "Go," Hacker said, without looking up.

Chapter 14

Taran had taken up a synchronous orbit over Houston. The crew began to relax. They were well above any conventional arms fire. Apparently the military had decided that Taran was indeed a civilian aircraft, not an enemy warship or alien invasion fleet. They would sit and wait awhile. The commercial radio and television stations were alive with speculation. All the anchor men were called in to report on the latest events. When Taran had gently elevated to orbital height without booster rocket assistance, everyone became aware that a new era of space travel had just begun.

The networks were thrashing around violently, trying to find experts who could tell the public what was happening. Beatrice was tuning into foreign broadcasts. With her knowledge of languages she was able to report that governments all over the world were trying to quell panic.

Still, there had been no instructions from Houston. Malvane was not available, according to ground control. They were advised that Mr. Charn would be back shortly with orders. They were to stand by.

Candie turned off her commercial TV pickup. "You know, I still have a funny feeling about this whole thing. Something isn't right."

Dandy put on his game face. "I think before we do anything, we'd better make sure things're what they appear to be. That Charn doesn't ring true. Beatrice, have you found out anything about him?"

"There's very little in the files about him. I was able to pick up his personnel file. I'll put it on the screen."

A standard personnel file appeared with Charn's picture and pertinent information. He was a recent addition to the board. By reading between the lines Dandy guessed that Charn had made it there because of money and contacts.

Dandy's eyes were out of focus as he stared through the screen. When he drew his attention back to the printed material before him, he momentarily saw double. It was then that he noticed two tilde marks. As he regained his binocular vision they became one at the end of Charn's name. He would have dismissed it as a typo had he not seen the same thing before.

"Beatrice, do you have my personnel file, too.?"

"Yes, I can get it."

"Will you put it on screen five?"

A moment later his file appeared. Dandy scrolled the material forward looking for the mark. There it was, right after his college roommate's name, Daniel Pugh. "Does anyone have any idea why a tilde would be after those two names?" Dandy asked the rest of the crew.

"What's a tilde?" inquired Corky.

"It's that little squiggle that goes over the letter 'n' in Spanish. It also has meaning in math. Neither use would apply here. I can't see any relationship between Charn and my college roommate." No one could offer anything, so Dandy turned his attention to other matters.

Candie was shaking her head vigorously enough to cause light to flash off her dangly earrings. "You'd think that Gal X would be burning up the airwaves with questions and instructions. No one has inquired about the condition of the ship. No concern has been shown toward our well-being. They don't even know if we sustained any damage. Are all of our systems working? Can we land if we want to? I wish we could deal with someone we know. What happened to Cal Harder?"

"Oh, oh." Beatrice sounded worried.

"What happened?" demanded Dandy.

"I asked the computer what the tilde meant. I got shifted to a security file. I tried to enter, but I was denied. It takes some sort of high clearance. I must have triggered an alarm, because my access to the main computer has been cut. I shook someone up. It wasn't an automatic shutoff. There was too long a delay. Someone did it."

Candie was beginning to get nervous. "That doesn't sound good. Why would those two names be in the same security file? And here we are, sitting in Gal X's future, and they cut off the computer access. It doesn't add up. We may need something in the computer to keep this thing in one piece."

The main screen came alive. It was Houston Control. Candie's wise-ass young man had been replaced with an older male. "Taran, go to secure channel one-eight."

Candie did as instructed. Charn came on the screen. "Taran, you're instructed to move to a synchronous orbit over 42.3 N and 101.4 E. As soon as you have sufficient light, begin your descent to a location approximately 1000 meters north of the farm structures. We'll construct a large white marker you will be able to see from a considerable altitude. The company will have a force on site to repel any unwanted visitors. As soon as all turbulence has cleared, a helicopter will pick you up. We don't want you in the middle of what could become a battle zone."

"Mr. Charn," injected Candie, "We need to speak to Mr. Mal....."

The screen went blank.

"Damn," snapped Candie. "I hate being cut off. My feeling about this whole thing is getting worse and worse. Why have us put down in a secluded area where Centurion can get to us at all? Just announce to the world Gal X has a new experimental spacecraft. Then we could land on the Capitol Mall in full view of the whole world. Centurion couldn't touch us."

Beatrice came on. "Gal X has any number of emergency landing facilities, but Nebraska isn't one of them. As far as I remember, we don't have any operations of any kind in that vicinity."

Tom was a stickler for details, "Did you notice that neither the call from the communications operator or Charn came from the control center? Before, the com center was in the background on the screen, but this time there was just a plain wall behind them. They're broadcasting from another location."

Dandy flipped on the conference switch so everyone could see the rest of the crew. "Did anyone else notice anything unusual?" He didn't get a response. "Okay, does anyone find anything suspicious in what has happened since we leaped?"

Corky led off the response. "It's been over three hours since the attack. If this project is such a big deal for Gal X, I'd, expect all sorts of defensive action to protect it. It's no longer a big secret, so why act like it still is? Where are the big cheeses? Why isn't there someone we know dealing with us? Then we wouldn't be sitting here debating orders from headquarters."

"One little item strikes me as strange. How come Charn is at Headquarters at 1:00 AM?" said Tom. "What day is this?"

Dandy had to look it up. "Monday morning."

"Surely there wasn't a board meeting late Sunday night."

"Maybe he was staying in one of the guest accommodations," offered Dandy.

"He didn't shave and throw on a fresh white shirt and tie to come charging to our rescue."

Candie was still shaking her head. "This whole thing stinks. I think we need to confirm our instructions before we do anything. Have you notice that no comment has been made that we disconnected ground control. If it were plugged in, then they could override the on board controls and do anything they wanted with the ship. Maybe whoever's out there doesn't know that much about the systems."

The screen came on again. It was Charn on the secure channel. "Taran. Taran."

"Let me take this one," Dandy said. He acknowledged the call. "Yes, Mr. Charn."

"How come you aren't moving? You don't have long before first light."

"We're trying to locate a problem that appeared as we were moving into this location. We've developed a severe vibration which is getting progressively worse. We're trying to find the source now. I'll advise you when we have something to report." Dandy broke the connection.

"Hey, gang. It's my opinion we should just stay put right here until we know more about what's going on. I don't like the idea of landing in the middle of a remote battlefield. Furthermore, I don't like the proposition that we abandon the ship upon landing. Does anyone have any objections to waiting until we can confirm our orders?"

No one offered an alternative plan.

"Okay, I'll keep stalling Charn. The rest of you turn in for awhile. In a couple of hours I'll wake Candie to keep feeding Charn lies while I get a few winks. By then we should get some things straightened out."

Chapter 15

Dandy spent the quiet time after the others had turned in trying to make sense out of what was happening. He was getting nowhere. About half an hour into his watch Charn called again. The board member was trying to hide what appeared to be extreme agitation.

Charn's voice quavered as he asked, "Taran, have you found your problem?"

"Yes. It looks like we sucked up a Centurion jeep with a recoilless rifle mounted on it. The equipment's imbedded in the underside of the ship."

"Taran, do what you can, but in any case you'll have to start moving to your destination within twenty minutes."

"That won't be possible. Our engineer says we can't move until we remove the debris." Dandy had to check a smile as Charn looked like he was ready to choke.

Charn glanced to his side as if he was consulting someone. "Why can't you move?" he demanded.

"That gun barrel has penetrated the hull. The end of it's in the couplings for the main A-G distributions unit. Any further vibration could rip those couplings apart. Then we'd drop like a rock."

Charn was turning purple. "How long will it take to clear the material away?"

"It's going to be slow work. Because of the hole, that deck is depressurized so work has to be done in suits. It looks like someone's going to have to take a space walk to cut the vehicle away, but that can't be done until it's daylight. Some of the external lights have been knocked out."

All Charn could muster was, "Stand by."

Dandy recorded the exchange and played it back. The second viewing reinforced his opinion that Charn was not working for the best interests of the company. There had been plenty of time for others more intimately connected with the project to respond to the emergency. No one in the program would do anything to endanger the ship. The crew might be considered expendable, but not the ship. As soon as a problem arose there should have been all sorts of technical help available. Engineers would be demanding video pictures. They would want ground control restored so they could run diagnostics. Everything was wrong.

Periodically, Charn would demand a status report. Dandy would say they were making headway, but he didn't get precise. Charn became more insistent that they move. Dandy changed over to Candie's station, but left his com line open so Charn could see his vacant seat, making it appear as if all hands were working on the problem. And he wouldn't have to make up tales to tell.

After two hours, Dandy quietly got Candie up. He told her what had been transpiring. "Just let Charn stew in his own juice. He can think what he wants. What we need to do is to watch out that nothing's fired in our direction, so keep scanning. I wouldn't think Centurion would have that kind of hardware available on a moment's notice, but they might. See if you can find any of their radio frequencies that'll give us information. Wake me and the rest of the crew in exactly one hour. I have something I want to try at 7:00."

That one hour of sleep did nothing but pack cotton between his ears, but he had to get moving. He had Candie set a channel on the ham radio frequency. The rest of the crew gathered around with their cups of coffee. At 7:00 o'clock Dandy broadcast, "Rimlick, Rimlick talk to the Cat."

While Dandy was waiting, he explained to the group. "My proctor, Walter Hale, is an avid ham operator. He has a speaker in his bathroom, so he can listen in while he's showering and shaving. I don't want to call attention by using his call letters so I hope he recognizes the title to a poem, 'Rimlick, the Cat'. I wrote it for his little girl, Shellee. If I can establish contact, maybe he can find out what's going on."

Every three minutes, Dandy repeated the call. He was about ready to make a fourth attempt when the speaker said "Rimlick is here."

"Yea," said Dandy. He punctuated it with a clenched fist.

"Rimlick, the Cat is up. Who is in charge?"

The answer was two carrier waves.

During the twenty-minute wait there wasn't much conversation. Everyone was consumed by their own thoughts. Too much had happened too quickly. No plans could be formulated until some solid information was available. They were in a holding pattern just like their orbit.

Finally, Hale responded. "Round cube....Protect yourself. Wait for familiar face."

Dandy responded, "Tall ball. We're in Rimlick mode."

"What's that all about?" said Corky.

"Those were just words from that poem that I wrote for Shellee. There's only one copy and my memory of it, so that makes for positive identification."

Candie was suspicious. "What's the Rimlick mode?"

"The poem's complete nonsense, contrary to reason. It deals with the unexpected. I just wanted to let him know we aren't going to do anything predictable."

Chapter 16

Dandy looked around at the rest of the crew. Everyone seemed to be waiting. "Okay everybody," Dandy finally said. "Get refills on your coffee and meet back here. We'll let Charn continue to watch a vacant seat. We have some decisions to make. Candie, you stay on the screens so we don't miss something coming in. I'll get your tea."

Five minutes later everyone regrouped around Candie's station. She was in her seat. Dandy perched on the edge of the map console. Beatrice, Tom, and Corky were seated on the floor with their backs against the bulkhead.

Tom spoke first. "Before we can do anything, there's one item of business we have to take care of. I know it was never envisioned that this situation would occur, but it has. We need to establish who's in charge. There may be decisions that have to be made by someone when there's no time to get a consensus. I recommend that Dandy be designated as captain with all the responsibilities the title entails. Candie should be second in command. I think that's the way the regular crew will be constituted, pilot is the captain and navigator is the commander. I certainly have no interest in the job. How about you, Corky?" Corky shook his head emphatically. "Beatrice, you're in a completely different mode."

All eyes shifted to Candie. She hesitated only a moment. "That's a satisfactory arrangement."

No one asked Dandy. They waited for him to take control.

Dandy was a little embarrassed. "As soon as Gal X gets moving, this thing should end. In the meantime, there are some things that should be done. I think it's reasonable to believe that Charn isn't working in our best interests. So, since he wanted us to go to Nebraska there should be some good reason for staying away. Beatrice, start checking through the computer to see if you can shed any light on that location. Tom, test all equipment to make sure everything is on line in case we need it. Corky, make a complete inventory of the critical supplies we have on hand. I want to know of any deficiencies. With full capacity, we can stay aloft for months if we need to, but the lack of one item could bring us down. Beatrice, what would be the logical thing for us to do?" asked Dandy.

"To hang here until headquarters gives us landing instructions. It'll probably be at one of the company's larger bases where they have a lot a manpower and equipment to protect us."

"I don't think we can afford to be logical," Dandy said. "I'm in favor of a moving orbit. Most orbits go west to east, so let try south to north. I'd like to get a little further away from Nebraska and not be a sitting duck. Also, every time we're on the far side of the earth from here I want a random length burn to put us either in higher or lower orbit or to change our angle. That'll make tracking us difficult and aiming at us even more so. And I want to do some actual testing on this propulsion equipment in case we need it. Since we aren't headed anywhere in particular until we get satisfactory instructions, we might as well go sightseeing. Let's get things moving, then we can go back on shift so we can get some sleep. Does anyone have any objections to this approach or an suggestions?"

After a pause, Corky stood up and stretched. "That sounds better than waiting around here for that big, ugly bastard to try something again."

"If you'll get your butt off my desk, I will lay out an initial flight plan," said Candie with a grin.

Beatrice was the only one who looked doubtful.

Dandy knelt down beside her. "Come on, Beatrice. We need something else from you. We have to find out all we can about Centurion, that Colonel Tokla, and whoever is making the decisions at Centurion. I've heard rumors about some joker they call the Hacker. We need to know what we are up against."

Beatrice got to her feet. Dandy could tell that all she wanted was to get out of this tin tub, but she headed back to her computer where things wouldn't be quite as scary.

Dandy went back to his position. He turned off the camera so the ground couldn't see him. He left the channel open to hear what would happen next. Charn was no longer harassing him, but neither was anyone else.

Candie was entering course coordinates into the computer. "This'll get us going in the right direction. From here, we can vary speed, altitude, and direction by using maneuvering jets."

Dandy took over. "Okay, everybody. Secure your areas and strap yourselves in. We'll have a 90 second firing of the main engines at 20% capacity. There's no sense in making ourselves too uncomfortable. I'll start a 20 second countdown in one minute." With the maneuvering jets he rolled the craft over into the proper attitude. His board was green. As he started the countdown, he had no hold requests from anyone. The engines fired properly and they were off. Even at low power, the thrust slammed them into their couches.

When the engines shut down, Dandy turned up the artificial gravity and they turned to their assigned tasks. It was good to have something to do to take up the slack in one's mind. In 45 minutes he would goose Taran into another orbital configuration. He was going to avoid a discernible pattern.

When they were over Asia, Dandy fired a maneuvering jet to push them little further to the west to alter the orbit so they would pass over the east coast of the United States. He was still leery about Nebraska. A few minutes later, his fears were confirmed when Beatrice reported that the coordinate they had been give was the site of an old ICBM silo, supposedly controlled by Centurion. There was no information to determine whether there was an operational missile in the hole.

Dandy flipped the conference switch. "I suppose you all heard the word about Nebraska. Now we can be pretty sure about Mr. Charn. How are the rest of you coming on your work?"

"All systems seem to be functioning properly," Tom reported. "The boards are green, with only an occasional minor warning. We must still be under warranty. However, there are a lot of things that have never actually been fired up. We've simulated them, but the wheels have never turned."

"Maybe we won't have to test them," said Dandy. He turned his attention to Corky. "How are the stores?"

"We're in good shape for a little over a month. When they provisioned the ship, they were figuring five people for six months. We have enough prepared eatables for the full period, plus a little. Then we'll be squeezing toothpaste. We can manufacture that stuff for months, if you could stand to eat it for months. Problem'll be with air and water. They only loaded enough for our tour of duty. Water is the most important because we can crack it to get oxygen when we produce hydrogen for fuel. If we do any extensive traveling. we'll quickly run out of fuel." Our life support systems are generated by hydrogen, too."

"We have no immediate problems, right?" asked Dandy. He elicited the affirmative answer from Corky that he wanted.

"Okay, Beatrice, what about Centurion?"

"You were right. The head of Centurion is some young guy called 'Hacker.' He appeared on the scene about four years ago. It took him two years to eliminate everyone above him. He's a computer genius. He can come up with scenarios so fast he's always ahead of the game. He has no more compassion than the machines he uses. Nothing stands in his way of advancing Centurion. His main enforcement arm is Colonel Zan Tokla, an ex-soldier of fortune, who was badly disfigured in some sort of accident. Hacker had Tokla's face rebuilt. Then Hacker made him the head of the company armed forces. Tokla is the personification of evil, with a calculating mind that makes him extremely dangerous." Beatrice's voice began to trail off as she reached the end of her report and had time to think about the ramifications of what she had said.

Chapter 17

Hacker sat at his desk eating Chinese take-out from a paper carton with pull apart chopsticks. Usually, this was one of his few enjoyments, but now he was eating to keep himself going. He was hardly aware of what he was shoveling into his mouth. Nothing was going right. They should have taken Taran in that surprise night attack, but there had been two miscalculations. The first one was that available information had not indicated that Taran was operational. The real crew was still in some sort of training. Indications had been that Gal X was still researching certain systems that would not be installed until this six-month "habitat" experiment was concluded.

The second miscalculation was that the crew would actually lift off, even if they had the capability. That crew was composed of three college kids, a handyman, and a fix-it engineer. The only spectacular thing in the whole group was that Bell girl's brain. But her brain didn't function under any hazardous situation. She knew that brain had to be protected.

Grudgingly, Hacker had to admit, at least to himself, that Tokla had been correct. The problem had been in the information, not the actual raid. According to the scenario, the raid should have been a success.

The second attempt to get Taran had just been an improvisation. Tokla had been successful in severing communications between the desert station and headquarters. Likewise, Centurion techs had been able to isolate the Gal X bosses from the world so that they just slept through everything. Gal X had helped considerably by keeping such a tight lid on the project that few people knew anything about it, especially those on night duty.

Centurion had paid dearly to get Byron Charn onto the Gal X board. He had been one of the best sources of information in recent months. Hacker had put him on standby during the raid in case some assistance was needed inside Gal X. Fortunately, when the raid failed and Taran had radioed in, the night communications duty officer had known nothing about the project, giving Charn the chance to step in to take control. Because of his position as a board member, he had been able to clamp a security net over communications, but it could only last until the shift change in the morning.

It would all have been over by now if it hadn't been for the damage the crew had reported. If Taran had moved to the Nebraska site, it would have either set down or it could have been blown out of the sky by that ICBM.

Hacker set the carton down and wiped his hands on his grimy T-shirt before he turned to his computer. It was time to clean up some messes. Charn had to be extracted. He was now a liability and he had to be eliminated before Gal X got their hands on him. Since Centurion couldn't take possession of Taran it would have to be eliminated too. Centurion would eventually be able to gather the technical information to build one of its own. Gal X was too far in debt to build a second ship. To stay afloat, they would have to sell technology.

There were other messes that had to be cleaned up. The fiasco in the desert would take some doing. Normally, it could have been swept up quickly by picking up Centurion's own debris and denying any involvement. It could be dragged out in court for decades. But when Taran took off, it scattered Centurion bodies and equipment—evidence—all over that part of New Mexico.

Hacker glanced at the clock on the computer. He had a little less than an hour at best to get Charn out before the shift change. He probably didn't have that long, because the news services were starting to report on the various sightings over the desert. Certainly, anyone from the inner circle of Gal X would make the connection immediately. His fingers flew over the keys, issuing order to various departments and operatives. This was the way he preferred to conduct business.

Chapter 18

Everyone seemed relieved to be moving instead of sitting and waiting. Each was at his assigned task when the page signal sounded. Dandy hesitated before answering. It was probably Charn, who would demand to know the reason for their movement contrary to orders. Dandy decided to confront him directly, asking for confirmation of his authority.

However, the face that appeared on the screen was that of Wayne Percy, Candie's proctor. He was badly in need of a shave. He had just gotten out of bed from the looks of his hair. Dandy was not sending an image, so Wayne just continued to look at a blank screen. "They should be receiving you." The voice came from off screen.

"TC, are you receiving me? TC, please acknowledge. We now control the communication center, but we need to know what is going on. We know you are up and now moving. We can not establish contact with your former home. Tell us what happened so we can take appropriate action."

The whole crew was watching. Dandy threw a switch, smiled at Wayne and said "Good morning."

Relief was written all over Wayne's face. "Is everyone all right?"

"Sure. We're all fine, except we didn't get much sleep last night."

Candie came online. "Good morning, Wayne." She smiled at him. He broke into a broad grin.

Dandy got down to business. "Wayne, we're still suspicious of everything. First tell us why you're the one calling us."

"I happened to be staying in the guest accommodations. A few minutes ago I received a call from Walt. He told me he'd received a message that you were up and wanted to know who is in charge. Walt tried to call Malvane, but couldn't get a call through. He called the communication center and was told that there was a security exercise in progress. He'd have to call back in after 8:00. That is when he called me. I called security who knew nothing about any exercise so I picked up an armed detail and we found communications under the control of Byron Charn and some guy we suspect works for Centurion. We have both in custody now. That's all we know except that you'll be hitting all the morning news programs. They know you belong to us. The switchboard is jammed. Talk to me, but be careful what you say. This is supposed to be a secure channel, but we don't know anything for sure."

Dandy nodded to Candie, who began a brief narrative of the events as they knew them. When she was finished, Wayne said he wanted the crew to continue to do as they were doing until further notice. He would be back with them as soon as the picture became clear. Wayne stood up and a young man slid into the vacated chair.

"This is Hal," Wayne said. "You can communicate through him. Each operator will be introduced to you personally so you'll know you are talking to the right person."

Dandy went about entering into the computer the various altitude and course changes which would greatly reduce the predictability of their position. He also added another variable. Instead of moving every 45 minutes he varied the timing too. All this would be done automatically by the computer. A warning would sound two minutes before the event so everyone could be prepared for the slight disturbances that would result.

Once that was done, Dandy announced that it was his turn to get some sleep. He told Candie to work up a duty roster so they could get back on a schedule. He left instructions to be awakened if anything happened.

Chapter 19

Dandy woke up on his own. He was not completely rested, but he felt much more human than he did when he had crawled into bed. He was ravenous and spent as little time as possible making himself presentable. His first destination was the drink dispenser for a cup of coffee. En route, he noted Tom, Corky, and Beatrice's stations were unoccupied. Candie was leaning back watching a network noon newscast on TV.

"Can I get you something?" Dandy asked her.

"No, I feel like a sponge now. I was getting ready to call you. Hal said that Malvane would be in at 12:30 to talk with us. I wanted to bring you up to date before then."

"I'm starved, so let me pick up something to eat and then you can fill me in. "

He brought back a packet of wieners and beans and another of scalloped potatoes. Candie rolled her eyes. He was beyond help. As he ate, Candie talked.

"Since there wasn't much going on, I put the rest down shortly after you to start us back on our old rotation with Tom starting out. When Malvane comes on, we all should hear what he has to say. Hal's been with us all the time. Walter checked in a couple of hours ago to say we were doing splendidly and to continue our random maneuvers. We're worldwide news. It's funny. The only video footage they have of us is a speck in the sky when you turned on the lights to inspect for damage. There's been a steady string of experts on each channel describing who we are, what we are, and how we got here. Nobody is close." Candie snickered.

She checked the clock, then keyed the intercom. "Everybody up. In ten minutes the CEO is going to talk to us. This is for everyone, so move it."

At precisely 12:30 Hal moved out of his chair and Artis Malvane slid in. Dandy flipped on all five monitors so he could see each of the crew members on their separate screens. Malvane acknowledged them with a nod.

He smiled. "Congratulations, TC, on a magnificent performance. You've been a step ahead of a very competent adversary. You have no idea of what you've accomplished. Be assured, you and Gal X are inexorably bound together. Thank you.

"Let me explain what's been happening. Security's a major problem, so whatever is said should considered public knowledge. At the moment, we have no idea how deeply we've been infiltrated. Last night, prior to the raid, my home was surrounded with an energy field so that no communications could get through. I had no idea anything was going on. It appears that a similar energy field was established around New Mexico because no information concerning the attack came from that source. Since you were on a direct cable link with the command center, you maintained communication. Part of the problem was of our own making. Your project was so secret that few in the organization were aware of it. When you called the central communication center, you were thought to be a hoax.

"When things went wrong with the raid, apparently designed to take control of Taran, they improvised with Byron Charn, a

Centurion mole. Fortunately, you avoided that trap.

"By the time we got a team to New Mexico, many of our people were dead. There's nothing left on the surface because of your leap. We're finding some evidence of Centurion involvement scattered around the landscape. We're trying to get a local criminal investigation, but it seems all enforcement agents have disappeared. We don't know if this is a permanent condition.

"Even before we figured out what happened, Centurion attorneys were busy filing law suits claiming industrial espionage, patent infringements, and a whole host of other charges. They're claiming Taran is actually theirs. They demand its return to them or a minimum that the vessel be impounded pending the outcome of this litigation, which could go on for years. They know we'd be hard pressed to build a second vessel. We believe they think they can buy or steal enough technology to build their own while our ship is impounded.

"There is another problem which seems to be developing very quickly. You, Taran, seem to be a plum just ripe for the plucking by anyone that has the capability of doing so, including any number of international corporations or foreign governments. If they can get their hands on you, then they can steal enough technology to make themselves wealthy.

"Earlier, I mentioned company infiltrations. It's apparently much more extensive than we'd ever imagined. Centurion appears to have information from many different sources, which tends to indicate security breeches on a variety of levels. We're now running checks on everyone in the company and all those who deal with us.

"Under the circumstances, you're going to have to stay aloft until the situation stabilizes. You are not to take orders from anyone you don't recognize. I'll be the primary giver, but in case I'm not available, listen only to someone you can check on through your personal knowledge.

"You're going to have to be vigilant because everyone is gunning for you. Most would like to capture you, but shooting you down would satisfy others. You're doing fine without any instructions from here. If I were to tell you to do something, then someone else could be there waiting to ambush you . Continue Rimlick mode in everything you do.

"Do you have any problems we can talk about? Or any questions I might be able to answer, keeping in mind our communication situation? For all I know, we might be going out live over the midday news. We hope to have a solution to that problem shortly."

Dandy sat up. "Sir."

"Yes, Mr. Dawson?"

Dandy stood up at attention. "Sir, do we now qualify for flight pay?"

Corky got it first and guffawed. Malvane was a beat behind, but not far. A grin spread across his face. His expression reflected his growing admiration for the kid who could take command of a difficult situation. The tension evaporated.

"I think that can be arranged, providing you can bring your craft home safely."

The CEO continued in a lighter manner "This station will be manned constantly. All personnel changes will be specifically introduced to you. Remember the whole world is growing teeth. Take care of yourselves."

Malvane stood up and Hal slid into the chair.

Chapter 20

Hacker was gobbling Chinese take-out with one hand and pounding his computer keyboard with the other. He had been at it for hours. Empty cartons were strewn all over the place.

The CEO of Centurion had been trying to break the "Rimlick" mode. So far, all his attempts had failed, and failure was intolerable. There should always be a sequence of scenarios ready to implement in logical order to achieve a desired result. If one didn't succeed, then the next should take into account all of those variables that had flawed the preceding plan, and success was inevitable.

But something had gone wrong. Taran was still not his. Twice, reference had been made to "Rimlick." The first was the kid telling Wayne Percy that he was in the "Rimlick" mode. The second reference was Malvane telling the crew to continue in that mode.

Hacker had searched all the Gal X files he had stolen over the years for reference to it. He hadn't found anything. His computer was working overtime trying to break the acronym down into recognizable words. Since he was working from an audio source, he had tried all variant spellings in all known languages. None of these approaches had produced any results. So he was analyzing the actions of the craft to try to determine a pattern that would make it possible to predict something. Even with the full mainframe working, nothing had evolved.

Now that Gal X had been alerted, more and more of his sources were being cut off. Security was at a high level at Gal X, and he had already lost several spies. None of the others could get close to the internal workings because all the functions concerning Taran were in the hands of a select few.

Unless he could break the "Rimlick" thing, he would have to concentrate on two other fronts. First, he would have to keep Taran out of the hands of Gal X. The second phase would be to steal or buy the technical information on the new systems. With the heightened security, stealing would become more difficult, so emphasis would have to be on buying.

The computer screen was crammed with data, but no patterns were developing. He threw the remains of the chow mien carton across the room and belched.

Chapter 21

After Malvane left the com center, the Taran crew gathered their thoughts.

"It looks like it's up to us to save our own asses," said Candie.

"That isn't what I wanted to hear. What are we going to do?" Beatrice responded.

Dandy jumped in before she could panic. "What we're going to do depends on what you tell us. Right now we need to know who has the capacity harm us. Have a quick conversation with Hugh. We have to find out if we're the safest doing what we're doing, or if we should do something else. Which countries, companies, or consortiums have space capability? Who has a weapon capable of getting to us?"

"I'll find out what we have, but our on-board computers don't carry that much current data. I wish we could link up with the mainframe."

Dandy turned his palms up and shrugged his shoulders. "Don't we all, but until we're sure of having a secure link the company isn't going to expose all its knowledge to the world."

Beatrice immersed herself in the question at hand.

Dandy turned his attention to Tom. "Will you get together with Corky to come up with some projections as to how long various stores will last under a variety of scenarios? Where are we critical?"

He had three working and turned his attention to Candie. "Keep an eye open for any unannounced visitors. Are you ready for that cup of tea now?"

Dandy left his station for the beverage machine. With coffee and tea he returned to Candie's station and gave her a sign to cut the intercom. He handed Candie the cup as he perched on the edge of her map table. Between the distance and the hum of the machinery, they could have a conversation without being overheard. "I was thinking that it might not be a bad idea to have on hand a course plotted to the moon. It's the closest hiding spot available to us if things get hot here. Can you work something out that'll get us going in the right direction and a course correction we can use later?"

Candie furrowed her brow, but then she smiled. "With all of these Rimlick moves, the most I can do is give an approximate course, but we could be underway at a moment's notice. Adjustments would have to be made, but that's no problem. Is this a secret?"

"No, not really. But Bea has enough to worry about right now. Besides it is only a thought. Something to keep you busy so you won't fall to pieces on us."

Candie snorted. "I do like your idea. Things could get interesting around here."

It took Tom and Corky only a few minutes to come up with the information Dandy wanted. All of the figures were in the computer. It was a matter of correlating them with the consumption requirements under different conditions.

Dandy set everyone up for a conference. "What did you find?"

Tom began to go through the readouts. "Corky already told you about the prepared food. When that runs out we have enough raw materials to last a couple of years. We won't gain any weight, but it'll keep us healthy. If we stay in orbit without too much fuel consumption and we recycle everything, we have oxygen for six to eight months. If we use our water supply as an oxygen source, that gives us another twelve months. Water's our critical supply. We're down to 17% capacity because the vessel wasn't topped off for our mission. If we power up the main engines we'll have to tap into the water supply to produce hydrogen. Our free hydrogen supply is only 10% capacity. Any sustained usage will deplete it. Then we'll be converting water. There are too many variables to give an exact figures. Basically, we're in good shape if we continue what we're doing, but if we have to go anywhere, we'll be watching the gas tank."

Before getting into any discussion, Dandy turned to Beatrice. "What did you find out?"

"From the information we have at hand, there are seven countries who have their own proven space programs. However, twelve more belong to consortiums believed to be able to put a ship into space. The big question revolves around the companies. There are at least ten that might be working on their own programs. Everyone knew Gal X could put rockets up, but Taran was a secret. There may be hosts of others with similar programs.

"As far as I can find, there aren't any specific ship-to-ship space weapons. If they exist, no one is talking about them. However, any vessel can be equipped with conventional aircraft armament that could shoot us down.

"There are numerous surface launched weapons that can get to us. Most of them are rockets developed for intercontinental ballistic interception. For years, experiments have been conducted to develop ray type weapons, but no one has admitted to any successes. Of course, that information probably wouldn't be in our computers."

"Great," said Dandy disgustedly.

"Heads up," shouted Candie. "Something's happening."

Taran skewed sideways. Alarms started sounding.

"Hull breech," Tom yelled..

"We're being shot at," Candie yelled.

Dandy's hand was already on the engine throttle. "Buckle up." He gradually increased the thrust while the others secured themselves. He ran the pressure up to three Gs.

After 10 seconds he eased back to make breathing and talking easier. "What's happening?"

Candie's voice was tense. "My monitor showed an energy pulse coming from either North Africa or the southern edge of the Med. The first one I saw must have missed. The second scored a hit. There was a third, but we were moving by that time. It looked like it wasn't aimed at us, but at where we were."

Tom turned off the alarms.

"Uh-oh." It was Corky. "I'm reading a substantial water loss from the number three tank. We must have a leak, a big one. I've shut down the system so we won't drain off any more than what's in that one tank."

Dandy started issuing orders. "Candie. Let me know as soon as we're out of sight of North Africa. I want to find a safe place to park this bus. Tom, get on the external viewers. See what you can find. Corky, when we stop, I want you to go down to that tank to find out what kind of damage we've sustained. Be careful. Watch out for depressurized areas."

"I've found a parking space for you." Candie said. "It is on the far side of Antarctica. I've plugged it into the computer. We'll decelerate starting in two minutes and we'll be on station in seven. It'll be an abrupt stop, so everybody hang on."

The maneuvering jets turned Taran 180 degrees so that the main engine became a retrorocket. Even with being gentle as possible, the deceleration was a jolt to the human system.

Dandy was busy getting everything straightened out to establish a geosynchronous orbit. "What tipped you off?" he asked Candie as he maneuvered

"I was watching the screen and a streak of light seemed to stab at us. The first one was near but didn't hit. I didn't realize what it was. The second flash did the damage. There was a third, but it was behind us."

"I bet we left a hell of an ice cloud behind us. They probably shot at that," Tom said.

Dandy parked Taran and turned to Tom. "Can you see anything yet?"

"I know where it is but I have to maneuver a camera into position to be able to see it. I'm using the portable on a tether. Look at screen five. There it is, a nice, neat hole near the edge on the lower part of leg three. Whatever it was, hit at an angle because the hole is elliptical. It looks like it's about 6 inches wide and a foot long. I bet there is an exit hole, too."

Tom had the full attention of the crew as he guided the camera around to the other side. Sure enough, there was a duplicate hole.

"Since this is a double hull construction, there are four holes to be patched. There's also insulation to replace if we are going to do anything about it."

Corky stepped out of the elevator. "Everything is in working order down below but we apparently have a hole in tank three. I can't go in unless I have a suit on because it's a void. As far as I can see, there isn't any debris in the tank. That tank held 25% of our water supply. We've lost that much plus a little more that might have been drained before I was able to close the valves. The tanks were interconnected to maintain weight balance. There's a tank in each of the odd numbered legs."

Dandy directed his question to Corky. "Can we fix it?"

"Oh, sure. We have all the materials we need and the tools to do the job. No problem there. We just need people to do it."

Dandy watched the crew closely. "We don't have a choice. We don't know whether the weapon is mounted so we can avoid it by staying away, or whether it's portable so it can be set up anywhere to waylay us. We may have to do some power flying, which requires a lot of hydrogen. Corky, can we take on water from a natural source on earth?"

"Sure. Fresh water is best. It'd take some time to fill those tanks with our pumping system. We carry a hell of a lot of that stuff."

"Okay, this is what I have in mind," Dandy said. "We patch the holes. Once we get them plugged up we start moving as if we're in a decaying orbit that'll drop us at some predictable location. At the right time, we veer off to some secluded watering hole where we'll fill our tanks. While we're at it we'll take on all the oxygen we can get as well. I wish there'd be a food service nearby....but we can't have everything. When we're loaded, we'll go hide behind the moon where they can't shoot at us. That is, if Candie can plot a course that'll get us there."

"Oh, we can't go to the moon," whimpered Beatrice.

"Why not?" asked Dandy. "It's not different than circling the earth. Besides it'd be a heck of a lot safer. We've been hit once. The next time their aim may be better."

"I'd rather do that than sit here," Tom said.

"I'm game," said Corky.

Beatrice looked around at the group and nodded slightly.

Chapter 22

Dandy started to get things organized. "Corky, cut pieces of durathane large enough to cover the holes. Candie and I'll do the outside work. We'll be able to carry the metal in a non- gravity environment. You and Tom'll be working the inside of the tank. When we get into position, you pass the welding torch through the hole. We'll need at least two gas tanks. While we're working the entry hole, which appears to be clean, check the exit hole for any jagged edges. From the inside, you should be able to grind away any snags. If you can't, pass the grinder through for us to clean the edge.

"Once the outside is sealed, you'll have to spray the insulation material in. Then it's your job to patch the interior of the tank. By the time we get back in, we should be close to getting underway."

"How do you intend to get to the damage?" Tom said.

"Exit the shuttle bay on the underside. Then we can work our way down leg three and over to the top."

"There may be an easier way," offered Tom. "Each water tank

has an external clean-out hatch. I'll have to check the measurements, but I think you can get out wearing your life support systems. That would put you within 20 feet of the damage."

"Sounds great. Check it out. I hope everyone paid attention to the lessons on weightlessness."

Dandy left his station to talk to Beatrice. She was just sitting there with her hands in her lap.

"Beatrice, while we're outside you're going to be our eyes and ears. I want you to monitor everything and alert us to any hazards. We'll be in communication at all times, so don't hesitate to draw our attention to anything that might have meaning.

"I have a second job for you as well. I want you to search your files for a location for us to put down. I want it as secluded as possible. That means far away from any potential hazard, like guns, rockets, and airplanes. Besides privacy, we need as pure an air and water supply as possible. Find us a nice spot for a picnic."

Dandy glanced at the screen and Hal patiently sitting in front of the monitoring camera as if nothing had happened. "If someone inquires about what happened, just show yourself on the screen and tell Malvane or whoever it is to stand by. Then shut off your transmission. Do the same thing each half hour if they keep insisting."

Tom confirmed that they could exit through the clean-out hatch. Corky reported he had the patches and equipment ready. Dandy turned the bridge over to Beatrice. The rest assembled in the changing room to get their suits on.

Even under the influences of 70% gravity, the heavy, bulky space suits were hard to maneuver. The repairmen labored their way to the fourth deck. When they dropped through the upper portal of the water tank, they passed beyond the artificial gravity system and were weightless. At Tom's suggestion, everyone took time to get familiar with the sensation.

The inside of the tank was polished stainless steel. Corky was going to have to do a special welding job. Light from the working lamps bounced off all the surfaces brilliantly. The tank was enormous. Gradually, they made their way to the damage site. There were two holes the size Tom had estimated. Whatever it was, had shot through the ship cleanly. That would make their job a little easier.

Tom opened the cleaning hatch. They looked out into the vacancy of space. They had all seen it through their monitors or the viewing ports, but this was the first time they had confronted space without an intervening safety barrier. Little fingers of fear plucked at Dandy. It took each human some time to handle it.

"Let's get to it," Candy said.

Corky attached two tethers to the hinges of the hatch. The rest of the interior was completely smooth. Dandy snapped on a safety line, gripped the edge of the opening, and pulled himself into the void. He paid strict attention to what he was doing, not where he was. His tool bag was passed through and he attached it to his harness.

Candie came through the hatch. She anchored her magnetic shoes to the exterior skin of Taran and did a slow turn, taking in all the sights. Upon completing her inspection, she reached inside to collect a packet of two durathane patches. Taran had been positioned so they would be working in the shadow and Dandy would be able to see the flame of the welding equipment.

The pair began moving toward the damaged area. Without the magnetic devices, they would not have been able to make much headway. The skin was smooth and featureless. It was slow going. Dandy was glad Tom had found a shorter route than from the shuttle bay.

When they reached the damaged area, Dandy tried to kneel down to get within working distance. When he bent at the knees the rigid soles of his shoes came off the plating, breaking his magnetic contact. His suit was too bulky to permit him to bend at the waist. He tried holding onto Candie for stability, but he needed both hands for the task. Candie tried holding him in place, but he was unsteady.

Nothing was working. Dandy was ready to go back inside to get more equipment. "Wait," said Candie. "Hold onto my leg and get down on your knees in your working position."

Using Candie as an anchor, he got into position. She stepped over him, clamping his hips between her calves. He was firmly in position with his hands free. Once he could work, it didn't take long. Durathane needed more heat that most common metals to fuse. To achieve the desired temperatures, a paste composed of powdered durathane and a flammable chemical were combined in a tube. It was like squeezing toothpaste. The compound served as an adhesive to hold the patch in position. Then a bead was laid down around the edge. Candie handed him a torch and he fired it up. When the blue flame touched the paste it fused everything together.

They repeated the process and the second patch went quickly. Then they made their way back to the hatch. Candie went in first. Dandy looked around at his surroundings. The little fingers were gone. They were replaced with an exhilaration like he had never before experienced. The simulation period in Taran had been a great experience. The last few hours had been so busy he had not thought beyond the immediate crisis. However, seeing Earth framed by the arch of Taran's legs, he suddenly realized he was directly in the middle of one of the greatest adventures of mankind. A tug on his safety line brought him back to the moment.

Tom helped them in and secured the hatch. Corky was trying to get insulation into the area between the hulls, but he couldn't get the equipment to work. The material was a two part chemical. Its thermal efficiency was extremely high, but in the cold of space, the chemical thickened and wouldn't flow.

Dandy watched the futile efforts. "We need to heat that stuff up," he decided. "I'll go back inside. As soon as I'm in, open the clean-out hatch. I will turn the ship to the sun. Put the foam equipment in the light. It shouldn't take long to warm things up. It would take longer bringing it to temperature if we took it back inside. When you get the foam in, close the hatch. Then we can pressurize the tank and you can work without suits. While you're putting on the interior patches, I'll put us into that decaying orbit."

Dandy and Candie went back inside and quickly removed their suits. Dandy turned the ship so that the legs faced the sun, while Candie conferred with Beatrice. Hal was still sitting at his desk working crossword puzzles.

Candie and Beatrice brought their tea over to Dandy's station. Candie handed him a cup of coffee. "I think Beatrice is a genius. She came up with a beautiful picnic spot for us. Tell him."

Beatrice beamed at the compliment. "Lake Baikal,"

"Baikal, why Baikal?"

"You wanted something remote. This is very remote. It's in mountainous terrain where you can hide better than on a plain. It's vast—over 13,000 square miles and up to 5000 feet deep. It's one of the least polluted, major freshwater bodies left on the earth. There are no large population centers or military installations nearby. For any other country or corporation to get there, they would have to deal with either Russia or one of her former republics."

"It's sounding better all the time." He turned to Candie. "Lay in a course so that it looks like we're in a decaying orbit, headed down. Keep us away from North Africa, and after about three orbits we want to make an abrupt change to Baikal. Call up computer maps and aerial photos of the area so we can pick a nice secluded picnic spot."

Dandy called to Tom and Corky. "How are things going?"

"We have one patch on, and the second should only take us a few minutes more, Tom reported. "We had to improvise. Our magnetic shoes won't hold to this stainless steel. We had to change to suction, which means we had to pressurize the tank."

"Let me know as soon as you're out of the tank. We will be on the move again."

The paging tone sounded. Malvane was on the monitor. Dandy switched only his camera on.

"Is there something we should know?" Malvane asked.

Dandy thought a moment. "Someone was pot shooting at us from North Africa or the south Med. They got a luckly one in. We're trying to correct the situation now. We may have to perform a Rimlick maneuver."

Chapter 24

Tom and Corky completed their work inside the tank and the patches were checked. Corky rebalanced the remaining water supply. Candie had established a decaying orbit. If the ship didn't burning up in the atmosphere, the projected landing area would be the southern Atlantic. Dandy engineered a number of jerky, zigzagged bursts of speed to make it appear like they were trying to start engines. The gyrations did not alter the projected touchdown in the Atlantic. As the ruse progressed the crew turned its attention to preparing for Lake Baikal.

Dandy asked Corky to give him a time requirement for topping off the water tanks and taking on all the oxygen they could get. He didn't like the answer he got back.

"We were never designed to take on water ourselves. That function was to be done at a filling station. We do have pumps on board that can be altered to function in that manner, but it'll be slow. I figure it'll take two hours and forty minutes of pumping plus whatever time it takes to get hoses into the water source and then retrieve them."

Dandy hadn't allowed nearly enough time in his calculations .

"That two hours forty minutes may be the short end of the equation," Corky continued. "Remember what a mess we sucked up when we took off. Even if we come down slowly we'll create one hell of a turbulence that'll muddy any nearby water source. If we come down in shallow water we'll suck up all the muck off the bottom. The water would be pretty foul."

Candie went directly to the bottom line. "I bet we won't have that kind of time even at Lake Baikal. Russia can scramble something sooner than that. We'd be sitting ducks."

Dandy began toying with his empty coffee cup. He held it upside down. As he studied the cup he said "We know Taran is airtight because we have to hold our atmosphere against the external void. It has enough strength to withstand the forces of takeoff and reentry. Its skin is designed to take small meteor impacts."

He turned his attention to Tom. "Can you tell me how deep we can go in fresh water before the pressure will collapse us?"

Tom stared back at him. "I can't recall coming across any figures at all about external stress."

"Get together with Beatrice and see if you can come up with some sort of a projection. Corky, if we opened those clean-out hatches we used to exit the ship for the external patch, how long would it take to fill our tanks?"

Corky called up his calculator and his fingers flew over the keys. He came up for air with a smile. "If we're in water deep enough to submerge the tanks it will take us about 10 minutes. If we purge the air out of the tanks prior to opening them under water, it'll only take about 7 minutes."

Dandy smiled back. "That's more like it."

Candie had been studying the maps of Lake Baikal, but she had not missed any of the conversation. "It sounds as if I'm looking for the wrong picnic spot. Instead of a quiet little cove, it'd seem we need deep water away from land. Am I right?"

"I hadn't gotten that far yet, but you're right. We need some place deep enough so we won't stir up the bottom."

Tom and Beatrice were arguing about something. The librarian was no scared milquetoast when she was in her element. Tom threw up his arms,"Okay, okay."

When he got back to his station, Tom gave his report. "It's my opinion that we can descend safely to 500 feet before we run the risk of a hull collapse. However, Bea thinks we can handle 1000 feet because of the double hull construction, materials, and contour. I'll go along with her estimate only if we increase the atmospheres of pressure to three. It won't be comfortable, but it'll give more internal strength."

"How fast will we sink? We will sink won't we?"

"Oh, yeah," said Tom. "We'll sink all right, but not as fast as you might think. We have a lot of insulation and void areas to reduce the weight. If we have all the openings shuttered up, we should descend at approximately one foot per second."

Dandy did the figuring. "If all of our estimates are in the neighborhood, then we should fill the tanks with 80 feet or so to spare on your 500-foot figure. Anything we have beyond that is gravy. After we take on water, we can elevate high enough so we can collect air. I don't imagine we'll have the luxury of unlimited time."

Candie came online. "I think I have a nice spot picked out. It's as far away from population centers and military installations as we can get—this is, of course, according to the info we have available. When we come down it'll be just at dusk local time. The closest town will be looking into the setting sun. Of course, we'll have the twin sonic booms that'll alert anyone who knows anything about this business. I can get you into the neighborhood, but you're going to have to select the exact spot. I'd hate to put this thing down on the upper deck of a ferry boat."

She studied the crew for a moment. "Everyone has been working pretty hard. My work's just about done, but yours is about to begin. We have about an hour before we change directions. You guys get something to eat and then relax until we have to buckle in. I'll watch the monitors."

No one argued.

Hacker had been monitoring Taran's frequency when Malvane was told about the attack and the Rimlick maneuver. His sweet and sour shrimp carton went splat against the Centurion logo hanging on the wall of the office. A call went out for Tokla.

Before long Colonel Tokla was back in Hacker's office, just where he didn't want to be. The boss was in a towering rage. The place was a mess. The floor was littered with computer readouts, and two printers were manufacturing more by the minute. While Hacker's attention was focused on one screen, Tokla scanned the various sheets that were close enough to read. They all seemed concerned about a word or set of letters, Rimlick. One stack of papers contained sounds or letters occurring in a foreign language.

With a snarl Hacker swiveled to face the colonel. "I have two jobs for you. Someone shot at the ship and apparently hit it. The shots came from either the southern Mediterranean or northern Africa. That's all we know. I want that gun, any way you can get it. Be as clean as circumstances allow.

"After the ship took a hit, it changed velocity and direction until it took up a stationary orbit over the south pole. A little while ago it started moving in an erratic manner. Now it's in a decaying orbit that will bring it down in three days in the middle of the Atlantic. I want a force on the scene big enough to take possession of Taran if there's anything left. If it sinks to the bottom of the ocean, I want to know where it is so we can conduct salvage operations. For some reason, though, I don't think everything's as it appears. That Dawson kid said they may have to do a 'Rimlick maneuver,' whatever the hell that is."

Hacker stared at Tokla through hooded eyes. "I expect you to be more attentive to business this time."

Colonel Tokla dipped his head in assent before turning on his heel and heading for the door. He didn't trust himself to speak. The only thing he wanted to say was with a gun, but that wouldn't have been in his long-term self-interest.

Chapter 25

Everyone strapped in. Dandy changed the attitude of the ship with the retrorockets and then he engaged the main engines to shoot off on a new course. He didn't want to waste much time getting to a position for braking and descent. The faster he got to where he was going, the less time the others would have to give him grief.

This was the first time he had ever tried landing. He had been thoroughly computer coached on proper procedure, but that was to a solid base with all sorts of electronic aids and without the possibilities of hostile forces coming to do the ship harm.

The crew was tense. Corky and Tom were engaged in strained small talk. Beatrice was silent. Candie was dutifully and with precise efficiency, reading off course readings and times. As for himself, he was clenching the arms of his couch so no one would see his shaking hands. He was desperately hoping they would not shake at a critical moment when he was maneuvering. He didn't want to go left when he should be going right. In New Mexico, the computers would have done most of the work, but at Baikal it would have to be done manually. In one sense, time was dragging, but in another there was all too little of it until he would have to perform.

On Candie's mark he changed the inclination to position the heat shields at the proper angle. At the precise moment, he fired the retros, which decreased their speed for re-entry. They were now in a controlled fall. Since they did not have wings, they could not glide. They were under the control of gravity. At 8000 feet Dandy executed another maneuver to turn the feet downward. He engaged the A/Gs. Gradually, he slowed the rate of descent and sideslipping. In the evening light, he could see Lake Baikal on the monitor screens. Candie put a red dot on the area of the lake she had chosen. It was still a long way down. As he moved toward the target area he kept overcompensating causing the ship to slip one way or the other.

Candie's image came on an adjacent screen. She mouthed, "Relax" and winked.

Dandy's hands and arms were like steel bands. He tried to do as Candie had suggested, with limited results. Somehow he felt he had had this problem before. He realized he was going through the same learning experience he had during his first summer in college. He had been invited by one of his friends to go on a family outing on their houseboat. The father had let Dandy have the wheel for a while. Everyone got a big laugh out of the corkscrew wake he was leaving behind. He was compensating too late or too much. By the end of the week, he had straightened out his wake. Here he had a joystick instead of a wheel, but the principle was the same. Gradually, he got control of the situation and began zeroing in on the red dot.

Early in the discussion of setting down in the water, Tom had raised the question of whether or not the skin temperature from re-entry might be high enough to cause some sort of problem when cooled so quickly with cold water. Research indicated that the durathane should hold together under that much thermal shock. However, to be on the safe side, Dandy slowed the rate of descent to give more cooling time for the hull. The A/Gs would suck up lots of water that would also contribute to the cooling before immersion.

While Dandy was maneuvering toward the red dot, Tom was

closing the doors on all exterior openings. Corky had created a vacuum in the water tanks. As soon as the feet were submerged he was to open the tank doors. Since water was the more important item, they would take that on first, and if the opportunity presented itself, they would suck up as much air as possible.

Gradually, the surrounding landscape disappeared from the screen, leaving only empty water. At 1000 feet the water began to become agitated. Their rate of descent had slow appreciably. Air was already screaming upward around the ship. As the descent continued, a column of water rose toward the underside of Taran. Water vapor blurred the lenses of the their monitors. Everything went blank at 500 feet. They must have looked like a toadstool as Taran sat on a stem of water. Fortunately, the various instruments did not rely on visuals and they continued to function. Even above the lake level they were enveloped in water.

When his altimeter read zero, Dandy throttled back on the A/Gs. The column of water collapsed on top of them, giving Taran an unwanted shove below the surface. The craft began a sickening slide back and forth as it began descending. The turbulence subsided. Corky opened the tank doors and the precious water began flowing in. Now they had a seven-minute wait.

Candie had been monitoring all the external sensors, watching for company, but nothing showed up prior to Taran going underwater. Now that the bubbles had cleared,she could see the brightness of the surface overhead.

The crew held their breath. The hull was groaning and creaking like never before. A gurgling sound was discernible. Three minutes went by. Tom came on the audio. "We're descending at a rate 40% faster than we calculated. We had a push from that column of water. That'll put us close to the 700 foot depth if the tanks fill as projected."

"It'll take seven and a half minutes to top off the tanks," Corky injected.

Dandy was doing some quick mental calculations. "Since we don't have a depth meter we're only guessing. We were shoved under the surface by the geyser. It took a little time for the turbulence to clear so we could open the doors. We're descending at a faster rate, and it'll take a little longer to fill up. Since we're in unknown territory, we had better circle the wagons. Start building internal pressure. Tom, if any of the sensors start showing any signs of a problem, let me know. I can stop the descent, but I don't want to disturb the surface in case someone's looking for us, nor do I want to suck up anything from the bottom."

The groaning of the hull was becoming much more pronounced. Beatrice was moaning. The elevated air pressure was causing ear aches. Dandy wrinkled his nose at the smell of his nervous sweat.

Candie's knuckles were white as she grasped the edge of her metal work station. All vibrations were being transferred directly to her nervous system. She was staring at the monitor for the top side camera, which pointed toward the surface. She saw a ghost of a shadow appear in a circle of light, but it didn't register. The shadow swung back and forth in the surface glow. It wasn't a boat. It looked more like a mosquito looking for a spot on a juicy thigh.

"Helicopter," she shouted.

The others' heads jerked up violently.

"Corky, how much more time?" yelled Dandy.

"About two minutes."

"How deep is the lake here?"

"About 2500 feet," Candie responded.

"We'll have to take in the rest on the way up. We're leaving. Close the doors as soon as we're full."

Dandy engaged the A/Gs, slowly breaking their descent. Taran was under terrific strain already. He didn't want to add hull pressure unduly, but they couldn't hang around any longer. As soon as they came to a stop, Dandy move the control forward. The reaction was even more dramatic in water than it had been on land. When the column of water over them lost its weight the pressure from below jammed them upward. It was like being fired out of a cannon. They were coming up a lot faster than they had descended.

Corky was able to get the doors closed before Taran shot out of the lake. A great pillar of water preceded them, taking a military helicopter with it. Underneath, the ship sucked water two hundred feet into the air. The crew was slammed into their couches. At a 1000 feet the greater efficiency of water pressure gave way to compressible air. The ship lost velocity and hung drunkenly suspended in midair until Dandy compensated. They began rising again, but more slowly.

Candie was watching the view screens and the electronics. The helicopter had disappeared. Then radar told her something was coming in fast. She picked it up on a viewer. "We have company coming in fast from the northwest. It's a jet plane. It's fired a missile. I can see its tail. Hang on."

Everyone's eyes were glued to the screen. There wasn't much they could do in the few seconds left. The missile skewed one way then another for a bit before heading away. The aircraft got close enough to be caught in the vortex of the A/Gs. It struggled to claw itself free, diving toward the water. Dandy opened the door to the drive engines.

"Hang on." He engaged the rockets. Taran shot skyward. The drive engines were not designed to be used in atmosphere. They created a spectacular fireworks display as they seared the sky. In the void of space, it was believed they could reach a quarter the speed of light at full throttle. At idle, Dandy was beginning to heat the top of Taran. When he reached an altitude beyond the range of the jets, he returned to the A/Gs until they were at orbital altitude.

The acceleration pressure eased off. Tom was drawing off the added atmospheres of pressure. Dandy adjusted the artificial gravity so they could move around. Things began to return to their normal state.

"Why didn't that missile hit us?" Candie asked.

After a little silence Tom answered. "I suspect it was a heat-seeking missile. We were probably colder than the surrounding air after having been submerged in Lake Baikal. The A/Gs don't put out any heat, so there was no target."

Chapter 26

Taran had risen beyond the range of the jets. Dandy was careful to stay away from the Med, and Candie was feeding the computer a new course to the moon. The whole board was green. Taran didn't seem any worse for wear after her bath. Because of the added weight of full water tanks, Dandy had to compensate by boosting power to the A/Gs. Now they were under main engine power. It wouldn't take much time to reach escape velocity.

Since they were in no hurry to get anywhere except out of range of the gun that had punched a hole in their ship, Dandy shut down the engines. He activated the artificial gravity so the crew could move around normally. They were on their way to the moon.

As Dandy was unbuckling, "I think the boss wants to talk to us," Candie said.

Dandy looked up at the screens. Malvane was sitting in the chair in operations with his hand folded in front of him. He seemed to be waiting. Dandy keyed his viewer, which brought a warm smile to the CEO.

"We're glad to see you're still with us. You have been creating quite a stir all over the world. It seems Centurion dispatched a huge force to some location in the south Atlantic. Apparently, they engaged the European Scientific Co-op in a battle over some sort of scientific instrument. The Co-op was testing on a ship off the coast of Algeria. The Russians are agitated too. They're complaining over losing a helicopter or something of the sort."

Dandy chuckled. "We were stocking up for an extended vacation we've been planning. We find that it's not too healthy where we've been, so we figured we'd change vistas, unless someone has a better idea."

Dandy figured Malvane already had figured out their destination. On their current path there weren't any others.

"Have a pleasant vacation. We'll let you know when it's safe to come home. Put Tom on, please."

Everyone had been monitoring the conversation. Tom switched himself on. A man stepped into view beside Malvane. "Tom this is Tim. He has some instructions for you." Malvane got out of the chair and Tim sat down.

He opened a folder and began. "We're going to modify your radio so we can have more secure conversations. Record these instructions, because they have to be followed precisely. Each item will be known by the storage bin number in which it's found. First I want you to replace bin number F-16 with O-4. Following B-34 add two C-11s in series."

Tim continued to give precise directions in a clear, crisp voice that left no room for misinterpretation. He droned on and on. Everyone else lost interest.

Corky said he was going below to check out the water tanks. Beatrice unbuckled herself because she had to go to the bathroom and Candie was getting a cup of soup. Dandy checked the course again. Everything was fine.

Chapter 27

Colonel Tokla was feeling much better as he headed for the CEO's office. This time he would be reporting success rather than failure. The receptionist motioned him straight through. The electric doors closed behind him before he realized Hacker was in a towering rage again. Tokla wondered what had happened. He had taken care of his assigned tasks with the utmost efficiency and dispatch.

Hacker was furiously entering data into the computer. "Report," he ordered, without looking up.

Tokla bristled at the tone of voice and the abrupt demand, but he concealed it behind his steely exterior. "We'll have a crack force on station at the specified coordinates in the south Atlantic shortly. No one will be able to interfere with whatever we do. We have the gun ESC used against Gal X in our possession. We're also pressing them with piracy charges against our ship."

Slowly, Hacker swiveled around to face Tokla. "I have three bits of information for you. Number 1, the ship isn't coming down. It was a wounded bird ruse. It zipped off to Lake Baikal to take on water. So call your forces back. Number 2, now the ship seems to be headed for the moon. I doubt if the gun will do us any good unless it can shoot through the moon. Number 3, they're making communication modifications that may make it impossible to monitor them."

Tokla didn't alter his expression. He'd have liked to have pointed out where the flawed plans had originated, but he wasn't prepared to try to handle the consequences. He said nothing.

Hacker stared at him through watery eyes. "When NASA was privatized into NASA Corp., they took with them the old shuttles. Since then, they've built more modern versions which they're using to fabricate the new space station. I'm making them an offer that'll be hard to refuse. They'll provide a shuttle, minimal crew, a launch, and a landing at a reasonable fee or someone will shoot down their multi-billion dollar space station. I want you to deliver the proposal in your own forceful way. You'll mount the gun from ESC on the shuttle. Make sure you have a qualified spaceman trained as gunner for the mission. We'll need one more person to protect the gunner and our interests. Return tomorrow morning at ten to pick up the formal proposal. Give me your recommendations for personnel."

Chapter 28

It had been a hectic few hours. Now decisions had been made and they could do something, instead of nothing. The crew was busy getting the ship in order. Tom was muttering over his radio alterations. Beatrice was feverishly trying to record all of the known data about their swim in the lake.

Corky came up from below. He began thumping around in the food area. Dandy could see into the area through a reflection in one of the blank monitor screens. It looked as if Corky was doing some maintenance. He had the fronts of a couple of the machines open. Within a few minutes a tantalizing aroma began to waft throughout the area.

Candie came up out of her astral charts. "What's that I smell?"

"Dinner in five minutes, but no peeking ahead of time," Corky replied.

The next five minutes seemed to be about as long as they had been under water in Lake Baikal. No one realized how long it had been since they had eaten and nothing they had eaten since coming aboard smelled so delicious.

Corky called them to dinner. He switched on the screen so they could monitor the dwindling earth and everyone could attend his little dinner party. He had set the large table as formally as plastic utensils and paper allowed. In the center was a long covered object on a platter made of durathane. There was a huge bowl with steam escaping around its paper cover. The paper napkins served as place cards with the crew's names scrawled in Corky's nearly illegible handwriting.

When everyone was in place, with a great flourish, Corky removed the covering from the platter. The poached fish must have been better than three and a half feet, including head.

Everyone gaped in absolute wonderment.

"Where in the world?" Candie gasped.

"Lake Baikal." Corky beamed. "I have a whole school of these babies swimming around in the water tanks. After dinner I could use a hand cleaning fish. I can add them to our menu."

Corky took the cover off the large bowl. It contained rice covered with a stir-fry steamed in the microwave. He had raided the machine to get at the rice and the vegetable packets. He didn't explain where he had gotten the spices necessary to make the dish.

Corky did the serving honors. With a couple of broad bladed putty knives he peeled back the skin. He placed great chunks of flaky, white meat on each plastic plate and he served the rice and vegetable dish.

When everyone was served, Dandy lifted his cup of grape juice. "I think a toast is in order. To TC. We're doing things no one else has ever done."

"Let's eat," Tom said.

Forks began to fly. Even Candie didn't hold back.

Once everything was gone, Corky basked in the compliments of his fellow crew members.

Dandy offered that there was only one appropriate activity after such a meal, a nap. "I have to do some checking on our course to see if any adjustments have to be made. We have to get back onto a schedule. In two hours, I'll turn it over to Candie. I'm going to need some orbital information for the moon. Then two hours later it's Tom. Finish your radio modifications. Next Beatrice, then Corky. I'll start off by cleaning up Corky's Fish House."

Chapter 29

Everyone had gotten some rest. Tom made the changes in the radio equipment and he was waiting until the home office set up a testing program. In the meantime, he was helping Corky filet, cut, and wrap fish for the food processor. There was a bunch. The crew was happy to have another item added to their menu. Corky was pleased to have the fish carcasses for the waste recycler because materials could be extracted from them.

The tone sounded, calling their attention to the monitor. Linda, Hal's replacement, moved out of the way so Malvane could seat himself. Dandy flipped on all the monitors. He could sense Tom and Corky's approach in the elevator. He was getting quite a feel for the ship.

Malvane was reviewing papers. When all the monitors had a face he said, "Good morning, crew. Tom, switch on your new communication array. In 10 seconds we'll send you a voice message. Record it and send it back to us. Then we'll let our computer talk with your computer and vice versa."

The voice message was a complicated series of sounds, tones, pitches and utterances. Apparently someone in the command center was comparing the two messages because Malvane waited until he had confirmation. "That was great. Let's have the computers converse."

Everyone sat watching their screens. Malvane frowned. "We aren't getting through."

"Oops." Tom made a dive for the console under his station where he had pulled out the tray so Colonel Tokla could not take control of Taran from the ground. "Try it again."

Malvane nodded. "Perfect. Switch all communications over to the new com system."

The images on the screens blinked out and reappeared. "Now, that is better," Malvane said. "We believe we're on a secured system, at least for the moment. We have no idea how long it'll take Centurion to figure this one out or whether they still have agents that can furnish them with the new design. So we're going to take care of some important business immediately, before we run the risk of hostile ears. While we're talking, we will be feeding your computer new advanced training programs for each of you. These were the ones the flight crews were going to use. You might need some of the information, although so far you've been doing beautifully without it. They're completely self-explanatory, just like the first ones. That'll keep you occupied while you're behind the moon. As soon as that's complete, we want you to send us all the information stored in your computer since you took off. Beatrice, it'll be your responsibility to down load all of that material."

Malvane paused while the technicians started things in motion. Then he turned his attention back to the crew. "I'll try to bring you up to date on what's happening here. The criminal authorities have washed their hands of the whole thing in New Mexico. They were probably bribed. They're leaving it up to the civil courts. We have a good case concerning the raid on you. Centurion had some time, but not enough to do a thorough clean-up job. You scattered debris for miles so we're suing them for damages. They're counter-suing, saying that Taran was actually theirs and they were just trying to recover their property. It would appear that Centurion is trying to tie us and our funds up with legal battles. We think they're stalling for time while they try to get a ship of their own built. We know they stole a lot of our technology, however, we think there are several important voids. If they can shoot you down so they can get a look at the equipment, they hope to be able to fill in the blanks and keep Taran out of our hands. They know we can't build another ship now.

"With so much worldwide publicity, any government would love to seize you until ownership has been determined by the courts and that's causing complications. Of course, by then that country would be wealthy selling the technology.

"Your idea of getting out of harm's way was a good one. The outfit shooting at you was the European Scientific Co-op. They're a multi-government venture for peaceful scientific development. They claim they were testing a new piece of communication equipment. Centurion took it away from them. Now Tokla has a new toy, so watch out. We have no idea what range or power the thing has. ESC is not talking.

"So a decision has been made. Since you can't safely come down right now, we're going to put you to work. All of you have now been promoted to flight crew level. No one knows more about that ship than you. We will have to discuss the chain of command."

Corky broke in. "We have already decided that. Dandy's first chief, Candie's second chief and the rest of us are just Indians."

Malvane smiled. "We had it figured something like that, but if you are satisfied with your arrangement, so are we.

"We want you to go through the new lessons. When you've mastered them we'll conduct a batch of experiments like we had planned for the original flight crew."

"I want a report on all of your activities. We're especially interested in your Baikal adventure. The Russians are still huffing and puffing."

The crew told the story from each prospective. Malvane particularly liked the fish story.

Chapter 30

The crew alternated between watching the earth recede and the moon approach. At the proper time Dandy began slowing so that the gravitational force of the moon drew Taran into orbit. It was an easy ride. Only a few people had made this trip, which placed them in an elite group. On the dark side of the moon, Dandy brought them into a stationary position.

During the conversation with Artis Malvane, a mass of data and instructional material had been loaded into the ship's computers. A whole new bank of computers was brought online. These were the ones the flight crews were to use when they began their space experiments. Beatrice had downloaded all the new material that had been collected. She had also requested more library information from the mainframe. Tom had gotten all the technical details on the space-drive hoping to get them up to half light speed.

Gal X was confident that the new communication system was secure, at least for a short period of time. Since Taran's computers now held all of the company's industrial secrets, Tom was instructed how to build in a self-destruction capability to keep the material out of the hands of the enemy, or anyone outside of the five TC members.

Of course, communications were difficult when Taran was behind the moon, so a Rimlick schedule had been ordered. At random times, Taran would pop out from behind the moon. High speed messages would be exchanged, so Taran could dive back under cover as soon as possible.

It didn't take TC long to get back into the same routine they maintained while on the ground. They fell into the same learning mode that had occupied their first several months. The only difference was the periodic movement for message transmission.

Since the Taran project had started, there was much new research to apply. Tom was given schematics of new equipment that he could construct on board.

One of the new systems was an improved particle-sensing device that made the solar jets easier to find. It worked out better than they had expected. Without interference from earth, images were much clearer.

Tom activated the system and they saw a burst of protons and electrons coming from the sun. As the rain of energy got further from the sun, other forces began working, causing them to coalesce into dendritic patterns. Gradually, as they moved further toward the Heliopause, they formed rivers undulating through space. It had been thought that the solar winds lost their force when they met the interstellar winds. With the new sensors, it appeared that major solar jets penetrated the wall of plasma and magnetic fields where they met with interstellar jets, undulating in changing patterns in space.

Dandy was at ease. Everything was going smoothly. The crew had enough new and challenging work to do. They were well provisioned except for their prepared foods. Corky's fish had been a great boost to the menu and the overall larder. He decided he was going to have to see if Malvane could send them a food package.

As far as he could tell they were safe. With random appearances in random places, they could conduct their business before Centurion or anyone else could take aim and fire. In fact, no one was sure any of the weaponry could reach the moon. Gal X seemed content to have Taran sitting on the dark side of the moon for the time being.

Chapter 31

Once Dandy decided it would be in the best interest of the crew to ask for a food drop, he composed a message giving his reasons for the effort. He suggested Gal X send an unmanned rocket past the moon. Taran could hop out and snag it as it went past.

He included Tom's latest report on the solar wind sensor tests, demonstrating how valuable they could be for scientific advancement. Candie had some preliminary maps showing general propensities in the solar jets. Taran popped out from the southern pole while the Pacific faced the moon. He sent his signal and message. Gal X had enough stations around the the world that such communications were always covered. One second after a station received the signal, the return message was sent.

For this maneuver Taran was only exposed for less than three minutes. Dandy had developed an elliptical course so that when they appeared, they were already turning back into hiding.

After Taran had resumed a stationary orbit, Candie played the incoming message. It was routine information except for one item that caused speculation over coffee in the Fish House. Gal

X reported that Centurion was negotiating with NASA Corp. for a shuttle service.

From that information, arguments ensued. The older shuttles were designed to go up to space, orbit, and come down again. They weren't moon orbiters. Tom pointed out that they had a large cargo-carrying capacity which could be converted to fuel cells. Gal X already knew that Centurion had stolen the gun from the ESC. Maybe the shuttle was going to be used as a firing platform.

Three days later, Taran was again setting up for a message run. It was a longer interval than normal, but they were still on a Rimlick schedule. The operation had become routine enough that the crew strapped themselves in and continued their work. As Taran moved out of the communication shadow, Dandy triggered the signal, which was followed by the message burst. On the return message Malvane's image appeared on the screen. Apparently it was a recorded message. "Beware. You have company coming." The message kept repeating itself.

"On your toes, everyone." Dandy shouted. "Candie, find that vessel. Tom, checked the main drive. We may need full power."

"There's nothing between here and Earth," reported Candie, "unless it's close to the moon. We have to get further out to see anything in the near vicinity."

"The board is all green," Tom said.

The attention tone sounded. Haggard, but clean-shaven, Malvane sat down in the communication chair. "I'm glad to see you're still with us. The shuttle has just passed out of sight on the opposite side of the moon from your current location. We were afraid they were going to sneak up behind you. They have that energy gun mounted in the nose of the craft. The cargo bay's carrying fuel for their return trip. As far as we can determine, the gun is fixed so the ship has to be pointed at you before they can fire, but we're not certain."

"Thanks for the warning," Dandy said. "I think we'd better find the cat before it finds us." He turned his attention back to his control panel.

"Okay, everybody. I'm going to try coming up on it from the rear. I want to try baiting it to see how it maneuvers into firing position. I hope we have enough time to get out of range. Bea, call up the info we have on the older shuttles. I want to know all we can about fuel consumption, capacity of the cargo bay, and fuel requirement to return home. I want to know how much chasing they can do before they reach a point of no return. All of that should be in the archives."

The hum of the main engines became pronounced. The crew pressed back into their couches. Dandy figured the shuttle was moving at an orbital speed to conserve fuel. He did not want to overrun them. All he wanted was to show himself momentarily to see how they would react.

"There they are," said Candie. "They're sitting still on the dark side waiting for us to return. It looks like we're behind them."

Dandy started the maneuver to reverse directions. Then he keyed the radio on a channel he knew they would be monitoring. "Hey, Centurion. You looking for us?"

"They're turning." Candie monitored their every move. "They must be doing it with maneuvering thrusters. The main engines are firing."

With that, Dandy dove below the protective curve of the moon. With the thrust Taran pulled further away from the shuttle. Dandy would elevate enough for the shuttle to catch a glimpse, but the moment the enemy was in line of sight, Taran would drop down again.

Beatrice came up out of the computer to report that from her calculations, the shuttle could only make two circuits of the moon as they were doing now. After that, they would probably need all the remaining fuel to escape the moon gravity to return to earth.

As Dandy guided the ship on its undulating course, another

more devious part of his brain was working. "So far they haven't gotten a shot," he thought out loud. "They are running out of fuel and time. Colonel Tokla probably doesn't take failure lightly. Whoever's the gunner is probably getting trigger happy by now. If that gun is semi-fixed, then the gunner probably has control of the ship to aim. The ESC fired at an ice cloud the first time. Corky, do we have anything we could expel as a target without using any of our precious water?"

"I've got a whole tank of fish guts and other semi-solid waste I'm holding for recycling. That might do the trick."

"Great. Get it ready to jettison on my mark. We'll wait until we're on the dark side. The plan is to drop lower, dump the trash, and get out of sight as soon as possible. Hang on, because I'm putting my foot in the carburetor and wiggling my toes."

"We'll in the dark in 45 seconds," Candie reported,

Dandy was moving to an altitude too low to maintain a stable orbit. He waited ten seconds after passing into darkness. "Dump it. Brace yourselves." He waited for the jettisoned material to fall away so he wouldn't incinerate it, then he jammed the throttle open. The crew was flung into their couches as Taran shot forward.

By the time the shuttle came in view of the trash, Taran was over the horizon. The radar on the shuttle was old and it had never been upgraded. When the gunner approached the shadow side of the moon, his screen showed his quarry ahead and below. This was the closest he had been able to get. The allotted fuel for the chase was nearly expended. The gunner dove instead of using the thrusters to simply tilt the nose down. When the radar locked on, he fired. Nothing. It took 4 seconds for the gun to cycle. He fired again. Nothing. The shuttle pilot was screaming at him. The gunner's controls went dead as the pilot cut him off. Precious fuel had to be used to regain enough altitude so they would not spiral down to the surface.

As Dandy powered down, Candie gave her caustic assessment. "Litter bug."

Dandy moved to a position where he could electronically view the shuttle. It appeared that the pilot was attempting to nudge it into a higher orbit without using any more fuel than necessary. Although Taran was within radar view, the shuttle showed no interest.

Beatrice was watching the calibrations intently. She announced her verdict. "I calculate they're now too short on fuel to make the return trip. Someone's going to have to send a fuel truck."

Beatrice giggled at her own witticism. The crew smiled at her first attempt at friendly banter.

Tom threw a wet blanket on the victory. "Depending on the amount of supplies they have we're going to have to play hide and seek with them for days or weeks, and if a rescue shuttle comes we might be caught between two guns."

Chapter 32

Dandy matched Taran's orbital speed with the shuttle's, on the opposite side of the moon and convened a meeting in the Fish House.

"I don't like the thought of being this close to those guys," he said."

"We don't even have a brick to throw back," Candie responded.

"Since we have to orbit, we are exposed to earth. I don't know if anyone has anything that can get to us now, but you can bet they're working on it," said Dandy.

"We're going to have to change our work schedule," said Corky. "Someone's going to have to be constantly watching for the shuttle with one eye and any other visitors with the other."

Beatrice shivered. "I don't like it here."

"This isn't my favorite vacation spot either, especially with the company we have to keep," said Candie. "It's getting too crowded at this resort. Let's find something else further off the beaten path."

Dandy began to say something, then paused. He looked at each of the crew and shrugged. "Let's go to Mars."

"It's better going somewhere than going nowhere," Beatrice said.

"Candie." Dandy began to plan. "Can you lay out a course toward Mars using the most optimum window from this orbit? We don't want to telegraph our punch to the shuttle. Just before we get to the departure point, I will increase speed to put more distance between us and Centurion. We'll exit at high velocity. Hopefully, we can get out of range before they know we aren't around. I suspect that weapon of theirs consumes a lot of power, so they shouldn't be taking too many shots at us. They can't chase us."

He turned to Tom. "We're going to have to convert water into fuel. Let's do that now before we are under pressure. Beatrice, please write up an account of our meeting with the shuttle so headquarters knows what has been going on. You're now our official TC historian. Until now we've been reacting to outside stimuli, but now we're going to be taking an active role in our future. Lets go see what's out there until the boss calls us back.

"Corky, please figure out the best way to get our food package aboard when it gets here."

The meeting broke and everybody went back to their work stations.

It wasn't long until they would be on the proper side of the moon for their exit. Dandy nudged Taran ahead to give them more time to get out of range of Centurion's toy. At the ten minute mark, Dandy warned everyone to get ready for heavy acceleration. With 10 seconds left, he sounded the message tone for a transmission to the home base. It was brief. "Send our lunch to Mars." Then he aimed Taran in the direction of Mars, throttling up just short of giving the crew nose bleeds. It was going to be uncomfortable, but they had to get enough distance and speed so the gunner would choose in his self-interest to conserve fuel rather than try an impossible shot.

Even though that was the theory, the crew was holding its breath until the sensors told them the shuttle had passed the point in its orbit where a shot would have been possible. Dandy eased back on the throttle to achieve a better comfort level. Everyone was exuberant.

Despite the difficulty in moving about, Corky distributed free-fall packs of grape juice. When he got back to to his couch he proposed a toast. "To us and our coming adventures."

Chapter 33

Colonel Tokla was coffee-logged. He wished passionately for a big belt of tequila. There was one small consolation. He didn't have to drink the green tea that Hacker preferred.

He had been in Hacker's office for hours. They had been listening in on the NASA Corp communications with the shuttle. There was a code that would be used if the mission was a success, but the words never came. Then the shuttle commander put in an emergency call for a rescue mission. They had lost a quantity of fuel, which made return to earth impossible. Hacker scowled at Tokla as he picked up the phone to tell his secretary that under no condition was a call to be forwarded from NASA Corp until further notice.

"You failed again."

Tokla grudgingly decided it wouldn't aid his cause to point out that it was a lame-brained scheme from the start. The element of surprise had been lost when Taran popped out for its communication run. They must have seen the shuttle coming and there had been a broadcast from their home base, which probably contained a warning. The shuttle had limited fuel capacity. Taran could fly circles around it. It boiled down to it being the wrong tool for the job. Now it looked like Hacker was just going to write off his two men.

Tokla prepared himself to take another truckload of guff from that wimp. One of these day Hacker would be on the receiving end.

The proceedings were interrupted by an incoming message at a terminal. Hacker read the short announcement on the screen. He stared into space for some time. Tokla began to squirm.

Hacker turned to face Tokla. "You just got lucky. What you couldn't do, Gal X did for us. Taran is on its way toward Mars. They're taking themselves out of the game, which is as good as shooting it down. They can't use it. Now we squeeze Gal X so tight financially that they can't build another. We can turn our attention to getting their technology so we can build our own. Do you think you can handle that?"

Tokla just nodded as he headed for the door and Hacker sent an electronic order to the kitchen for Pork Bok Choy.

Chapter 34

Once Taran had traveled what they thought was a safe distance from earth, Dandy reduced speed so they were drifting. The crew was busy with housekeeping duties, studies, and scheduled relaxation. Tom and Corky were back to their gin game. Beatrice started watching the TV game shows. She was beating everyone. Candie and Dandy played electronic games and talked about what might be waiting on Mars.

During the second day of drifting, Candie picked up a launch from earth. She wasn't sure where it had originated, but it was heading up. They waited to see if it assumed an earth orbit but it kept coming toward them.

The message tone sounded. Malvane's appeared. "Bon appetit."

The crew cheered. No one wanted Corky as chef.

Malvane became serious. "We have reason to believe our communications have been compromised. We'll have to guard our words. However, we've decided to use what has been given us. Gal X is starting a public relations project to tell the world about Taran and the five of you. We'll make our court case over the airwaves. You're about to become famous. As time goes along we'll probably set up interviews with various news commentators, scientists, and maybe even politicians.

"We're in the process of advising your families and the list of friends you gave us so they won't be shocked when they find out over the media you're someplace between here and Mars. By the way, good thinking.

"Another news item. It seem the NASA Corp. shuttle miscalculated its fuel consumption. In a couple of days a rescue mission will be launched to get the ship home. I'll be interested in your thoughts on that matter."

"Standby." Dandy cut off the communication link. "Beatrice, have you finished the report concerning our encounter with the shuttle?"

"Yes."

"Are there any secrets we don't want Centurion to have?"

"No, not really. If their people are telling the truth, they should know most of it. Not about the fish guts, though."

"Get the report ready to transmit," said Dandy.

Dandy opened the channel again to Malvane. "Sir, in a moment we'll transmit a bedtime story. I hope you enjoy it."

Taran was out of reach of Centurion. After giving the vessel a thorough check, the crew relaxed back into their routines. They waited a week for the care package to catch up to them. No firm decision had been made on how to handle the transfer because they didn't have any idea of how big it would be or how the package would be wrapped.

The package turned out to be an old manned-mission nose cone with a tubular body that apparently had external rockets attached. Tom took as accurate a set of measurements as he could, using Taran's sensors. He calculated that the forepiece of the cargo vessel could be put in the bed of the utility shuttle. Then the shuttle could pull the whole thing into the cargo bay.

Normally, the launching and retrieval of the utility shuttle could be conducted from the main consoles, but because of the added length and bulk, someone would have to be in the cargo bay to direct operations.

After considerable discussion, it was decided that Dandy had to fly Taran, in case something went wrong. Tom would handle the shuttle and Corky would do the external work. Candie would also have to be in a pressure suit to be in the cargo bay to direct loading operations.

Beatrice was left to watch the bridge, while Dandy went to help the others suit up.

This was their first attempt at using the shuttles. Everyone knew all the manual material, but it was an adventure taking on the real thing. Before they tried to hook up, Tom made several practice runs to get the feel of how the craft reacted to the controls. Finally, he said he was ready to try. He maneuvered into position in front of the missile. Then he gently braked to allow the cargo pod to close the gap. As they got near, Corky went out the air lock into the cargo bed with a long rod with a hook on the end. It took considerable effort to get the two lined up. Tom had to be careful that his maneuvering thrusters did not hit the target, pushing them apart.

After two attempts, Corky made contact, but there was nothing to hook. The fourth time he waited until the craft was close enough to use both hands to direct the rod. He was able to exert enough pressure to bring the two objects together. He gently led the nose of the rocket as far into the cargo bay as he could.

"Any ideas how I'm going to tie this thing on?"

Beatrice came up with an answer. As soon as she found out the vehicle designation, she called up its specifications. "There's a small access panel in the nose with four hand nuts. Inside is the loading ring that was used when these things had to be lifted out of the ocean."

The cargo pod was tied off. Tom brought the shuttle around to its loading ramp. The shuttle and the rocket were going to be too long. Tom brought it up part way. Corky and Candy lashed the pod to the ramp. The freed shuttle was parked to the side. The rocket was then moved up the ramp so that it didn't protrude beyond the edges. Candie raised the ramp sealing the cargo bay. The interior was pressurized so that Tom could exit the shuttle.

It was going to take a some time for the bay to heat up enough for them to work. Dandy used that fact to hold the excitement in check so the crew could get some needed rest before starting the next phase.

In an attempt to portion out the physical work, Tom and Dandy would work in the cargo bay unloading the pod. The temperature of the cargo bay was left at 30 degrees so any frozen food stuffs wouldn't thaw. Items for which temperature didn't matter would be loaded on the elevator and sent to the next level. Beatrice and Candie would receive and sort the material.

When Tom and Dandy stepped off the elevator, they were both struck with the size of the pod. Before, everyone had been concentrating on the job without really considering the object. Against the enormity of space, objects are without scale. When something is weightless, it seems less significance. But that tubular structure was now securely grounded with artificial gravity within a closed structure. Viewed against the scale of the shuttles and the ship's interior, it became gigantic.

In the bottom of the pod was a hatch secured with bolts. Tom removed the nuts, and the two men carefully lifted off the cover. They turned their attention back to the pod and were confronted with a red paper seal. It was imprinted with a bold-faced lettered "WARNING." Under it was a hand printed message. "Inside is a destruction device. Immediately disarm it by removing the receiving unit." Specific instructions followed. Dandy stepped aside and with a sweep of his hand, he invited Tom to handle the technical matters.

It was a very simple procedure. Following directions, he clipped two wires and loosened the mounting so he could remove the unit from an explosive charge.

"What should we do with this little baby, jettison it?"

Dandy considered it for a moment. "No, I think we should save it. There's no telling when we may need a brick to throw at someone. Can you store it safely?"

"Sure, no problem. Why do you think it was there?"

"I'd guess there's something inside that the company didn't want to fall into unfriendly hands."

They began unloading cases upon cases of food items. According to the labels they were going to have new entrees to sample. Since the crew had come aboard, one of the most bitched about items had been the food. It looked like the food designers had taken some of the suggestions to heart. Along with some of the newly preserved foods came a processor to add to the mechanical array in the Fish House.

Dandy was inside the pod when he came to another barrier. Behind it were items that didn't need to be kept cold. He started shoving out boxes of items—toilet paper, plastic plates, a resupply on all the utilitarian items they used. Then came big boxes with the individual names of the crew, containing personal items.

Tom opened his. It was loaded with uniforms, underwear, and toiletries specific to him. Candie and Beatrice had been watching on the monitors. When they saw personal items had been included, they erupted into cheers. Dandy turned to Tom. They shrugged at each other.

"Uncouth savages," said Candie over the intercom.

Even working at slightly reduced gravity, to make the job easier, the boxes were beginning to feel heavy. Dandy called a halt to the unloading. He had Tom load the personal boxes onto the elevator and at the next level they picked up Candie and Beatrice.

The women immediately disappeared into their rooms with

their boxes. Tom had already seen what was in his. It didn't excite him much, so he told Dandy and Corky to stow their gear while he watched things.

After they had unpacked their gear, they assembled in the Fish House to sample the new edibles. Corky cooked ten different items to serve family style so everyone could have a taste. The fare had improved considerably.

After the meal, they relaxed over drinks, until Dandy stood up. "As much as I hate to break this up, we have a lot of stuff to secure. We can't leave anything floating loose. Beatrice, you stay up here to watch things. Candie, you and Corky start filling the food dispensers. Tom and I will finish unloading. We're just about through, although we don't know if there's anything in the nose cone. We'll secure the pod, then come up to help you."

Beatrice started cleaning up the dinner mess. The two Andys glanced at each other before moving out of the area, not wanting to interrupt an historic first event.

The few remaining boxes were removed from the cylinder. Tom opened the hatch to the nose cone. "Hey, Dandy. Look at this."

Just inside the hatch was a holographic Christmas tree glittering brightly under the work lights. "What's the date?" Dandy said.

"Twelve-nineteen."

"Six days until Christmas."

The nose cone was crammed with brightly wrapped packages complete with name tags.

Dandy grinned. "Let's stage our own little surprise."

They loaded everything onto the elevator and secured the pod. They pinned the Christmas tree in front of the packages. They took the stairs to the command level. Via the intercom, Dandy asked Candy and Corky to use the stairs to come up. He gathered the group together in front of the elevator in the Fish House and turned on the viewers for the home office to see.

When the elevator door opened, the rest of the crew gasped at the sight of the paper Christmas tree and the huge pile of packages.

"Today is December 19 on Earth." said Dandy. "However, we're six days out which makes it December 25 here. Merry Christmas."

Everyone sat down on the floor in front of the elevator and the cameras.

The first item took both men to handle. It was a huge box as big as a coffin. It was for Candie, signed "AM."

"Open this one first. Our curiosity won't wait."

Candie crack the lid to peer inside and threw it back to reveal a chest of fresh vegetables and fruits. Candie was ecstatic. She grabbed a radish and popped it into her mouth. With a flourish she offered everyone access to the treasure with a hearty, "Merry Christmas."

The fun began. Paper flew everywhere. There were presents from all sorts of people. One of Candie's favorites was a beautiful pair of dangly earrings from her proctor, Wayne Percy. Beatrice cried over a CD collection of chamber music from her mom. Corky could hardly wait to get to his workshop. Mr. Lombard, the unsmiling personnel director, had sent sets of plans for miniature Congreve clock. Tom had a new cribbage board from the engineer he had worked with during some of the training. Dandy's favorite gift that he showed the crew, but not the camera, was a crayon drawing of the strangest cat ever envisioned entitled "Rimlick Cat." It was signed Shellee, Walter Hale's little daughter.

There was one box to the group. It contained a 2-litre bottle of cherry cola for Beatrice, fresh-squeezed orange juice for Candie and one of those high-powered sports drinks for Dandy. However, the items which got the biggest cheer were two quart bottles of premium beer for Corky and Tom. Attached to the beer bottles were photos of the back of Malvane's head.

On the more serious side there were 9mm automatic handguns for each person and an assortment of long guns for different purposes. Included in their armory were a variety of hand grenades and a half dozen shoulder-fired rockets.

When all the gifts had been opened, the crew waded through a sea of wrapping paper to stand arm-in-arm. To the camera they sang a raucous rendition of Jingle Bells. Candie flipped her head back and forth so her dangly earrings flashed in the light. In unison the crew wished everyone a Merry Christmas and a Happy New Year.

Chapter 35

No one had the guts to get anywhere near Hacker's office unless they were commanded to appear. Once the Centurion technical people had compromised Taran's communication systems again, Hacker installed a receiver in his office so he could monitor any messages directly. Everything was being recorded in an attempt to find any hidden elements.

Hacker had been privy to the celebration of Christmas aboard Taran. He had raged when he had found out a launch had been made to the ship without any word getting to him early enough to intercept it. What was he paying all those idiots for?

When he picked up the Christmas party, he saw the crew as flesh and blood creatures for the first time. They had been pretty much disembodied shadows occupying something he wanted. Now his hate was personified—that cute, bouncy blonde with the dangly earrings and that good-looking, well built Dawson. That crew had thwarted his every move.

His disposition got even uglier when a message on his screen advised him to turn on one of the national network news casts. Artis Malvane was being interviewed by the news anchor. Gal X was publicly acknowledging ownership of Taran. There were photos of the ship and Malvane explained it was Christmas Day on board Taran and he showed selected footage of the celebration.

Such a publicity ploy was going to seriously damage any court case Centurion might try to make. Even worse, it could make his company look foolish.

To cool off enough to think about the next move against Gal X, Hacker pulled up his personal black list. He began crafting the most excruciating purge he could devise. He wouldn't just fire people. He would destroy everything they held dear.

Chapter 36

It took a couple of days for things to get back to normal. All the new gear had to be stored. Decisions had to be made about things as to where the guns and ammo should be kept. Everyone was relishing the fresh fruits and vegetables. Corky and Tom saved their beers until the next night when they were both off shift. They made a big play of setting up the cribbage board on the main table of the Fish House. They made token offers to share their brews with the rest of the crew, but of course they were turned down.

Another item in the Christmas package had been disks of all the first run movies. Dandy and Candie watched them together. At first, Beatrice tuned into them in her room, but later she joined the group in the Fish House.

On the third day after Christmas, the crew was at their stations and Dandy called for their attention. "It's time we get back to work. I've been going over the new material the company sent up while the com net was secure. Our main engine's a small version of a larger design. It's believed that this has about half the speed capacity of the bigger edition. With the full scale one, they hope to ride a solar jet at about half light speed. With our little engine we should be able to do about a quarter of that. These are all theories, of course.

"We have nearly a full load of fuel. Our tummies are full. We don't want to just sit around waiting for someone to figure out how to do us harm. We know more about this ship than anyone else in the world. Let's put Taran through her paces to see what she can do. Any objections?"

Everyone approved of the plan. Even Beatrice offered no resistance.

Dandy activated the command station and started issuing orders. "Candie, find the best solar jet to take us into the vicinity of Mars. Give me a course, too, so we can hook up with it. Beatrice, get ready to record masses of data concerning every particle of information we can gather from this trip. From here on out, we're scientists examining a whole new frontier. Tom, you and Corky check out all the equipment to make sure it's in top working order."

By midday, Candie had located the best jet not too far from their present location. It undulated through space as it swung in the direction of Mars. She laid in a course that would put Taran into the stream. However, since there were no firm estimates on how much speed would be achieved, she could only hazard a rough guess as to where deceleration should begin.

Dandy set course for the solar jet. He adjusted his speed to give Tom and Corky a full day to complete their equipment checks. Dandy needed the time, too. It was becoming increasingly clear that caution was going to be needed. There were too many unknowns.

Dandy spent his time going through the instructional disks again. When he had first learned the material, it all sounded so logical. But, after the little flying he had done, he could see gaping omissions. The reviews produced more questions than answers.

He got together with Candie. She was facing some of the same problems. She brought up a question that hadn't been answered. Should the slowing be done in the solar jet, or should Taran exit the stream? Would leaving the stream abruptly, be like jumping off a speeding train? There was no way of really knowing whether or not the solar jets were two way streets. Could one go upstream? If so, would it be as fast, and which way was upstream? Or would it be faster to move outside the jet? Just as the planets move, the jets are continually in a state of flux. Finding one going in the direction Taran wanted to go might be a problem. From earth, little could be seen of the solar jets. When the new sensors got above earth interference, they produced much clearer information. The jets were far more complicated than the crew originally thought.

Dandy and Candie made long lists of questions. They tried to anticipate situations that might arise out of a lack of knowledge. These were highlighted so care could be taken to try to avoid such problems.

Everyone kept a positive attitude, but anxiety was building behind the facades. Before, they had been reacting to greater dangers by taking action. Now they were intentionally stepping into the unknown.

Chapter   37

Dandy was moving Taran to enter the solar jet that Candie had selected at an angle to the line of flow. That way they could enter gradually with limited course adjustments. Without any jets, Dandy had already gotten speeds sufficient to exert very uncomfortable G forces on the crew. No one knew what would happen to the forces when they were traveling in jets. They had no instrument to measure the speed of the particles in the stream. It was obvious they were flowing very fast.

Dandy gave everyone a warning call so they could take care of any personal needs. Once the crew was strapped into their couches, he advanced the throttle so they were actively thrusting ahead. Holding that speed constant, he eased into the solar jet.

Tom was taking exacting speed readings. They felt nothing strange as they entered the particle flow, but before long Tom detected a gradual increase in speed. In three minutes it had increased 7%. At six minutes their speed had gone up 16%. Tom began calling out the speed in 5% increments. There was an increase in the G-pressure but not in the same proportions as their increase in speed.

Corky was monitoring other systems such as the hull pressures. So far he had not encountered any problems.

When Tom's readings reached 50%, Dandy upped the engine output by 10%, which resulted in a 30% increase. He planned to continue increasing thrust until they got to three Gs. Then he would back off to evaluate the performance. At the moment, speed relative to other objects was not being interpolated and they were not yet sure of how fast they were going.

Suddenly, there was an unsettling feeling that Dandy had just left his stomach behind. "What was that?"

"We came to a junction in the solar jet, Candie reported. We're in a larger trunk."

"Our speed has jumped 23%," Tom said.

The G-pressure was building without increased engine thrust. Then Corky broke in. "Hey, guys. we are building a severe magnetic charge that could affect all onboard systems."

"Should we get out of the jet?" Dandy shouted.

"In or out, it's already happened," replied Corky.

"Tom?"

"I can send an electrical charge through the ship like when they degaussed the old iron ships."

"Do it," said Dandy. He was holding everything in a static state. The Gs had reached 2.5. He wanted to get to 3 before he backed off.

"I'm building a charge," Tom said. "In eight seconds I'll release it. That should reverse the polarity. Four, three, two, one."

Everything went mushy. Dandy looked around his station. Surfaces seemed to flow. He felt horrible. The image of a soft shell blue crab when the face is torn off and the rest of the creature is fried, shell and all, haunted his thoughts. He didn't have time for that. He had to power back and get out of the stream. He reached for the throttle, against horrid forces that were pressing against him. With his right hand he eased back on it. With his left, he set a new course that would slip Taran out of the solar jet.

On his monitor, Dandy could see Tom struggling to reach a switch. He looked like a bowl of gelatin. He touched it just as Dandy eased back on the throttle. There was an abrupt slowing that ripped at the crew's bodies. The straps, although heavily padded, tore at them. Under the G forces they were crushed against their couches. Now they were being torn away from them. Without restraints they would have been splattered on the ceiling. Any unattached objects became missiles. Things were no longer mushy. Then it was over. The forces became manageable.

Candie and Beatrice ripped off their restraining straps and struggled to their rooms. Dandy had a strong urge for a rest call too, but he held on until the ship appeared to be under control. Candie emerged from her quarters.

"Take over," Dandy yelled. The guys bolted for their bathrooms. He felt lousy. He ran his hand over his face. A mirror confirmed what his hand had told him. He was sporting more whiskers than he could ever recall having, outside of those grown on camping trips.

He went out to look at Corky, the heavy-whiskered one of the bunch. Corky looked like he was trying to grow a beard.

"We have something strange here," said Dandy. "Did everything look like it was all mushy?" Everybody nodded. "Now, here is the question. How long were we in that condition? That would have been from when Tom threw the charge to degauss and the time we started to slow."

"I just flipped the switch on and then turned it off," Tom said. "It was a couple of seconds. Well, maybe a little longer because there was a strange surge that forced me back into the couch."

"So how do you explain your beard, and mine, and Corky's?

Why did everybody have to go to the bathroom so urgently?"

Candie wandered over to her fruit and vegetable box for something to chew on. She opened it up and stared at the contents. "Look at this."

The crew gathered around to gaze at all the mold that had formed over the riper and softer items in the box. Everything had been good just before they headed into the solar jet.

Dandy turned to Beatrice. "Your computer was storing information. It's all automatically dated, isn't it?"

"Yes, all of it," she replied.

"Call up our current time and date."

Beatrice went back to her terminal. "Information is still being recorded. There's a ton more data that couldn't have been recorded in the time element I recall. I started recording at 1000 hrs. on the 23rd. The current entries are be time marked 1200 hrs on the 25th. Fifty hours later."

"Candie, find out where we are."

She jumped on her computer. Before long it was obvious she was not getting the answers she wanted. She switched to radio and TV frequencies. All she got was static. The various external cameras produced images on her monitors. She swiveled around to confront a bunch of anxious faces. "I haven't the foggiest idea where we are. The only thing I do know is that our solar system is nowhere in the vicinity. Given time I can probably find it, if we are still in the same galaxy."

Dandy saw what might have been a glint of panic in his navigator's eyes. Tension showed on every face. Dandy stood up to stretch the kinks out of his body. After some elaborate gyrations, he commented casually, "At least Tokla can't bother us here." He was rewarded with a couple of nervous snickers. He continued his pantomime by rubbing his stomach. "Is anyone besides me hungry?" He looked at each of the crew members and they nodded. "Let's eat." He headed for the machines.

Dandy waited until everyone was involved in their meal. "I think we've just made history. If we are indeed outside of our solar system. Such an important event should be recorded for posterity."

Dandy walked over to Beatrice's station to start a recorder. "This is the Starship Taran at a currently unknown location in space. According to shipboard chronometers, it's December 25, at 1230. I'm Andrew Dawson, pilot." He nodded his head toward the rest of the crew, who in turn gave their names and titles.

Dandy continued, "At 1000 hours on December 23rd I steered Taran into the flow of a solar jet stream to test engine speed." He continued to relate his actions and sensations during the time period. One by one, each of the crew members told the story as he or she lived it. The accounts were similar, with only minor variations, primarily depending on perspectives and assigned duties.

When the stories were finished, Dandy turned off the recorder and began assigning duties. "Candie, find out where we are. Beatrice, help her with any of the information that you may have stored in that computer. Tom, get to work trying to figure out what happened. It'd seem that the event was triggered with the electrical charge. Get to the physics behind it. We'll probably have to pull that little trick again to get back home, so check our supplies. How much fuel did we use? Then go over the ship for any physical problems that may have been caused by this flight. I'm going to review the flight logs to see what they can tell us, and I'm going to scan our surroundings for any hazards. If there aren't any, I suggest we squat here until we have some answers."

No one had any objections.

Chapter 38

The weather man was calling for a freeze. Artis Malvane was in the yard with the gardener working out a defense for some of the less hardy plants. Mrs. Malvane interrupted the proceedings by tapping on the window. She held her hand to her ear indicating a phone call and pointed to his study. That would mean a business call on the com link.

Malvane was a little surprised to find an agitated Calvin Harder waiting on the viewer. "What is it, Cal?"

"Sir, Taran has disappeared."

"What do you mean disappeared?"

"That's what I mean."

"Okay, Cal. Back up, and slow down. The last I knew Taran was hanging in space after their Christmas party. Pick it up from there."

"After they picked up our package, they drifted. They did that for two days. We figured they were probably stowing supplies. Then yesterday morning they got under way. Although things are confusing from this distance, we suspect they were heading for a solar jet. We had a faint reading of one, but we couldn't tell if it was going toward their destination. When they got to a point, the craft veered off in the direction of the flow of the jet.

"It appeared they moved into the stream. The craft began picking up speed. It was a constant rate of acceleration for three minutes followed by an increased rate of speed.

"The boys theorize that Dandy sought out a jet. Then he entered the flow at a constant speed. The jet augmented his speed considerably, and at the end of three minutes he boosted engine output, which accounts for the rate change, followed by constant acceleration for another period of time. There was a lateral motion which suggests they came to a confluence in the stream"

"Suddenly, the image disappeared from the screen. We've played the tapes over and over. One instant it's there, and the next the screen's blank. There was no hazard observed in the vicinity. There's no debris. We could have picked that up if it had been blown into little pieces. It just disappeared."

Malvane stared through the image on the screen. Harder squirmed.

Malvane finally said, "Can you still track that solar jet they were apparently riding?

"Yes, I think so."

"Fine. Look at the end of it and you should find Taran."

Chapter 38

Candie was getting frustrated. She was trying to reconcile her star charts with what she was seeing from their present location. She had shot new astral photographs and now she was trying to find a visual correlation. The computer had already said it didn't know where they were. Until more data was available she got the same response each time she asked. This had been going on for hours.

Beatrice was at Candie's terminal doing mysterious things with the computer. She was completely oblivious to Candie's rantings. Maybe that was because she was wearing huge, padded earphones she'd gotten with her Christmas CDs from her mother.

Finally, Beatrice draped the earphones over her neck, stood up and unplugged the phones from the console. She tapped Candie on the shoulder. Before the navigator could snarl, Beatrice pointed across the room to toward the base of one of the tables. "Earth's in that direction." Then Beatrice headed for the bathroom.

A few minutes later she came out of her room sucking on one of her treasured hard candies. She had everyone's undivided attention.

Candie was leading the pack. "How do you know?"

"Years ago there was a governmental program that was looking for intelligent life in the universe. It was called CETI. They broadcast a repeated message for years until someone decided it might not be too smart to send a homing beacon to possibly hostile civilizations. Maybe we caught up with that broadcast. I started a search pattern on the proper frequency."

Candie started setting up a new star shot back along the reading Beatrice had given. She printed it on transparent film so she could read it from the reverse side. She called up the file chart on one monitor and entered the reversed view of the retroshot on another. With Tom's technical assistance she was able to superimpose the two charts on the same monitor. There wasn't anything close to an exact match because the two shots had been taken at slightly different angles.

Then Candie started eliminating what didn't appear on both photos. Those stars located between where the two shots had been taken remained. With that much sound information she was able to ask the computer again. This time she got an answer, but she didn't want to believe it. While everyone waited, she checked what the computer had said against the sandwiched star charts on the monitor.

"Well?" asked Dandy.

Candie swiveled around to face the four concerned faces and turned back to the monitors. She separated the images. "This is the view from earth. See this little dot?" said Candie. Then she pointed to the second transparency. "Okay, now see this large blob on the shot taken from here? Watch."

She superimposed the two images. "Look at the arrangement of bodies around the two dots. See the triangle there? The same triangle shows up here. Project a line along the hypotenuse and you find three stars in a row. There are other identification points."

Tom was getting impatient. "So?"

"That little point of light and this big one are the same. That is Tau Ceti. We're somewhere beyond it. Tau Ceti is 11.8 light years from earth."

There was a stunned silence. There seemed no reason to doubt Candie's conclusion, but how could that be?

Corky was the first to speak. "Hey, driver. Aren't we a little off course for Mars?"

Beatrice pointed out, in a small voice, that it would take a dozen years for a message to get back home.

"That is only if we send it from here," Dandy countered. "Corky, how are we doing on fuel?"

"While we were in the jet, the miles per gallon was fabulous. We used more in going from the moon to where we entered the jet. If we keep Taran in the jet, we can cruise all over the galaxy. Moving between the jets is where the rub is going to come in. As of now we still have 83% of capacity."

Dandy turned to the Candie. "Will you scan the area to make sure we won't run into an asteroid belt or a comet for the next few minutes, then join us in the Fish House?" He led the way to the beverage machine.

By the time everyone had served themselves, Candie had joined them. Dandy took charge of the meeting by perching on the edge of a table instead of seating himself.

"I'd guess everyone realizes that if we set a course for home, fired up the engines and headed off, we'd never make it. Our fuel would run out. Even if we could get all the fuel we wanted, we wouldn't live long enough to make it back. So we'll just have to go back in the same manner as we came."

Dandy looked at Tom. "Have you figured out what happened?"

"I can say what happened, but how it happened is another thing. I think I can duplicate the event, but I don't know the physics behind it. Decades ago someone designed a train that travelled in a vacuum tube on repelling magnetic fields. It would travel from coast to coast faster than an airplane. It accelerated at one G to Denver before it had to start braking. In our case, we were traveling in a vacuum. The solar jets are composed of a condensed stream of protons and electrons, which are emitted by stars. As we moved along the stream we started to build a magnetic charge. When I tried to break up the magnetism, I must have set up a repelling magnetic field, which propelled us at tremendous speeds."

"We must have done something to time also," Candie said. "We reduced years to minutes and I'd swear that from the time you switched the charge on and then off, it was just a matter of seconds."

"I had the feeling everything turned to jelly," noted Dandy.

Corky wrinkled his nose. "I thought everything turned slimy."

"Our chronometers, watches and various auto devices didn't seem to be affected, just us." said Tom. "If we find a jet going in the direction of earth and do everything we did before, I'll make one change. I can set the duration of the electrical charge on a timer so that it'll automatically shut off, independent of our concept of time. That way we can take a jump without ending up in the next galaxy."

"That sounds reasonable to me," Dandy responded. "How long do you want the time interval?"

"I think ten minutes would be enough to tell us if we're going in the direction we want to go."

Dandy glanced around the team. No one seemed inclined to object. "Let's do it. Candie, find us a jet going in the other direction."

Dandy turned to Beatrice. "Are you recording all of this?"

"I'm recording how many cups of coffee you're drinking and what percentage you let get cold and throw away."

Chapter 39

The apprehension was high over whether they could duplicate the event that had put them 11.8 light years from a home cooked meal. Dandy kept everyone as busy as possible without forcing issues. Candie had found another solar jet going in the general direction they wanted to go. Taran was heading for it, but at a comfortable speed. Tom had some work to do on the timer. Beatrice was setting up cameras to record everyone's activities during the "mag lev," as Tom called it. Corky was rigging up a device he hoped would log the path of the flight.

Dandy gave ten minutes warning before he was going to enter the solar jet. Everyone headed for the rest rooms.

With constant attention to every known detail, Dandy entered the stream. He was working from a script taken from the ship's logs. It wasn't long before it became apparent that their speed was in part determined by the size of the stream. He was using the same engine output as before, but the speeds were not increasing at the same rate as on the first flight. The stream was not as large at the first one. The question arose as to whether they should stay in the stream longer or accelerated more to reach speed.

Dandy had the problem in his lap. His mind was racing furiously to devise the right strategy, when Tom made it a moot question.

"The magnetism is growing rapidly."

"When the levels reach the same as before, throw the switch."

"It will be in less than a minute," reported Tom.

They watched the viewer as his hand rested on the toggle switch. All eyes saw him throw it. Things seemed to shimmer as if they were made of gelatin, but in what seemed like a heartbeat later objects regained their solidity. The automatic timer had turned off the current after ten minutes. Dandy eased them out of the stream.

Candie was already taking readings before Dandy asked for a relative fix. It didn't take long for her to smile at all the eager faces. "We did it. We're much closer to Tau Ceti. At the moment I can't tell how fast we were going because the jets meander all over the place. Maybe Corky's readings will give us a better idea."

"I can tell you when we zigged and when we zagged," said Corky. "We did a lot of that, but I can't tell you the distance between the curves."

Candie spoke hesitantly. "Since we don't know how far we were past Tau Ceti, nor do we know what kind of undulating course we took, I can only give a rough estimate. It looks like we were traveling at approximately .25 light years per hour."

Beatrice gasped. "That's about 1.5 trillion miles per hour. Impossible."

"I can't even begin to comprehend that," added Corky.

"We're sitting on the far side of Tau Ceti from Earth, so it's possible," said Candie. "The thing is not to think of it as miles.

Think of it as light years. Eleven or twelve is easier to handle than trillions."

Before the positive elements of their experiment could fade into some sort of hopelessness wrapped up in unintelligible numbers, Dandy jumped in. "Candie, take a look at this ten minute exercise. Using it, give me a ballpark estimate of the time needed to get in the vicinity of Tau Ceti. Also is our solar jet still going in the right direction? I want to be the first to visit another solar system."

Chapter   40

They found that outbound jets were far more numerous than the inbound ones and it took the better part of a week to get into the Tau Ceti solar system. An important discovery was made while getting there. Trying to go upstream in the jet was entirely different. It was like trying to paddle upstream in a swift river. Furthermore, the magnetic field did not build in the same manner. Inward flights used considerable fuel.

Dandy pointed Taran toward the star and let her cruise. This was becoming a scientific venture. They set out to map the system. Along the way, they were going to record every scrap of data they could. Beatrice was in heaven.

They ran into one problem that neither they nor the designers of Taran had anticipated. A mass of sensing equipment was aboard the ship, but the raw data was to be transferred by telemetry to equipment on earth, where it would be analyzed. The analyses were then to be sent back to Taran. The system was designed to be used within communication distances of the ground base. Taran had sensors to read the mineral content of a planet or asteroid, but it had no way of analyzing the information aboard. Tom didn't have the parts aboard to construct such a complicated piece of equipment to handle that amount of data. They were going to stuff the suggestion box when they got back.

Candie was delighted. She had found a new way to identify the physical structure of the solar system. With her enhanced solar jet sensor she could locate planets, moons, comets, and asteroids by the influence they had on the jets. She could extrapolate size, velocity and direction by how the space objects bent the jets.

On the wall behind her station, Candie had created a huge map of the Tau Ceti solar system. As observations were made concerning the composition of the system, she entered the data. The picture continued to grow and change. Periodically, the crew members would wander over to see what new entries had been posted. So far she had identified five planets. She suspected there were at least two more, but they would be on the other side of the sun. It would be a while before they could be observed. These were the two that held the most promise of being inhabited. They were within the acceptable parameters of distance from the star and speed to sustain life.

Dandy was particularly interested in those two. His specific concern was water. The travel between solar jets and now into the solar system was consuming a lot of fuel. He was hoping that one of those planets held water. So far he hadn't expressed any concern to the crew. He had talked privately with Tom about fuel supply and consumption rates. Their figures were about the same. There wasn't enough fuel to get home in their current manner of travel. Neither man had stated the obvious.

They had two possibilities. They could locate a fuel supply: water, ice, or frozen hydrogen. Or they could try a long jump back toward Earth. The problem was that they could not be sure the jet would be going where they wanted to go.

For the time being he planned on keeping an eye open for some source of hydrogen. Tom had said he thought he could rig up one of the sensors so they could operate it aboard without the telemetry link to the ground. With it, they could search out hydrogen at considerable distances. If they found some, he hoped it would be in some form that they could use.

They were moving on an intercept course with the fifth planet of the Tau Ceti system. The assumption was that it would be a frozen planet, too far from the sun to sustain anything that they might recognize as life. However, the composition of this planet might give some indication of what to expect on the others. Taran was going to consume a lot of fuel to get to the two other planets. He wanted some indication that the trip would be worthwhile.

P-5, as Candie designated the fifth planet, was getting closer and closer. It appeared to have some sort of cloud cover, but without the sensor analyzing equipment that was on earth, they couldn't tell if the cloud was water vapor or methane. On the map, Candie had just added a moon to P-5.

Dandy picked up a coffee for himself and a tea for Candie. He perched on her map table while they sipped their drinks. He had never seen Candie so invigorated. She had always been a live wire , but now she was doing what no one had ever done, or probably ever thought of doing. She was charting other solar systems. This wasn't theory, but the real thing.

"If we only had the sensor array operational," she lamented. "We're getting close enough to P-5, that we could do a pretty good survey of its geography and geology. We could map the climate, too. We could do all that in a fly-by without costing us any particular time. I really am more interested in the other two planets. That's where we might find life."

"If we find life, what do you think we should do?" asked Dandy. "Should we extend our hand and say 'Howdy'? Or do you think we should be more circumspect? You know, we've never done much thinking along these lines. Until Taran, we only considered what we'd do when an alien ship entered our space. Now we may be in someone else's space. We'd be the invading aliens. How does that strike you?"

"You certainly know how to break a mood," Candie said. "But you're right. It might be a good idea to throw the problem out to the crew so that we have some time to ponder the question. There's nothing in our training tapes to give us any guidance. Malvane can't give us any input. We're on our own."

Dandy stood up. "Later today, when everyone is up, I'll call a meeting so we can toss the problem out for everyone to chew on."

Candie turned back to her instruments as Dandy went to check his board. Everything was green. Dandy didn't have much to do so he wandered back to Candie's station. She was intently studying four different windows on one screen. She slid aside so he could get a better look at the images which showed P-5 and it's moon.

"See anything odd?" she asked.

Dandy knew there must be something, but he couldn't find what warranted the question. "The whole thing's amazing, but I don't see anything that seems out of step."

"When the first observation was made, the star was lighting the right half of the planet. The moon was just crossing in front of the P-5 so the dark side of the moon is silhouetted against the lighted side of the planet. The bright side of the moon is still against the black of space. Look about 2 mm off the moon at about 4 o'clock."

"It looks like a star way out in space," Dandy said.

"Now look at the next image. Of course, the moon and planet are changing relative positions, but look where the star was."

"It's not there, but it could be covered by the planet."

"Maybe, but on that same window, look about midway across the moon on a line between 4 and 10 o'clock. There's your star against the dark side of the moon. Look at this black dot at 10 on the third shot." Candie pointed at a tiny dark point about 2mm off the edge of the moon. "It's in the shadow of the moon against the lighted planet. It doesn't show up at all in the fourth picture. Something is orbiting the moon."

Dandy shrugged, "So the moon has a moon."

Candie gave him one of those "Dummy" smiles. "How does it maintain an orbit against the mass of a planet that size?"

"Are you trying to tell me that whatever we're seeing isn't natural?"

"I wish we had those sensors working. I would suggest you have that crew-talk sooner rather than later," said Candie.

Chapter 41

Dandy stared at the screen for a while before heading back to his own station. He leaned back in his couch, crossed his ankles, and knitted his fingers behind his head.

After ten minutes, Dandy snapped his couch into an upright position. He started reviewing his flight plan. Once he had all the figures he wanted, he turned to Candie. "Is there anything more you can say about that object?"

"No. Not really, until we get closer."

"I think sooner is now," said Dandy. He struck a tone on the intercom and he announced, "We have something to discuss. Meet in the Fish House in ten minutes."

Corky was the only one who had been asleep. He came out sleepy-eyed. Tom had been watching videos. Beatrice came out with her earphones draped around her neck. Candie reappeared after a brief retreat to her quarters.

When everyone had settled down, Dandy began. "All our lives we've lived with the UFO stories. Science fiction has concocted all sorts of invasions of earth by aliens. Our approach has been constructed around how we'd react to beings coming into our space. Now we're placed in a unique position for human beings. We have to consider ourselves as aliens. We may be entering the space of other sentient beings. I think this takes a preplanning so we have at least some sort of guideline to help direct our approach instead of ad libbing on the spot." Dandy sat back.

There was a prolonged silence as the proposed idea sank in.

"No matter how much thought we give the question," Candie finally said, "there's going to be a lot of ad libbing. I think the basic premise must be that we'll be met with hostility. How this plays out depends on relative stages of development. If we locate a species who is at the hunter/gatherer level, we might be taken for gods, but feared nonetheless. If they're more advanced, some would want to extend the olive branch, while others would want us destroyed before we contaminate or destroy them. Everyone would want our technology. To more highly developed orders, we'd be a curiosity, even if we don't pose a threat."

Tom chimed in. "Don't forget that we have no way to defend ourselves outside of running. We're pretty quick in a solar jet, but we may not be all that fast, comparatively speaking, under regular engine power."

"But we don't mean any harm to anyone," said Beatrice.

"How are you going to communicate that to other beings?" asked Tom. "We certainly won't be able to tell them. Even trying to get your point across with signs has its own problems. Just stick up a fist in Texas with the index and little fingers raised and it means 'hook em horns,' but in Mexico it means 'I know who's sleeping with your wife.' Maybe the beings we might run into don't even have hands."

Corky had been sitting back taking everything in as he sipped his coffee. "Is there some reason we're discussing this particular problem now?" he inquired.

Dandy smiled. He nodded to Candie. "Show them what you've

got."

Candie stepped to her station to switch the four views of the P-5 moon on the Fish House screen. No one could see anything strange until Candie pointed out the orbiting object.

"Candie has a number of reasons to believe that it is not a natural object," Dandy said.

Candie had everyone's attention. "For one thing, because of the relative sizes of the planet and the moon, I think the planet would snatch away any real moon. The orbit doesn't seem compatible with the arrangements of the bodies, direction and velocity. It's also much more reflective than the moon. Under maximum magnification it appears to be uniformly angular. As we get closer, I should be able to tell more about it."

"Do we want to get closer?" asked Tom.

Beatrice was in her research mode. "We can't pass up our first chance to learn if there's other intelligence in the universe."

"It wouldn't do anyone any good to find out if we can't communicate that information back home," Tom pointed out .

"As soon as we find out, I'll send a message home. It may take a dozen years to get there, but they'll get it."

"You know," said Corky, "it may be 'alien-made', but that doesn't mean it constitutes a threat to us. We have thousands of pieces of space junk circulating around our solar system. Maybe it's a probe of some sort. It could be debris from a long gone intergalactic war."

"It could also be a military outpost just waiting to repel invaders," Tom said. "Don't get me wrong. I'm as curious as anyone, but I counsel extreme caution in approaching anything alien."

Dandy entered the discussion. "At the moment, we don't know what we're looking at. If it's a manned alien vessel, then they've had days to sight our approach. If they have space travel, then they should know we're here. So far, it's just a strange object orbiting a moon. I'm for continuing on our present course. That'll bring us close enough to get a better look. If we get some indication that it's something other than an orbiting pile of galactic rock, then we can alter our plans. We need to know more about that planet than we can get from this distance. Do I hear any objections?"

"I'm curious," Corky said.

Tom, who apparently didn't want to be the sole dissenter, said, "All I'm saying is let's play it on the cautious side."

Dandy nodded. "That sounds prudent to me. From now on we want a round-the-clock observation of that thing. We must know if there's any deviation at all that could indicate an intelligent presence. Corky, you've had your sleep, so you take the first watch."

Chapter 42

Two day's travel gave them a much better look at Candie's mysterious find. They accepted that it was not a naturally occurring object. It appeared to be a flat, equilateral triangle. Tom and Beatrice had their heads together. They came up with tentative dimensions of 100 yards per side, with no major projections breaking the smooth surface. There had been no signs of activity. Beatrice had been scanning the various frequencies to detect communication activity. At least the object was not broadcasting on any channel Taran was capable of catching.

The crew was curious enough to press on. Everyone was apprehensive, but not sufficiently so to suggest an alternative action.

As might be expected Corky came up with a name for the object. He dubbed it "Nacho," like the triangular corn chip.

For two more days Taran proceeded on its fly-by course. Speculation ranged widely as to the object's origin and its reason for orbiting the moon. All indications were that the P-5 would not sustain any life form that could create space travel. They still couldn't tell anything about P-3 and P-4. The greatest likelihood was that if the object was some sort of space ship it would have come from one of those two planets. The only other alternative was that it had come from another solar system, but judging from the size of the craft, that would be far-fetched. It appeared to be only a little bigger than Taran, but, of course, Taran was not supposed to be there either.

Tension built as they got closer to Nacho. Dandy had tired of playing solitaire on his computer, so he turned his attention to wandering through material on hydrogen, looking for anything that might aid in resupplying the ship. He already knew the scientific data. Now he was looking for anecdotal material that might reveal variant sources.

Candie rapped her knuckle on the console, which was her signal that she wanted to speak to him without an audience. Dandy made a drinking motion to which she nodded. He stepped over to the machines for coffee and tea. Dandy handed her the tea as he perched on her map board.

Candie sipped her tea. "A while back I took time readings on the orbit. Yesterday it seemed like it didn't take as much time to get around the moon as it used to, so I took some more readings. Also, our angle has changed so we aren't look straight down on the orbit anymore. Now we're viewing it from the side. I've been taking distance measurements. Nacho's in a decaying orbit. As closely as I can figure it from this distance, it'll take a dive in four days. It is spiraling down to the moon in ever steeper angles. Since there isn't any atmosphere it won't burn up. It'll just impact the surface."

Candie brought up an animated diagram on her screen. When she set it into motion it was obvious that Nacho was going down.

"It looks like it's about time for another meeting," Dandy said.

Dandy relayed Candie's new observations. "The question is what to do now. We can get to it in one day under power. So far, we've seen nothing to indicate any activity. If there was life aboard, I'd suspect they would be trying something to save themselves. If they can't do that, you'd think they would be yelling their heads off trying to get help or letting their home base know what was happening to them. We haven't picked up any broadcasts at all."

"Maybe they are broadcasting on some frequency or wave we can't hear," Tom said.

"They could be playing wounded grouse like we did with Tokla over the south Atlantic," Corky commented.

"We could let it impact the moon. Then we could go down to inspect what was left," said Candie. "At least we wouldn't be in any danger from aliens."

Beatrice jumped into the fray, horror spread over her face. "We can't do that. If that's an alien ship, just think of what we could learn. All might be lost if it crashes."

Candie winked at Dandy, who said, "She's got a point. Why don't we jump in there? We'd have a couple of days to look around before it drops. I doubt they've left a hatch open. We might have to cut our way in. At the first sign of danger of any kind we head for cover."

"I'll go for that," said Corky.

The rest of the crew nodded. "Okay," said Dandy. "We power up in 10 minutes. Secure everything and get yourselves ready."

There was a scramble, and ten minutes later everyone was in position. They had been through the drill enough to know what had to be done. The anticipation of the impending event heightened their reactions. Dandy kept the speed low enough for the crew to function without undue discomfort.

Every screen on the ship showed Nacho. Details started to become visible. It was the thin, equilateral triangle they had taken it for. Tom's and Beatrice's estimated length of the ship at 100 yards was confirmed. Engine ports lined one edge. The opposing point had a triangular bubble raised slightly above the skin. It was probable the bridge. The rest of the ship was smooth. No recognizable armament could be seen.

Constant observations continued to reveal nothing indicating life. No cohesive energy radiated from it. There were some minor traces, but it was hard to determine if they came from the ship or from the moon.

Dandy switched on the intercom. "Hang on. I am going to do some maneuvering. I want to orbit parallel to the ship, but higher and slightly to the rear. If it wants to come at us, it'll have to turn, giving us a little warning."

The vessel was clearly visible on the illuminated side of the moon. When direct observation was impossible, sensors kept track of it. Beatrice was busy recording every detail.

Once Dandy parked, he convened another conference over their screens. "Our hypotheses have been confirmed from the information we've been able to gather at this proximity. Tom, can you tell anything about the propulsion system?"

"Not really," Tom answered. "I have never seen anything resembling it. Our external apparatus is for thrust and exhaust. Those on the alien ship look like multi-faceted lenses. It must be a whole different principle. I don't seen any signs of a landing capability, so maybe it can't operate in atmosphere. Maybe they're equipped with shuttle craft."

"Maybe the crew evacuated in their shuttle craft," said Candie.

"Maybe. But where would they go?" Dandy said. "There isn't much around here that seem hospitable to life....no matter what form. That ship may be full of bodies, too. Of course, they may be a thousand years old, too."

Candie wrinkled her nose.

"We can't tell anything from here," Dandy said. "We can record what our sensors say, but we can't read them. I'm going down there to have a look around. Corky, will you drive the pickup?"

Corky beamed. "Sure."

"Beatrice," Dandy said. "I am going to have my radio on all the time. Record everything I say. I'll also carry a video camera on my helmet. I'll try to explain what I'm seeing."

Candie looked a little miffed.

Dandy explained his reasoning. "Candie, you take over my station in case of emergency. You may have to make a split-second decision. If a hazard develops, it's your responsibility to save the ship. If it becomes a question of Corky and me or the ship, there's no question, save Taran. Get this information back home. You and Tom can fly this baby. Tom, come help us suit up."

It took an hour to get ready. Finally, Corky took control of the shuttle. He opened the ramp and nudged the vehicle into a free fall. Dandy's stomach was queasy at the thought of it being a long way down to a barren moon. Once they were far enough away from Taran, Corky fired the engine.

Their approach to Nacho was from above and behind. Dandy started his running commentary for the record.

"We're coming in from above. As Tom estimated, it's very close to 100 meters per side. It is about 7 or 8 meters thick. The edges of two sides round off. The third side has what looks like three huge rectangular lenses fitted into the hull. The skin of the hull comes out far enough to protect the lenses. That must be part of their propulsion system. There are no obvious exhaust ports showing, nor are there any carbon-type stains. The area on the opposite point rises about two meters above the surrounding surface. It looks like there are shuttered ports. Everything's buttoned up tight."

"Corky, take us underneath," Dandy said.

"We're close enough to go to maneuvering thrusters. Hang on. Here we go."

The shuttle nosed over and it dropped below the craft. Dandy continued his talk. "We're in the shadow now, so things are not nearly as discernible, but it appears to be much like the upper surface. It's blue-grey in color and glossy looking. Hey, Corky, doesn't it look like this thing was designed with aerodynamics in mind?"

"Yes, I think you're right. . It doesn't make any difference in space, but I don't see anything that would serve as landing gear. It certainly can't land on its end. It'd fall over."

"Maybe it's not designed with the capability of working in atmosphere. You know, it's pretty small to be used for interplanetary flight, unless it has a lot more speed than we do."

"Look. There's a huge circular line on its underside," Corky pointed out. "Could that be a shuttle launcher, like our ramps?"

"It could be anything. Maybe it's a weapons array. It looks like everything's locked up tight. Are you finding any energy radiating from it?"

"There's a little, but it is so small that nothing major could be operating. What we're getting could be a background reading. Of course, there could be a lot going on and it's shielded so we can't detect it."

"Let's go back up top for a closer look," Dandy said. "Do you think you can set down on this thing?"

"I can put it down, but keeping it there may be tricky. I could probably maintain contact as long as I kept the maneuvering jet operating. It depends on the hull composition. If there's iron in it, the magnetic shoes will hold, but no iron, no grip. Suction doesn't work in a vacuum. There's probably something we could tie to. It won't take much, because we are weightless."

Corky slowly brought the shuttle hovering behind the forward raised triangle. With the utmost care, he brought the shuttle down on the ship and threw a switch.

"The magnetic shoes won't hold," Corky reported. "You'll have to find a hitching rail. Hook yourself up to the shuttle winch so we don't lose you. That line is light, but strong. I can reel you in if necessary."

Dandy put on his helmet. They had been in a pressurized cabin. He had wanted to conserve his suit's supply of air. He tested the radio with Corky. Then he called Beatrice. "How are the helmet pictures?"

"They are coming in fine, but look at things long enough so we have a chance to identify them. If you move your head too fast everything is blurred. When you hesitated on objects, we can get a clear shot that can be enlarged or enhanced."

"Okay, gang. Here it goes," said Dandy as he stepped into the airlock.

When the air was purged from the chamber, Dandy swung the side door open. The shuttle was being held to the surface of the ship by a tiny jet from the maneuvering thruster. That kept the shuttle in place, but it wasn't going to do him a bit of good. He was far enough from the edge of the ship that he couldn't see the moon underneath. That made keeping his composure easier.

Dandy began a careful, slow scan of his view of the alien ship. "The surface is a muted blue-green with the appearance of glazed ceramics. We know already it's non-magnetic because the shuttle shoes won't hold. It's smooth and featureless. I am about twenty feet from the raised area, which rises about 6 feet from the surrounding deck. The sides are slanted at approximately sixty degrees. These may be shuttered ports. There are seams along the edges. There are what appear to be handrails on both sides of one of the sections. Maybe, if I can get there, I can tether the shuttle to that rail."

He reached around the edge of the door to release the cable for the side winch. He snapped the fastener into a utility ring in his belt. Using the edge of the door he pushed himself down onto the skin of the alien ship.

"I'm not going to be able to walk on this smooth surface. There's no way to hold myself down. I just float away or drift off in reaction to one of my movements. Corky, can you ease me over to that rail?"

"Yes, I think so. Get back inside so I don't run over you."

"I'm in."

Slowly the shuttle swung around so Corky could see where he was going. Gently, he urged the craft forward. "You should be able to reach it now."

Dandy slid the door open again. "Good. I can make it now." He pulled himself down to the surface and made his way along the side of the shuttle. "I'm within arm's length of the rail. I'll tether the shuttle to it with a light line in case we need to break away." Dandy reached the rail. "Okay. Corky. You're tied off. Do you have any of those sticky strips you use to keep machine parts from floating off when you are working on something?"

"Sure."

"Pass a couple through the handout window."

Dandy took the strips of material. They were three feet long, double-sided, self-adhering material. One side had a light adhesive so the strip would stick to a surface. The other side was a thick, tacky substance into which parts were impressed. Dandy tore off the protective covering the back side and, with great difficulty, put the tape on the heels of his boots and up the sides of his legs. He removed the outer cover and, keeping close to the shuttle he took a couple of tentative steps. The adhesive kept him firmly in contact with the skin of the ship. He rocked forward onto his toe and the adhesive grudgingly released. It would be slow going, but it would work.

Candie had been watching through the images relayed by the helmet camera. "Well done."

Dandy moved out in front of the shuttle. "I'm standing on top of an alien spaceship and there isn't much to see. Everything's featureless. Maybe we should have taken a closer look at that large circular mark on the underside. We're going to have to get inside to gather any significant information."

He turned to examine the inclined plane of the shuttered parts. He could see rectangular outlines, but there was no way to pry one open. He rapped his knuckles on the surface. "Anybody home? I wonder if I can cut a hole in this stuff. I'll put a torch to it to see what happens." He began to make his way back to the tool bin of the shuttle.

"Uh, oh," said Corky. "You better look behind you."

Dandy had to take three steps to turn himself around. "Uh, oh, is right." In front of him, one of the panels had started to descend into the deck, revealing darkened glass underneath. The blackness was broken by sparkles of bright color, like gem stones. Some were blinking. As Dandy studied the 4-by-6-foot void in front of him, he began to become aware of a shape. He could not actually see the shape, but it broke up the patterns of the gem lights behind.

"I think there's something standing right in front of me, but I can't see anything." Dandy raised his empty hands to the side and slowly turned around.

"There is a creature in there," Beatrice said into his earphones. "I pulled up an enhanced view. In fact there are several creatures in there. I can't make out details, but what I do see doesn't make sense."

Dandy turned to face the open portal again. Slowly, he gave a formal bow from the waist and then stood straight with his hands hanging at his sides. "Corky, stay out of sight, but be ready to jerk me out of here on my command. Just take off. Break the tether. You can reel me in later. First, I'm going to try the friendly approach.

"Something is happening," Dandy said in a strained voice. "Lights are coming on inside the ship. I can see the bridge. One of the beings is silhouetted in front of a working area. It looks like a turtle with two heads on long necks. It appears to have two legs and a tail and two arms with hands in about the same position as our arms. Between their heads is some sort of structure that looks like a fence post. The tail looks like the bottom end of the post.

"The lights are getting brighter in front of the figure. I can see its faces. Each one has two eyes. They are set well off to the side of the head....kinda like a heron's. They're looking straight at me, but one swiveled around to the side to look at the other head. There is a protrusion between the eyes like the head of a fish. I can't see if there are any nasal openings. It looks like it has a mouth without lips. It's just a round orifice and both mouths are talking."

The frontal light illuminated the figure entirely. The two hands, which had been hanging at the sides moved to the front where they clasped with a third hand-like appendage in the middle of the body. The figure bowed forward in the same way Dandy had done.

Dandy kept up his commentary. " He's wearing a uniform with emblems on it. Maybe they designate rank. He is returning my salutation. When he bowed he was standing on two legs. Now he has settled back to a three point stance. It looks like he is sitting on that fence post. I can see three other creatures propped on their third leg at various consoles. They must not need chairs."

In the background, Dandy could hear Tom say, "Gee, they'll never believe us back home."

"Yeah, they will. Bea's getting it all," said Candie.

"Shhhh," hissed Beatrice.

The figure in front of Dandy slowly raised his right hand with the palm up. Dandy could see two fingers and one opposing thumb.

Off to the left, the panel between the rails started to move downward into the ship. Behind it was an alien dressed in a space suit. The top was a clear dome containing the two heads and the post. The heads were looking in all directions. With long necks, the heads could swivel almost all the way around.

The alien straightened its two legs, raising itself off the post into a standing position. The alien advanced until it was standing on the hull of the ship in front of Dandy.

"They have some way besides stickum to keep them on the

deck," observed Dandy. "He can walk a lot better than I can."

The alien stopped ten feet from Dandy, where it began giving an assortment of hand signals. None of it made any sense to Dandy. In turn, Dandy tried to indicate that he should slow down and repeat. They weren't going to be doing much communication.

"I don't even know how to say yes or no," said Dandy. "Corky, do you have one of those large pieces of chalk we use to mark crates?"

"Yes."

"Put it in the handout window."

Dandy waved both hands at the alien trying to get him to stop. Dandy held up a finger hoping the alien would wait for a moment. Dandy swung around and headed for the shuttle without looking back. "Corky, what's he doing?"

"He's beginning to fidget. Both head are talking up a storm."

Dandy opened the outer hatch of the window and pulled the chalk out. Before turning around Dandy marked a big, white X and made a squiggly line on the side of the shuttle. Then he turned around. The alien was standing on his two feet and quartered toward the opening in the ship as if to flee should the necessity arise.

Dandy moved to the edge of the opening so he could use the handrails to lower himself down to the deck. He wrote the numbers one through ten in column on the hull. Using his fingers, he held up one and pointed at the appropriate numeral, going through to ten. Then he drew the signs for addition, subtraction, multiplication and division. He wrote one plus one equals two and then looked directly at the alien. In an exaggerated manner Dandy nodded. The alien looked at him. Both mouths were going. Dandy wrote four minus two equals two and nodded again. The alien did nothing. Next he wrote one plus two equals four and in the same exaggerated manner he shook his head. Then he rubbed out the number four and replaced it with three.

As he bobbled his head, the alien made an inward motion with each head.

"Maybe we're getting somewhere. It may be possible that it's motion is affirmative. Let's see if I can get the negative."

This time he wrote two and three equals four. As Dandy shook his head, the alien thrust its long necks toward the outward side of its body. To check on his results, Dandy pointed at the alien and marked one. Then he pointed to himself and wrote down another numeral one and then one plus one equals two. The alien immediately thrust both heads outward.

"Maybe I've gotten something wrong."

The alien reached for the chalk and Dandy surrendered it. Next to Dandy's line of numbers he wrote figures of his own, stopping at nine.

Continuing on, the alien pointed at Dandy and wrote one. Pointing at himself he wrote plus two, equals three. He then moved his heads inward.

Dandy just looked at the alien without comprehension. "Does he mean he's twice as big, twice as strong or twice as smart?"

Corky injected, "They are lighting the window again."

The alien extended a hand toward the window. Dandy had to turn to see it. Just inside the glass an alien wearing only some sort of waist wrap instead of the uniform sat down on the post-like structure. The figure wiggled and split down the middle into two figures. Each half had a head, half the post structure, a leg and foot, an outer arm and half of the huge center arm and gripping device. The parts move away in an awkward manner, like a man walking with a peg leg.

"Amazing," stated Dandy. "Instead of bipeds, it's bipersons. For the record, the skin reminds me of an elephant's. It is blue-grey in color. The hands and faces seem darker. I don't see any hair anywhere. The outside hand seems to be the dexterous appendage while the middle arm seems to be extremely powerful, a holding device."

The two figures moved back toward one another and sat side by side on the center structure.

"The matching sides looks like it has all sorts of connectors to hold them together. I'll bet a lot of them are sensory so that the two can act as one."

The pair jiggled a little and seemed to suddenly grow together. The figure stood up on its two legs to walk back into the bridge.

Dandy nodded. He pointed to himself and held up one finger and pointed to the alien and held up two fingers. Then he held up three fingers. The alien made the affirmative motion.

"I'd better get down to business before I run out of air," said Dandy.

He moved over to their chalkboard. With his glove, he erased his computations. He pointed to the ship under his feet. He drew a triangle to represent it. Then he pointed to the moon below. The alien kept nodding affirmatively with Dandy. Next Dandy drew a circle and shaded one half. The alien pointed to the planet and Dandy nodded. Off to the light side he put the star. The alien was following him. Slowly Dandy drew three circles around the planet. Then he put the chalk on the triangle. He drew a spiral down to the moon. The alien looked at Dandy for a considerable time before nodding to the affirmative.

Dandy held out the chalk to his space companion.

The alien accepted the chalk. First, he wrote the alien equivalent of the numbers Dandy had inscribed on the hull. Then he drew on the triangle representing, a shaded edge. He pointed to the side which Dandy and Corky had already determined to contain the engines. Behind the engines he made marks. From the front of the triangle he drew an arrow headed up and away from the moon. Then with a finger he rubbed out the engines and the upward rising arrow.

The alien moved to a clean part of the hull. He drew Tau Ceti with all the planets. From the fourth planet he inscribed a line to the fifth. Along the line he drew a larger object, of two pyramids hooked base to base. Next to the double triangle or diamond shape he made a tiny triangle. Pointing at the triangle with one hand, he stomped a foot on the hull, and pointed with another hand at the ship on which they were standing. He erased the small triangle and redrew it by P-5.

Dandy had been giving a running description of all that was going on. "Anyone have any idea what he means?"

"I think something is coming from P-4 to P-5," Candie offered. "It would have to be another ship."

"I bet he drew the little triangle to show scale," said Beatrice.

"If that's true, that big ship has to be enormous," said Dandy. "Do you suppose it's the mother ship of this one?"

The alien moved back over to Dandy's drawing of P-5, where he had indicated the three days until Nacho goes down. He inscribed five circuits of the planet. He stepped back to his galaxy diagram where he drew a line from the diamond to P-5.

"I think he's trying to tell us that in five days another ship arrives," said Dandy.

"That'll be too late," said Candie.

Dandy took the chalk back. He pointed at the diamond and then P-5. He wrote the alien equivalent of five beside it. While indicating his own diagram showing the alien craft spiraling down to the moon, he wrote three. Then he subtracted three from five. When he looked directly at his companion, the aliens moved their heads toward center.

The alien pointed at his ship, then the moon. His hand made a diving motion toward the moon.

"They know they're going down in three days," said Dandy. "They also know they'll be killed."

He didn't have time to dwell on this revelation because Candie cut in. "Dandy, you should be getting short on air and we have ten minutes before we enter the dark side of the moon."

Dandy looked at the star position before checking his gauge. Candie was right, he was getting low. He turned his attention to the alien. He held up a finger. He then patted his backpack tank. He made motions with his mouth of taking in and expelling gas. He made a sign of an extended index finger and thumb coming together to indicate a diminished supply. The alien moved its heads inward. Then Dandy held up two fingers. He pointed at the sun and then the moon. With the chalk Dandy drew a picture showing Nacho moving into the shadow. He tapped himself on the chest and pointed at the shuttle, making a motion with a hand toward Taran, which was just a spot in the sky. On his drawing of the moon, he moved the alien ship through the darkness into the light again. He made motions showing his return to the same location.

The alien made motions to the affirmative. He clasped all three hands together as he gave a little bow. He stood up on his two legs and moved toward the opening. As soon as the alien stepped into the chamber, the panel slid closed.

Dandy untied the tether and Corky reeled him in.

Chapter 43

It wasn't until Dandy was back aboard Taran that he realized how tired he was. Candie was there to help him while Tom assisted Corky. He was glad there was no need for explanations. Beatrice called down to the dressing room to see what they wanted to eat. When they arrived at the command level she had food waiting.

The crew was in awe of the realities of the day. Lifelong beliefs were going to have to be amended. They had suspected and even hoped that such a day would come, but they were still unprepared for the events that had just taken place. Not much was being said.

Dandy was more interested in sleep than in eating. "I'm going to bed for about four hours. Then we can meet to decide on our next plan of action. You know the situation as well as I do. When I get up, be prepared to offer suggestions." He staggered off to bed.

The crew conspired to let Dandy and Corky sleep for 6 hours. The rest of the crew got some rest, too.

When he arose, Dandy was so groggy he didn't realize he had been asleep for a couple of extra hours. After two cups of coffee he began to function more efficiently, and the crew gathered in the Fish House.

To get things going, Dandy turned to Beatrice. "You've been recording all of this. Give us a recap of what we've learned and what you can extrapolate."

This was not the same Beatrice that had come aboard a few months earlier. She wore coveralls like everyone else. She no longer fussed with her hair, but rolled it up out of the way. Now she stood up to see everyone and to be seen.

"The beings appear to be from P-4. Candie postulated that that planet had the best chances for life. If that's true, then they're used to a climate cooler than earth, with a gravity a little greater than we experience."

Candie interrupted. "How can you tell that? We can speculate about P-4, but we haven't seen it yet. We don't know anything more than it exists. The drawing the alien made only shows that its on the other side of Tau Ceti. That drawing was probably on a general scale."

"That's not the basis for my belief," Beatrice said. "Remember that skin you said looked like an elephant's? The way it rolls, it looks like there's a uniform layer of fat under it, which would keep a body warm. Instead of an elephant, it's more like one of our sea-going mammals covered with blubber. That third leg looks like a device to handle heavy gravity. The other legs are sturdy. Unless it has to move, the being is tripedal. That would conserve a lot of energy in a high gravity environment."

"Why do you suppose they showed themselves to us practically naked?" asked Tom.

Dandy suggested a possibility. "We were trying to establish some form of primitive communication. A problem was arising when I tried point at it or they." He hesitated. "Or--."

"Bip."

Everyone looked at Corky. "Bip?" said Dandy.

"Yeah, Biperson. That's one double. Two bipersons are two Bips and so forth,"

"Okay." Dandy started over again. "A problem arose when I tried to point at Bip and then at myself to come up with the sum of two. I think to avoid confusion at that crucial juncture, they demonstrated their duality."

"Do you suppose they were born like that?" asked Candie.

"No, I don't think they're twins," Beatrice said. "There are slight differences in structure. Their skin color is slightly off. I'd guess that it's some sort of symbiotic relationship. Each half wouldn't function nearly as efficiently as a single. Mobility would be severely restricted. Think of trying to get around with a short, wooden leg. That center hand is no more than a strong vise, giving a single unit very little hand dexterity. It appears that when joined, they share, at least in part, a nervous system. The right hand continued to perform tasks while only the left head was watching what it was doing. Did you notice that while drawing or writing, Bip used hands interchangeably?"

"Do you think the Bip we saw was male or female, or one of each?" asked Candie.

"Husband and wife?" said Corky. "That would be carrying togetherness much too far."

Beatrice had had time to study all the filmed records as she cataloged them into memory. "I think those two were both of the same sex, whatever that may be. For that matter, they could be neuter drones of some sort, but since they went to the trouble of covering parts of themselves I'd guess they were being modest."

"We can speculate until the sun comes up," Dandy said, "but we have another more pressing question. They are going to crash two days before their mother ship arrives. What do we do? It appears they're powerless to prevent the crash. They must not have any escape mechanism or they wouldn't have indicated they were going down before the cavalry rides in."

"If they can't do it," Tom said, "maybe we could shuttle them to the moon's surface where they could be picked up. We don't have time to take them to the planet and get away before the big ship arrives, and I have the feeling we shouldn't be around when it gets here. From the scale Bip gave us, that ship's enormous. All present indications are that they don't have starships. Since we aren't from this system, they might suddenly covet our technology. That's another good reason for not bringing the Nacho crew on board Taran."

Candie stood up to get another tea. "I'm with Tom. We'd better be careful. Even though they don't seem to have starship capability, I'd love to see what kind of drive Nacho has. There's another problem. We know the rescue ship is going to be a couple of days late. How far has it to come and how long does it take? We know Nacho has been in orbit six days, because that is when we first saw it. Maybe it's been in orbit a while longer. But where was the rescue ship when the call went out? If it was on P-4 when they got the call, we had better fire up now and get out of here. That ship would be fast."

The discussion continued through a meal period. It was coming up on time to go back to Nacho.

Dandy called a halt to the discussion. "Are we going to try to help the crew of Nacho or let them go down? My opinion is that we try to help them, then get the hell out of here before the mother ship gets here."

Corky and Dandy went to get dressed for their next space walk. The same routine applied as before. When Dandy stepped out of the shuttle on to the alien spaceship, he had new stickum on his boots and a full tank on his back. As soon as he had tethered, the shuttle the panel opened revealing the turtle-like figure. The alien advanced onto the surface of the ship, clasped all hands in front and bowed. Dandy was unsure if the bow was a copy of his own actions the preceding day or if it was part of their ritual. Dandy clasped his hands and bowed in return.

"That is the same Bip you talked to earlier," Beatrice said in his ear.

Dandy was glad to hear that. He got down to business. He had a new piece of chalk in his hand. He moved to the drawings remaining from the first encounter. To review, he indicated that there was one more day before their ship dove to the moon. He got an affirmative nod. Dandy held his hand up to indicate a stop. He pointed at the alien before him and then made an encompassing motion toward the other beings in the craft. He gathered his hands as if to usher them toward the shuttle. With the chalk he drew the shuttle going to the moon. Again with the diagrams, he indicated three days and the arrival of the rescue ship.

Dandy stepped back to see if he had gotten the message across. Both heads were talking to each other and into their communication system. Finally, the figure indicated himself and the others in the cabin going to the shuttle. Then he pointed at the shuttle. With his hands he made motion of travel to the moon. Dandy nodded "yes."

The creature stood immobile for a little while, then indicated "No." One of the heads started miming the act of breathing. One hand reached down to pick up the trailing air-line and held it out for Dandy to see. Then there followed a series of motions, which Dandy was having trouble understanding. "Does anyone know what he's saying?"

" I think," said Candie, "they're saying that they don't have air or gas enough to keep them alive for three days on the moon."

Dandy replicated their breathing motions as he pointed to the moon with three fingers raised. Then he shook his head. The alien immediately motioned "yes." Dandy huffed and puffed again. Then he pointed to the ship on which they stood. He held up three fingers to again signify the three days. He got an affirmative motion for his efforts.

"If I am reading them correctly," Dandy said, "they don't have air enough to go to the moon, but they can hang on for three days in the ship. If that's so, we need another plan. Any suggestions?" There was silence over his earphones.

"Tom, you there?"

"Sure am."

"If I recall correctly," Dandy said, "the exterior dome of Taran is pure structural material where all the leg struts come together. Is that right?"

"Yes, that's the strongest part of the structure. Everything ties together at the apex."

"What do you suppose would happen if we put that spot on the underbelly of Nacho then gradually turned on the A/Gs? Do you suppose we could lift Nacho back into a stable orbit?"

It took a few seconds, but Tom came back. "It might work. There really wouldn't be much strain on either ship, because Nacho would be within the shadow of our A/Gs and it would lift, too. It wouldn't be a fast process, because the gravitational attraction of the moon isn't particularly great. Our reaction is proportional to the amount of pull. I don't know what kind of tensile strength the other ship has. We might damage it, but I can't see where we could harm ourselves. Because of all the structural members coming together at the top, most of the sensor ports are lower down."

"Do I hear any objections?" Dandy asked.

Candie spoke up. "I'll go along, provided that at the first sign of a problem we back off. There aren't any repair facilities in the vicinity, and we have a long trip ahead of us."

"We can't just sit by and let them crash," said Beatrice.

Corky finalized it. "I think you'd better do the flying. You're the pilot."

"Candie, bring Taran closer so they can get a better look while I try to explain this. And figure out how much higher Nacho has to be to gain a stable orbit."

During this conversation, Bip had been patiently seated on his third leg. Dandy moved off to a clean part of the control room wall. Bip followed. Dandy drew a circle while pointing at the moon. Bip understood. Then he drew a triangle as he pointed to the alien ship. From the ship he drew a spiralling line to the moon. Next Dandy pointed at Taran, which was moving closer.

"Candie, turn Taran so we can see the legs. From here it looks like a tennis ball."

As Candie brought the ship around Dandy drew Taran touching the underside of the triangle representing Nacho. He had the aliens' undivided attention. Below the two ships, he drew an arrow pointed up and away from the moon. He then redrew Nacho further away from the moon with a line indicating a stable orbit.

The heads started talking. There was a lot of animation. Both mouths were going at full speed.

Bip turned to Dandy and pointed at Taran followed by a motion indication Taran would go beneath their ship. Using both outer hands in a lifting motion, Bip raised them above head level until they pointed skyward.

Dandy nodded. "It appears they're confirming what I said."

There was more alien consultation.

Bip raised a hand the way Dandy had done to get attention. Then both heads nodded.

Dandy raised his hand in turn. He drew a triangle and made a motion to indicate the underside. On the triangle he drew the large circle he and Corky had spotted earlier. He added the dome of Taran against the bottom of Nacho. After putting in the thrust arrow, Dandy drew Taran denting in the hull of the ship.

When he looked up, Bip reached for the chalk and sketched a platform that lowered from the hull. They made a small mark as they pointed at the shuttle.

"That must be their launching bay for their shuttle. I wonder why they aren't using it."

"I'd say they have had some sort of massive power failure," said Tom. "They have enough air aboard to sustain them, but apparently they can't pump enough into bottles to sustain them on the moon. I'm picking up virtually no energy reading from the ship."

Bip continued making motions, but no one aboard Taran was getting the idea.

Bip walked to the Taran shuttle to touch the sensor array in the nose.

Then Bip held their hands on the outside of their helmet above eye level. The heads started to peer around while their hands shaded their eyes.

Beatrice got the prize. "Those things on the platform are sensors looking around, down, at the moon, the planet."

Bip started pointing at metallic objects--the hull of the ship, the shuttle, the handrail, metal objects on Dandy's space suit.

"This is a mineral survey ship," said Beatrice. "Everything fits, the size of the ship, the small crew. It doesn't have to land. If they want to go down, Nacho is left in orbit while the shuttle does the atmosphere work. They were probably in a low orbit surveying the moon when they had a power failure."

Bip was going through a bunch of other motions, but no one understood what was being said. Bip rubbed out the sensor array, then clapped one hand against the back of the other hand. Bip seemed to be getting anxious. Finally, they stopped everything by sticking one hand up like Dandy had done. They pointed at Taran, motioned it to the underside of Nacho. Then they made the lifting motion.

"I think we've been told that the sensor array isn't important. Get us out of here," said Dandy, as he duplicated Bip's motions. He got an emphatic nod from Bip.

Dandy bowed before he moved off to untie the tether. Bip returned the bow before backing into the airlock.

Chapter 44

It took a while for Dandy and Corky to get back aboard, change and ready things for the rescue attempt. Tom had checked all systems to make sure everything was in top working order. Beatrice was frantically recording all the data that she could. She was also copying the alien material in case something went wrong with the computers.

Dandy brought Taran to a position directly under Nacho. "I wish we had some sort of communication with them. I could have at least set up 'yes and no' sounds. Do we have a theory on how they communicate?"

"Whatever it is, it's something completely different from any of our technology," said Tom. "We aren't picking up a peep."

Dandy was trying to watch four screens at once as he attempted to line up the two ships. He nudged Taran to center on the disc shape on the bottom of Nacho. With Candie's help to watch the gauges he got everything together.

"Okay. I hope everyone's strapped in. Here it goes." Dandy brought the A/Gs on line. Slowly Taran advanced toward the underbelly of the alien ship.

The initial touch produced a heart-stopping grinding sound. Dandy gave Taran a little more thrust to keep the two hulls together. There were more creaks and groans.

"We're gaining altitude slowly," announced Candie. "We'll have to do better than this or we'll still be at it when the big ship arrives."

"Patience, patience," Dandy said. "The rate of acceleration will continue to increase. I'm not getting much resistance. Nacho seems to be moving with us."

Dandy continued to produce more A/Gs thrust and the speed continued to increase. However, acceleration was excruciatingly slow, especially with the persistent groaning of the ship. Periodically, Tom would reassure everyone that the hull was not showing any undue stress. Candie was giving percentages of completion....10%....15%. When she reached 50% the crew began to relax.

Finally, Candie announced, "This orbit will hold them even if the mother ship is late." A cheer went up.

Dandy drew back on the A/Gs, but the ships remained together traveling at a common speed. Using maneuvering thrusters, he was able to brake enough to permit Nacho to move on ahead. There was a light grinding sound as the ships parted. Carefully, so as not to disrupt the flight of Nacho, Dandy moved away into a parallel orbit.

"Corky, let's go say our goodbyes," said Dandy. "Candie, while we're gone can you find us a handy solar jet?"

Chapter 45

For the third time, Dandy tethered the shuttle to the hand rail. The panel began to open, immediately. Bip stepped out onto the hull. They stood straight on their two flexible legs. With exaggerated slowness the alien clasped both anterior hands in the center of the dual bodies. Both heads inclined while the figures bent at the waist in a low bow.

"I take it this motion means 'thanks'," said Dandy.

Corky said, "Look to your right."

The Bip straightened. He stretched his left hand to the side. The panels on the control room were opening. Lights illuminated the whole interior. Standing behind the windows was the crew. There were five other Bips. Two appeared to be about the same size as the one dealing with Dandy. They all wore similar uniforms.

Beatrice broke in. Her voice conveyed her excitement. "There are two sexes. Look at the three smaller figures. They have some sort of hair around those long necks. Keep your camera trained on them until I get good pictures."

All five Bips in the control room duplicated the bowing of the figure in front of Dandy. Dandy returned the bows. He clasped his hands in front of his chest. Then he bowed at the waist.

Dandy returned his attention back to the alien standing before him. Bip reached into a pouch in the side of the space suit. They drew out a box-like object the size of a small brief case. The exterior appeared to be metal similar to that of the hull of the ship.

"Heads up," Corky said. "If thing starts to get funny I'm going to jerk you out of there."

"Hang on. Let's go a little further before we panic."

Bip apparently noticed the signs of uneasiness. They used Dandy's hand sign of the finger in the air to indicate a change of subject. Slowly, it placed the box in the grip of the center hand. With deliberate motions the other hands unfastened two clips on the case. Bip opened the case, carefully. There appeared to be some sort of book inside. It had pages covered with printing and drawings. The alien flipped through all the pages as if to show that there was nothing else in the box.

Beatrice came on. She was excited. "That looks like an illustrated dictionary or encyclopedia."

Bip closed the case, bowed, and presented the box to Dandy.

"I think they are giving that to you," Candie said. "It might be a thank-you gift."

"I think you're right, Dandy said. If that's a dictionary, it'd be incredibly valuable to us. I'm going to accept it."

Dandy took one of his awkward steps forward to receive the box. It had the appearance of considerable heft. Dandy returned the bow. Bip bowed again, then held up a finger to change subjects.

Bip pointed at the writing on the hull and made a motion to indicate writing. Then it held out a hand as if it was holding the chalk.

Dandy shifted the case under one arm while he fished into a closed pocket for the chalk. He handed the chalk to Bip. The aliens moved back to their previous drawings. They indicated the three days until the big ship arrived and Bip moved to a clean area. They drew a small triangle and pointed at the hull and stomped a foot showing the drawing represented Nacho. Then they drew a huge diamond shape twenty times or more taller than the triangle. That, he identified as the incoming alien ship.

Tom gasped, "That ship is gigantic."

Bip continued on and drew Taran. They sketched a triangular opening in the big diamond shape. With one hand Bip reached toward the Taran figure with a picking action of the fingers. Then the arm was withdrawn. It emphasized the action by drawing an arrow from Taran to the opening, then rubbed out Taran and the opening in the big ship.

Bip stopped to look at Dandy. Dandy was getting a good idea of what was being communicated.

Candie did too. "I think it is time to get out of here."

Dandy nodded.

Bip raised one finger, another topic. They pointed to Tau Ceti, then they stuck out a hand so that a shadow was cast on the hull. The aliens pointed at the shadow with a negative movement of the heads. Then they pointed at the lighted area, pointed at the star and then back to the lighted area.

Bip again pointed at the source of the light. With a darting motion then pointed at the light on the hull. This motion was repeated when Dandy didn't respond.

Corky supplied the answer. "Light speed."

Dandy nodded and Bip drew an arrow from the big ship. At the end they wrote what Dandy recognized as the alien number for one, a slash to the left. To emphasize the message they held up one finger. With the other hand it pointed at the ship before making a motion from the star to light on the hull.

Corky's voice was dull. "The mother ship has light speed capacity. That's at least four times our proven speed with a solar jet."

Bip held up a finger again. Bip pointed at Taran and then made a motion as if flying back the way they had come. They pointed at the right head. The mouth was making motions like speaking. With the other hand they indicated the big ship. The mouth was still going and they pointed in the opposite direction.

"I think they're indicating that they'll tell the mother ship we went in the other direction," said Dandy.

Candie came on line. "That isn't going to help us. Right now there isn't a solar jet close enough. They could overtake us before we could get to one."

"If we make an all-out run for it," Tom said, "we'll consume too much fuel."

Bip was waiting for Dandy's reaction. Dandy held up a finger. Then he pointed at the alien, made the talking motion as he indicated the mother ship. Bip nodded affirmatively. Dandy indicated Taran going off in the direction from which it had come. Bip repeated the message. Dandy nodded. The alien nodded. Both figures bowed to each other.

Dandy stepped back toward the tether line. Bip retreated into the airlock.

Chapter 46

Dandy and Corky wasted no time getting back to Taran. Dandy left Corky to secure the shuttle while he stripped off his space suit. Without taking the time to clean up and dress, he headed for the control room. The others were at their stations. As he slid into his chair he told Candie to lay in a course for the shadow side of the planet.

"Our only hope appears to be deception," said Dandy. "We can't outrun them, we can't fight them, and, after what Bip said, we'd better not try to be friendly. I'm going to head for P-5 at a slow speed until Corky gets everything secured. Once we're underway I'll get cleaned up, then we need to talk. In the meantime, Candie, chart any solar jets that may come our way. Even a small one might be of assistance. Tom, find out everything possible about that planet. Beatrice, extrapolate all you can about the Bips and their mother ship. I want all of you to give thought to their method of conversation and propulsion. Be creative."

Dandy turned Taran toward P-5 and engaged the engines. He kept the thrust low enough to allow the crew to move around. On his way to the showers, he took the alien gift to Beatrice. It was a lot heavier than it looked. "Glance through this to see if there's any possibility of gleaning useful information, but don't spend too much time in it right now."

When Dandy came out of his quarters he felt a lot better.

He didn't bother sitting down at his station, but he opened a channel to the crew. "Tom, conduct a sweep to see if we have any other company within sensor range. Candie, what's the situation with Nacho?"

"In about a half an hour, Nacho will disappear behind the moon. It's still in the same orbit. I can detect no change."

"I can't find anything else within our sensor range," reported Tom..

"Good," said Dandy. "Let's gather in the Fish House. We can talk as we eat. As soon as Nacho gets out of sight it will get uncomfortable. We'll be going to 3 Gs or better."

When everyone was seated with their food, Dandy opened the conversation. "Without a handy solar jet, we haven't a chance of outrunning the mother ship, if it does have light speed. As far as I can see, our only hope is to try hiding. We need a plan. To formulate a plan, we have to get all of our information together in one pile. Beatrice, is there anything else you can tell us about the Bips?"

"Besides what we've already discussed," said Beatrice, "I would say it is a male-dominated society. The ones you talked to are bigger than the other forms. The ones we took to be males had the dominant position when they all bowed to you. There are insignias on their uniforms, and the larger figures have more elaborate designs. The uniforms and insignias indicate either military or government. The big brass will be on the mother ship.

"I'd suspect that the Nacho crew is grateful to us for saving them from crashing. That's why they gave us a gift. Secondly, they warned us about the intentions of the mother ship. Then they told us the speed capacity of the rescue ship. And they indicated they would lie for us about the direction we took. The last three items are, at best, just suppositions. The last one's the most tenuous because it involves a lie to superior officers. Will they take the risk? Will all tell the same story? Can the mother ship find out for itself which way we went? What kind of sensing equipment do they have? What is its range? Can they detect residual elements of our passage? There are lots of possibilities."

"If that big ship has light speed, how come it's not here already?" said Tom. "P-4 can't be that far away."

Candie nodded. "I've been wondering that, too. But it could be that the ship wasn't at P-4. It might have been on the other side of the solar system. When Bip drew it coming from the planet, they may not have meant it literally. It may have been on another more important mission. Maybe it needs something like a solar jet to reach those speeds. Maybe that something wasn't coming in this direction, so the mother ship has to slug it out like we do. Perhaps the ship wasn't ready to fly when the call for help came in. Besides, we just have an alien's word for it that the rescue ship is three days away. It could be coming around P-5 right now."

Dandy nodded to Tom. "Have you come up with anything about their communication system or propulsion system?"

Tom shrugged. "Just one big blank. I've played around with all of the receiving and transmitting equipment we have on board and I haven't raised anything. There should be all sorts of transmissions from Bip's home world. I can pick up natural transmissions from all over the solar system, but nothing local. They must use some other force than the ones we use. I can read a weak electromagnetic field around Nacho. I suspect they're on minimum battery power. If they were on their regular power system, maybe we could determine something, but right now they're as silent as a tomb."

"Any guesses about their propulsion?"

"All I can tell you is that it's not a combustible system like ours. A wave energy must be producing a thrust of some sort. None of our science has even wandered in that direction yet. Of course, no one back home has the foggiest idea that we can ride a solar jet the way we do."

Dandy thought for a moment. "Just keep the problems in the back of your mind until we can come up with some more information. More importantly, we need to find out all we can about P-5. If we can't outrun the mother ship, then we are going to have to find a hole and pull it in after us. I want all of us turning our attention to P-5. So far, all we've seen is that it's a large cloud-covered planet."

"It looks as if it may be a rather strange planet," said Candie. "I've been trying to chart this system. It appears to have an elliptical orbit that takes it far enough from the sun to cause it to become a lump of ice and then it passes close enough to vaporize everything but solid rock. Nothing could live with such temperature extremes."

"What phase are we in at the moment?" asked Tom.

"Cold heading toward warm," Candie answered.

"That would account for the clouds," Tom said. "Elements with the higher temperature melting points are beginning to change into vaporous materials. That type of action would set up convection currents that would produce the swirling patterns. I've been able to cobble some equipment together to read our sensors so we can get a better idea of what's down there. One good thing is that I'm reading a lot of hydrogen. It is pretty much universally distributed. I can't tell what form it's in. There's a bunch of it. There seems to be a soup of various gases....methane, oxygen, nitrogen, as well as hydrogen."

"Does anyone have any thoughts on what kind of surface we're looking at?" asked Dandy. "What I want is a hole. I would also like to investigate that hydrogen source."

The crew seemed to be focused on their beverage containers.

"Since we can't see through the clouds," Candie said, "we have no way of knowing for sure. At this distance our equipment doesn't show much. The only thing that I can surmise is that there should be one heck of a northern polar cap. The planet's axis puts the north pole away from the sun most of the time. There must be a huge accumulation of ice."

Dandy stood up. "Everyone knows the questions. Now we need answers. While we're under acceleration you will have time to consider our problems. Try to come up with some way of solving them. We have to hide until we can get to a solar jet ahead of the Bips. I think we can figure that they are going to come looking for us. We have no idea of what kind of sensing equipment they possess. We have nothing with which to fight them. I don't think it'd be a good idea to try shaking hands with them.

"In ten minutes we'll make our run to P-5. I am going to decelerate so we can swing around on the opposite side of the planet. We don't actually know from which direction the mother ship will be coming, but it'll eventually end up alongside Nacho. It's possible the mother ship doesn't know about us yet. That'll change as soon as they find Nacho still in orbit."

Everyone strapped in, and Dandy threw on the power accelerating to 3 Gs. It would be uncomfortable for a while, but he wanted to be out of sight before Nacho came out from behind the moon.

At the appointed time Dandy flipped Taran around for deceleration, but let the velocity continue a little longer. He would rather bypass P-5 and come back than be caught in between Nacho and the planet.

Chapter 48

Dandy brought Taran into a stationary position on the side of the planet opposite the alien vessel, but they couldn't stay there without chancing detection by the incoming ship. A synchronous orbit would expose Taran on every revolution. A standard orbit would periodically bring them into view. Tom was scanning the rotating planet for physical features. Beatrice was recording the sensor information so the computer could work on topography charts. Candie was studying the surface. At closer range, storms could be seen sweeping around the planet in much the same manner as the wind patterns move about the earth. However, the movement did not indicate the land and water distribution. There did not seem to be major physical barriers to deflect the gaseous flows.

Eventually, Tom, Beatrice, and Candie came up with the conclusion that the entire surface was relatively smooth. It was probably covered with ice. That was not what Dandy wanted to hear. He had been hoping for a deep canyon where Taran could set down within protective walls. Taran couldn't stay in orbit. They couldn't hang in the gas mists. Undoubtedly, the mother ship's sensors could pick them up.

Candie had located a small solar jet, but it was three days away at maximum speed. It was slowly undulating in their direction, but not fast enough to do them any immediate good.

Dandy was beginning to get nervous. He felt it was his duty to the crew, the company, and to humanity to put Taran somewhere safe. But he couldn't find anything that met the minimal demands. There seemed to be very little contour to the planet. There were no continents or oceans as he knew it. Outside of trying to make a run for it, their only option seemed to be trying to hide in the mists and they seem just too ethereal to afford much protection.

Now it was a matter of where to put it down. It didn't make much difference. The mists seemed to be uniformly dense.

"Does anyone have any preference where we vacation?" asked Dandy as he started his descent.

"In the absence of a physical barrier it might be useful to hide at the north pole," said Tom. "The electromagnetic fields of the planet may help confuse the mother ship's sensors. Candie says the pole's in the shadow due to the angle of the axis. Maybe we'll get lucky. They'll come, pick up their distressed ship and leave while we're on the back side."

Dandy moved to a position over the north pole. He was getting pretty good at maneuvering the craft. He decreased the main power source until they were hanging against a heavy gravitational pull. When he cranked up the A/Gs, he transferred the lift to them. By slowly backing off on the power, Taran began settling into the mists. The external cameras went blind. Everyone held their breath as Taran noisily came to rest on the surface. There was a slight tilt but insufficient to call for a leveling procedure. Dandy closed down everything he could so they wouldn't radiate any more energy than necessary.

"Too bad we can't go fishing again," said Corky. "We could use a few hundred feet of water to hide in....and we could take a big drink at the same time."

"I'm not sure the fish here would be edible anyway," Tom said, smiling.

The crew felt vulnerable and anxious. And there was nothing to do, since power was shut down to a minimum.

Dandy got up to get a cup of coffee and drew a tea for Candie. As Dandy sipped his coffee he leaned against Candie's map table. His gaze wandered over the map that Candie had been putting together of the Tau Ceti system. Dandy nodded approvingly at how much information she had added to the solar chart. It showed seven planets.

"I thought Tau Ceti was only supposed to have four planets," said Dandy.

"That was all we could count from Earth, but there are at least three more. The fourth is the inhabited one. No one at home knows it even exists."

Alongside the chart were printed computer readouts of the scans of P-5. Beside each was a radar view of the surface. There wasn't much configuration there. The polar views looked like a billiard ball.

"How thick do you think that polar cap is?" said Dandy.

"Probably between five and six thousand feet deep near the pole, but it could be two or three times that."

"Have you any idea of the chemical composition of that ice sheet?"

"An uneducated guess." Candie shrugged her shoulders and tossed her head.

"Guess."

"When the planet is closest to the sun, everything that can change into a gas does so. As it moves away, the various chemicals and compounds will precipitate in the order of their freezing points as they pass from gas to liquid to solid."

"So, what do we have underneath us?"

"Ice."

"What kind of ice?"

"Water probably freezes first. Then the various gases like oxygen, hydrogen, nitrogen, etc, depending in their freezing points. I'd have to look them up. There may be elements we don't recognize."

"Then the various elements could be layered," said Dandy, "graded by temperature, so to speak."

"There would probably be some mixing, I suppose, but basically that sounds right."

Dandy leaned over to toggle the intercom. "Tom, could you step over to navigation?"

Tom sauntered over.

"What would happen to the ice beneath us if the exhaust from the main engines hit it?"

"Oh, boy. We'd dig a hell of a crater under us and make a whale of a snow storm above us."

"What do you mean?"

"Outside it's closer to absolute zero than it is to zero. That engine produces several thousand degrees of temperature. It would instantly vaporize the ice. If we didn't immediately generate enough thrust to lift off, we'd drop into the pit. The confined heat would probably melt Taran's legs, and as soon as all that vapor hit the outside temperatures, it would become snow."

"Okay." said Dandy. "If we used the A/Gs to hold us off the surface could we bore a hole through the ice?"

Tom gazed off into space for a bit. "Yeah, we could probably do that. If we had some distance between the craft and the surface, the temperatures shouldn't build to a critical point. The A/Gs would push the re-freezing material up the tube to the surface where it would be deposited like a volcano cone."

"Candie thinks there are water deposits under the surface." Dandy said, "If we could burrow down to them, maybe we could liquify enough to fill our tanks. That would solve our fuel problem, and it would give us a hole to hide in."

Candie had been following the exchange. "What kind of activity do you think could be seen on the surface, in case someone was watching?"

"There might be a bubble in the mists while we were actively working," said Dandy, "but I expect that it would level off quickly once the A/Gs were shut down. Or there might be a disruption in the surface flow patterns, but we'd still be in the darkness. Maybe they wouldn't see it, or if they do, maybe they wouldn't recognize it as being extraordinary."

"Maybe, if we dig deep enough, their scanning gear won't be able to find us," said Tom.

Corky had come up from his work area. He had been listening. "If we're going to do this, shouldn't we get going before the mother ship is supposed to arrive?"

Dandy looked around the group and they nodded. Dandy glanced in Beatrice's direction. He didn't bother to try talking to her. She had her head buried so deep in the Bip dictionary, she hardly came up for air.

"Okay, lets do it," Dandy said. "Candie, keep track of what's happening overhead. Work all the sensors. Sound off if anything looks strange. Tom, I'll need constant elevation information. Don't let me get too close to the engine backwash. Monitor the temperatures so we don't burn up. Corky, it'll be your job to take on any water we can find. We're going to be playing this by ear, but I think we'll have a better chance than if we sit on the surface and wait for lady luck to smile."

The crew moved back to their respective stations. "Beatrice," Dandy said. "Strap yourself in. We are going to do some maneuvering."

She nodded absently and lashed herself to her couch as she

continued to read.

Dandy switched on the full intercom, "I'm going to lift us 100 feet of the surface. Then I'll start the main engine. It'll idle and I'll hold everything steady until we see what's happening. Here it goes."

As Dandy engaged the A/G generators, Taran eased off the ground. At 100 feet he brought it to neutral buoyancy. A distinct roar resounded through the ship.

"I think that's the sound of ice crystals hitting the underside," said Tom. "I can't open the camera ports. Those crystals would frost over the cover plates. We'll have to fly blind."

Dandy didn't open the engine doors until the second before ignition. He kept the engine at its lowest setting.

"We're digging a hole," said Tom. The ship's temperature is holding. Bring us down a little."

Dandy nudged the A/G generator back. As the ice melted away, the altimeter said Taran was getting higher.

Gradually the ship eased down.

"Keep it at 300 feet," Tom said. "We'll see what happens."

Dandy fussed with the generators to keep the ship at a constant height.

"We're really creating a blizzard up there," said Candie.

"We're two hundred feet below the surface." Tom was making the instrument readings. "The hull temperatures are beginning to rise. I think it's all that live steam coming under us. Take us back to the surface. Hold us there while you step up the thrust of the engine. We need to blow the hole bigger. It is only about 150 feet wide. It's like being in a rifle barrel. If the hole is wider, the steam will rise further away from the ship."

Dandy did as Tom suggested. He made the descent slower. The pit widened, permitting the heat to dissipate. Gradually, they settled further and further into the ice cap. Tom kept sounding off the depths.

At five hundred feet Corky shouted, "We're in water ice."

"Is there any liquid water under us?" asked Tom.

"I don't think so. It looks like the engine turns it from a solid right into a gas."

Dandy broke in. "Be ready to take on water. I think I can produce some." He shut down the engine as he held the ship in position with the A/Gs. There was a lot of crunching and rattling on the underside of Taran. When the noise settled down, Dandy eased the ship down. He shut down the A/Gs.

Moments later, Corky came over the intercom. "I'm taking on water just like we did at the lake. No fish though. How did you do that?"

"The engine produced super steam," Dandy said, "which was being carried up the tube by the A/Gs, our snow storm. Without the A/Gs, the snow is falling back on the hot hull. There should be enough heat to keep the water flowing for a bit. It'll freeze pretty fast, so if you run out, we can heat up some more. Let me know as soon as you're finished. We can't let too much ice build up around Taran's feet."

After what seemed like an eternity, Corky came on the intercom again. "The tanks are topped off. Ice is beginning to form. I think we're building an ice shell over us."

Dandy cranked up the A/Gs. He built up a field and chunks of ice could be heard banging the hull. He lifted the ship to make sure it wasn't stuck. They heard ice crystals hitting the hull again.

"I'm beginning to see light over us," Candie said. "You must have blown the tube clean," announced Candie.

Dandy set Taran back down on the bottom of their burrow. He shut down engine functions and things became silent.

Candie turned on the external lights. Then she activated the cameras. Taran was situated in the center of a huge, hollowed out cavern two hundred yards across. The wall glittered under the lights. Flakes of snow that had not been blown out began to fall.

Corky stared at the spectacle. "It looks like we're inside one of those winter wonderland paper weights that you shake to make it snow."

Chapter 49

There wasn't much for the crew to do. The projected time of arrival for the mother ship was still a day and a half away. They were running on minimum life-support power to keep energy radiation down. They checked various systems for readiness, but couldn't actively engage in any sensing probes because of their location and the desire to remain hidden. The passive radar sensor was on, which wouldn't give them away and it was hooked up to an automatic alarms system so no one had to tend it.

Tom and Corky were back to their gin game. Beatrice was still deep in the dictionary. Candie was below working out, trying to make up for lost time.

Dandy cleaned up his tiny quarters, did his laundry and even scrubbed up the coffee rings around his work area. Needing something to occupy his time, he had tried to watch a movie, but he couldn't concentrate on it. He wandered down below. Candie was soaked in sweat from working out in the heavy gravity. She was not to be deterred from her program, so Dandy left before he got exhausted watching her. He ended up on his couch with a cup of coffee, staring at nothing.

As usual, he let the coffee go cold. When he got up to get a refill he found the gin game still going on. Beatrice came up only long enough to change the disk in her CD player. While he was drawing a fresh coffee, Candie came out of the elevator.

"While you're there, will you get me a double orange juice?" she asked as she headed for her quarters.

Dandy collected his coffee and the two juices containers. Candie's door was open. He found Candie in the middle of the tiny room stripping off her soaked workout clothes. Dandy had to juggle the beverages to keep them in the cups. He was too far into the room to back out. They had seen each other naked before in the line of work, but somehow this seemed different. He was beginning to have problems maintaining a clinical detachment. Under the circumstances, any change in their current relationship could be troublesome. It might be enjoyable, but it was too dangerous.

Nonchalantly, Candie stepped over to him to take one of the juices, leaving him holding the other. As she turned toward the hygiene booth, he caught the flash of a smirk reflected in the mirror. She was back to her old tricks, teasing him again.

"Working on those saddle bags again, huh?"

Candie whipped around to find an angelic smile on Dandy's face, and she laughed.

Candie waved her arm in dismissal. "Get out of here. I'll be out to have lunch as soon as I get cleaned up."

Ten minutes later, Candie emerged from her room scrubbed and shiny. They went the machines to get something to eat. The gin game broke up and Tom and Corky joined them. Dandy selected the big table where they all could sit. He invited Beatrice over.

Table conversation was mainly revolved around the mother ship and when it would arrive, how long it would remain, and how they would know when it left, if it didn't find them.

They finished eating, and Dandy asked Beatrice what she had found from the alien book.

"Actually, quite a bit," she said. "The box appears to be a thin sheet of the same material as the ship's hull. It is non-magnetic and it is strong. The pages don't appear to be of any sort of natural material, like paper. They're tough. I think that it's an old book, from the stains on the pages. It's been well used."

"So far I've identified thirty-two letters. There are at least seven diphthongs, probably more. I'm still working on vowels or consonants. Some of the vowels seem to be doubled for some reason. It doesn't look like it's a polysyllabic language. I wish we had some spoken references. It could make things a lot easier. There are some pictures of weird animals, plants, tools, and architectural devices. I can learn the written forms, but I have no idea how they would be pronounced. I could use a Rosetta Stone."

What's a Rosetta Stone?" asked Corky.

"It was a stone on which was carved the same texts in three languages, Greek, demotic, and Egyptian hieroglyphs," she said. "Since Greek was known, the others were eventually translated. That still wouldn't tell us how it's spoken. Can't we pick up some sort of radio transmission?"

Tom shrugged. "So far, I've stomped through all our known communication devices, but they're silent. Maybe they use telepathy."

The conversation ebbed and flowed for a while.

"We need to set up another watch routine," Dandy said. "Not only do we have to concern ourselves with the mother ship, but I think it would be a good insurance plan to keep an eye on our surroundings. We wouldn't want to ice ourselves in this deep. We need to monitor all the external conditions. I can switch all the necessary functions to your own stations and I'll put a half-hour timer on so you can do other things until it beeps you."

Chapter   50

Two days passed and nothing happened. Speculation ran from the idea that the mother ship and its chick had long gone, to the thought that it was sitting up top like a fox waiting for the rabbit to stick his head out. Tension was building. Dandy had been counseling patience, but the only person who seemed to be paying any attention was Beatrice, who was still stuck in the dictionary. Candie was working out her frustrations by running laps on the lower deck and pumping iron with a vengeance. The card game took on a new, more aggressive dimension when poker became the competition of choice.

Dandy was left to his own devices. Candie worked herself into an exhausted lump, leaving insufficient energy to contemplate the future. She wasn't much company, so to pass the time Dandy formulated scenarios ranging from no problem to ending up in an alien zoo.

By the fifth day, pressure was mounting to do something. Peeking over the edge of the hole had the greatest appeal. They didn't have any type of probe that could do the job from a distance, so Taran would have to go up the shaft. Dandy pointed out that the A/Gs would throw great volumes of gas and ice into the atmosphere. It would also give a loud energy signature. Any radar search through the clouds would instantly give them away. Candie argued that she wanted to get up high enough to find a solar jet and her instrument didn't radiate a recognizable signature.

Corky threw another element into the pot. Snow had been accumulating around Taran. The heat radiating from the vessel was turning it to ice around the feet of the ship. Too much of an ice build-up could trap them there forever. That thought brought Beatrice out of her book. She began to get scared.

Dandy talked everyone into another day of waiting, but that was all the patience they would willingly grant. He was on duty. Everyone else had retired to their compartments.

A loud thump brought Dandy sitting straight up. The ship had been hit by something. The crew came pouring out of their rooms. Dandy turned on all the external lights and cameras and gave a quick scan of the ship, but could not find any damage or anything that could have caused the impact. They watched the monitors as Dandy began a second, more careful look. They still saw nothing.

"Could it have been something in the ice underneath us?" Tom said.

Corky had been checking the hull integrity and announced that he hull was intact.

Dandy surveyed his instruments. "We haven't changed attitude at all."

"There. Leg six," yelled Beatrice.

Everyone looked, but no one saw anything.

"Look at the shadow on the left side. There's something up against the outer side of the leg. See the multiple shadows being cast by the lights?"

Dandy started changing light arrangements until he had a

single source coming in from the right. Sure enough, an elliptical shadow was cast beyond the leg. Something was there. It appeared to be much too regular to be a chunk of ice. There was no camera to see into that area.

"Someone has to go see what that is," said Candie. "I think it's my turn." Without waiting for a reply, she headed for the elevator, motioning for Dandy to help her suit up.

As Dandy got up to follow, he instructed Tom to maintain a watch above and Corky to keep an eye on the underside of the ship and the object.

In the changing room, Candie stripped while Dandy laid out the suit. He thought how different it was from when he had seen Candie shed her clothes in her quarters.

Candie was suited and all systems were tested. She stepped into the elevator. Dandy was going to equalize the internal pressure with the external pressure so there would be no rush of air in either direction.

From Corky's lower control panel, Dandy monitored Candie's progress. The exterior door opened and moved inward a few centimeters before it slid into the wall. There was a ridge of ice about two feet high outside the door. Candie had to climb up over the edge. She tried to get to her feet, but she could not get traction on the ice. She was still close enough to the doorway to catch the edge of the ice, and she pulled herself back into the elevator.

"I need something to give me traction," she said.

Corky had been watching the operation and came on line. "I'll be right down. I can solve the problem."

Candie came back up as Corky came down. Working rapidly, he traced the outlines of Candie's boots onto a thin, flexible sheet of durathane. With electric metal shears, he cut out the shapes and drove stainless screws through the durathane. With cargo straps he fastened the plates onto the soles of Candie's boots making a serviceable pair of climbing irons.

When Candie ventured out for the second time, she had no trouble moving on the ice. A tether line was added as a second safety feature.

To get to leg number six she was going to have to traverse some eighty feet. She took a circuitous route so she could see the object from a distance.

"It looks like an overgrown basketball with whiskers. It's lying against the leg. It is definitely not a natural object. I think we've been discovered." She had her helmet camera operating so the crew could see.

"Any guesses as to what it may be?" asked Dandy.

"I presume it's some kind of probe. It looks like sensors are penetrating the surface. There's something on it that looks like a lens. The whiskers are sensors or antennas"

Tom came on line. "If I could take it apart, maybe I could answer a lot of questions. Can you bring it onboard?"

"I don't know how heavy it is," Candie said. "but I'm sure it could be handled. Do we really want to bring it on board?"

"It could be a bomb," Beatrice pointed out.

"If it is a bomb, it really doesn't make any difference whether it's out there or in here. It'd probably do us in anyway," said Dandy. "I think we can assume that the Bips want Taran. They might be more reluctant to detonate a bomb if it was to blow up what they wanted to get. I'm in favor of bringing it aboard."

Candie was closely inspecting the device. "It's a little large for me to carry. Besides, I wouldn't want one of whiskers punching a hole in my suit. However, I think I can drag it with my tether."

She untied the line from her belt and carefully wrapped it around the object several times. When it was tied off, she backed away. The object was not too difficult to slide over the ice. Once it was clear of the leg, Candie retreated to the air lock, dragging the object.

"In case that's a lens, can you put something over it to blind it?" Dandy said.

Candie slapped a hand full of snow in the opening. "That should do it until I can find something better."

Before long, she had it in the elevator. After pressurizing the compartment, she went up to the work level. Dandy and Corky met her with a wheeled work bench to take the probe to Corky's tool room. The lens was covered with metal tape. Tom joined Corky while Dandy helped Candie out of her suit.

Tom and Corky stayed below trying to open the mechanism to inspect its innards. Dandy and Candie went back to their stations to watch and wait. They knew the Bips had found their hole. The crew had to find new options.

Dandy opened communication channels so those in the control level could watch the progress of the probe investigation. Corky made a tool to open the casing. Work progressed with great care as if they were defusing a bomb. Hours went by and finally the two technicians had to take a break.

The crew gathered in the Fish House. As they ate, Corky extolled the magnificent workmanship of the mechanism. Tom agreed, but more importantly he admitted that he had absolutely no idea of the principles involved. They had determined that there was a battery power source, but even that was somehow different. It was probably made of a different metal-chemical relationship. Most of the whiskers were springs to cushion the mechanism. However, two proved to be some sort of antennae. There was a camera behind the lens, but the image didn't seem to be translated into electromagnetic energy and there was some sort of audio pickup, but again they couldn't see how anything was sent. The thing was loaded with completely unknown components. Nothing made sense by earth's standards.

The discussion of the device waned. Not much more could be said until the fundamental investigation had been completed. The problem was that Taran lacked a lot of the basic tools needed to conduct the investigation.

Dandy switched topics. "I think we can safely assume that the Bips know we're here. It may have been a guess to drop that probe down the hole, but unless it was damaged, it would have sent back enough data to confirm their suspicions. They undoubtedly know we found the probe and we're fiddling around with it.

"We need to arrive at a governing, operational policy. The question is simple, but the answer may be a lot harder."

"Okay, let's have the question," said Candie.

"Can we permit the Bips to get their hands on us and Taran?"

There was a long silence. No one seemed willing to broach the question. Finally, in a timorous voice Beatrice suggested, "They may be friendly."

"There is just as good a chance that they are not friendly," Candie pointed out . "In fact, the weight would be on the unfriendly side, since in gratitude for saving their lives, the Nacho crew warned us about the mother ship."

"Friendly or unfriendly doesn't make any difference," said Dandy. "Let's look at this from a personal point of view. Do you think that if we ever lose Taran we will see home again? Can you envision the Bips passing up interstellar technology? They seem to have advanced technology, but apparently they're still limited to their solar system. Would they simply look us and our ship over before wishing us bon voyage to return to Earth? Even if they were kind to us, we'd be probed and prodded from every conceivable direction. And there are other considerations, can we breathe their air, eat their food, function in their gravity, and survive their diseases? We have only limited supplies. What happens when they run out.

"Then there's a larger consideration than just us. What happens if they get hold of this technology and all the information we've stored on Taran? Earth could well be in peril. They would know a great deal about our species, while our people don't know they exist. Besides our people don't even know we're here or how we got here. Long before our message home would arrive, an invasion fleet could be sitting on the lawn of the White House."

Dandy had investigated the various possibilities that they might confront. His thoughts on the matter had gone beyond the rest of the crew. It took them time to catch up.

"We can't give the Bips the keys to the city," said Corky.

The crew nodded.

Dandy stood up. "Okay, we do everything we can to avoid capture. When all is lost, we do what we have to do." Looking at Tom and Corky, he said, "Find out what you can about that probe. The rest of us will keep the watches. Beatrice, you're up."

Chapter 51

For the next three days, Tom and Corky worked around the clock trying to make sense out of the probe. They could watch various parts function, but they couldn't find any results. Corky periodically would make the loud proclamation that it was a widget sent by an insidious alien to confuse them, or that it was some form of an IQ test to see whether humans were worth the bother. Then he would go back to work.

Their original working assumption was that the probe was to collect information to be sent back to the mother ship. To prevent the relay of data, Tom and Corky unscrewed the antennas. After hours of tracing circuits they found one antenna connected to a peculiar tube three and a half centimeters in diameter and close to eight centimeters long. The first quarter was solid, but the other three quarters were cut to make long, fine filaments. The tube was a bi-metal composition, silver outside and blue inside. Neither was magnetic.

They decided that they should hook up the antenna. Then they proposed to feed the probe various stimuli to see if they could find out, by monitoring the output at the antenna, what function the sensor performed. They discussed the situation. They were willing to try almost anything to figure some way out. The test proceeded, but they found nothing.

"Maybe our hull dampens or blocks any signal," suggested Corky.

"We should be able to tell if the darn thing is broadcasting even if the signal can't get outside," objected Tom, who's patience was getting frayed.

Corky shrugged. "Maybe that's our logic, not theirs."

"Okay, let's hook it up to one of our antennas."

It took a while, but they made the connection. Still they found nothing. They had been trying to test everything without dismantling it. Dissection seemed to be the only option left.

Suddenly, a jumble of sound started from the bi-metal tube. The filaments were vibrating at frantic speed within a very limited pattern. The racket was terrible.

Corky shouted above the din. "It's a receiver. The case is probably the speaker." He grabbed the face of the sphere. As soon as he enclosed the mechanism there was a pronounced change in the character of the sounds. It became a speech pattern.

Beatrice came streaking out of her room. "Record that. Record that," she shouted.

Dandy threw a couple of switches, but five seconds later the sounds stopped.

"They're trying to communicate with us," Beatrice said. "We need to record everything that comes through. Maybe I can match up some sounds to letters."

Five minutes later, the receiver broadcast the same message for 3 minutes. Beatrice determined that it was a recording which was being repeated at regular intervals.

Even though they had no idea of the principles involved, they knew that the mother ship was there. That knowledge kept the crew from being over anxious to do something. Dandy was content to stay in their hole for the time being, but Corky was getting more concerned about the buildup of ice around Taran's feet.

The crew spent hours speculating on the broadcast. It seemed logical that the broadcast was an attempt to get them to surrender. It could be couched in any number of ways, but the ultimate result would be the crew's loss of their ship and their freedom. That was not an acceptable situation. Neither was endangering the security of Earth.

Another three days passed. Everyone was on edge. The only thing that broke the monotony was Beatrice's discovery that the Bip's spoken language was tonal. She had recorded the probe's message onto a continuous tape that ran repeatedly through her headset. Although some of the sounds were difficult for her, she could give a fair recital of the message with all of its inflections.

She had been trying to break down the sounds into letters and to distinguish between consonants and vowels. She was also trying to figure out where words and sentences began and ended. Then there were compounds to identify. Nothing seemed to be coming together until she turned her attention to the inflections. While she was looking through some of her notes taken from the dictionary, she was humming the message. She was staring at one of the words as she hummed one of the inflections and enlightenment came in a burst. She gave a yip and after a flurry of activity to confirm what she suspected, she put her work aside to get a cup of tea. She was celebrating. The rest of the crew joined her in the Fish House.

Candie couldn't take Beatrice's smug expression any longer. "Well?"

"It's a tonal language."

Beatrice got blank expressions, which pleased her even more. With a grin she proceeded to enlighten the lesser. "Let me use the word 'man' to explain. I've found many words that have two spellings—'man' and 'maan.' I had no idea of whether they were two different words or one word with different features, like 'bat' and 'batted' or 'bat' and 'bats,' or 'to,' 'too,' and 'two'."

While listening to the inflections of the taped message I realized that 'man' is spoken in a high level tone like the Chinese Mandarin first tone. 'Maan' starts high, descends and then hooks back up. The significance of this is to differentiate between a single entity and a double, or a Bip, as Corky would call a paired unit. Apparently, the same distinction is made for activities that can be carried on either singularly or in pairs, because there are many words with this duality. Maybe there's a lot of this pairing on their world. Even the fauna and flora might be the same."

Although Beatrice's discovery didn't change the situation any, the crew was pleased for her sake. Dandy was particularly satisfied, because he had been concerned about how she would react to the crisis they now faced. He didn't want to be burdened with her if she fell apart.

After everyone had a bite to eat, they wandered back to their stations. For the moment, the tension had waned. But it didn't last for long. A sharp vibration ran through Taran, followed a few seconds later by a muffled sound of some sort of blast. Then there was a second shudder in the ship and another blast. At the periphery of hearing a roar began to build. The roar grew louder by the second.

"They're trying to bury us," shouted Dandy. "Buckle up."

The noise was tons of ice cascading down their tunnel. Upon descent Taran had skewed about as it dug its hole, so the shaft was not straight up.

Dandy started the generators for the A/Gs. He eased the power to the gravity deflectors. He didn't want to leap upward, crashing either into the roof of their cavern or meeting the oncoming ice. He also had to worry about getting Taran's feet out of the ice. An anguished, electronic-type of squeal came from below. Dandy flipped on the monitors. The Bip probe was in its death throes. Circuits were blowing and smoke billowed out of the casing.

"Gravity. Their systems are based on gravity force," shouted Tom.

Dandy didn't have time to think about that. Taran hadn't moved. It was still icebound. The roar was coming but running into resistance instead of free falling. Chunks of ice began to rattle off the underside of the ship. Another explosion reached them, shaking Taran even more because the floor of the cavern was coming up in chunks. With a lurch the ship broke free. The falling ice had stopped roaring. Dandy kept advancing the thrust of the A/Gs and their speed increased appreciably. They were in the tube now. They scraped the wall with piercing screams as the durathane ripped the ice. Dandy accelerated as fast a he felt he could. Taran was like a bullet coming out of the barrel of a gun. The pressure pushed the crew into their couches.

As soon as Taran cleared the tunnel, Dandy ignited the main engine. A tail of flame disintegrated an enormous chunk of the icy surface. The enveloping gas clouds swirled in a huge eruption. Taran streaked up through the P-5 skies. A great column of ice and snow preceded the ship. The flame from the powerful engine was like colorful feathers on a speeding arrow.

Dandy activated the radar. There was a huge blip right overhead. Apparently, the mother ship was in a synchronous orbit above the tunnel.

Dandy didn't dare shut down the A/Gs because he would have crashed into the tons of ice that had shot out of the tunnel ahead of them. He could sheer off away from it, but for the time being it formed a shield between Taran and the mother ship artillery. He adjusted his course slightly so the blip of the alien ship disappeared behind the ice. They were accelerating so fast it was getting hard to breathe.

A concussion reverberated through the ship. "They're shooting at us," Candie shouted.

Whatever weapons they were using were not penetrating the ice. The arrow streaked upward. Several more concussions came in quick succession, each getting more pronounced as portions of the ice column were blown away.

"They're getting nervous," Corky said grating through the acceleration pressure.

"So am I," gasped Candie. "We're getting awfully close."

Then there was no more firing. Dandy expected the mother ship to try maneuvering out of harm's way, but it stayed stationary. It was huge. Radar was able to see it and Dandy was beginning to get distance readings. His impulse was to veer off, but he knew the closer he could get, the better chance he had of hitting them with his snowball. He waited almost too long. When he did sheer off and shutdown the A/Gs, he nearly traded paint with the alien ship. The exterior cameras were operating but it all happened so fast that nothing registered to the eye.

"Find me a solar jet, the closest one, no matter how small."

Almost immediately Candie entered a new course. Dandy made the changes.

"Tom, keep an eye on the mother ship. I don't know if they were firing at us or the ice. I hope it was the ice."

Dandy backed off on the engine a little so everyone could breathe more easily. Beatrice was rerunning the camera tapes of the passing of the mother ship. She ran them at ultra slow motion. It showed a great puff of white as some of the ice impacted part of the ship. They got only a glimpse as they passed, before the tail of flame flicked across the surface of the alien vessel.

Minutes dragged by and no more shots were fired at them. The mother ship remained in orbit of the planet, which would take it out of sight behind P-5 in fifteen minutes more.

"What do you think happened?" Candie said.

"Maybe we caused some damage with either the ice or the exhaust flame," Dandy suggested.

"Maybe they didn't mean us any harm in the first place," Beatrice speculated.

"Then why were they trying to cave in the tunnel on top of us?" said Corky.

"It might be that with light speed they don't have to chase us until they are good and ready," said Dandy.

"I don't think it was any of that," Tom said.

"Well, what was it then?" said Candie.

"Remember when we first powered up the A/Gs in the tunnel? That alien probe squalled at us and then puffs of smoke came out of it. We haven't been able to figure out what physics the Bips are employing. I think they base everything on the low force of gravity. That may explain why we haven't been able to pick up any communication signals in an inhabited system. Remember the Nacho's propulsion system? It could be based on some sort of gravitational wave. Our A/Gs blew out the probe's circuits. Maybe it does nasty things to their whole physical base."

"Then why didn't it do nasty things to Nacho when we used the A/Gs to push it back into orbit?" said Dandy.

"We speculated that they were operating life support off batteries," Tom said. "There was so little energy leaking from the ship, we could hardly detect it. They probably didn't have any systems powered up for us to blow."

Candie entered a slightly altered course as the solar jet undulated. The mother ship disappeared behind P-5.

"We must have dinged them up some," said Corky. "They haven't moved since we came out."

"Maybe they've decided to let us get further out into space."

"No, that's not it." Dandy looked up from his computations. "They don't know what sort of speed capability we have. It wouldn't be too much of an assumption to figure we have light speed, too, since we came from some other solar system. I think Corky was right. We damaged them some way. It's going to take us several hours to get to that jet. That gives them a lot of time to effect repairs. A ship that large should be able to maintain itself in space. They still have time to catch us."

The crew was uncomfortable at the speed Dandy was maintaining. Every few hours he backed off long enough for the crew to move around and take care of personal needs.

The mother ship appeared and disappeared in its P-5 orbit again without showing any activity. Taran was still a couple of hours away from the solar jet when Candie sounded the alarm.

"It's not there anymore. It should have come out three minutes ago."

"Do you suppose it crashed?" said Tom.

"I don't see any disruption of the gaseous layer that would indicate any large event happening. Radar isn't picking up any indications of a ship on the surface."

"Hey, Tom. Can our sensors pick up anything going at light speed?" said Dandy.

"I doubt it. Of course, it's never been tried. But I don't think we have to worry about it. They can't use that kind of speed to chase us. Think of how far they would go per second. We're too close."

"If they have zero to light speed capability, they can use any fraction of it they want," said Dandy.

"I don't imagine it is quite that simple," said Tom, but he didn't elaborate.

"There she is," said Candie. "At least there's a ship coming at us on an intercept course from a completely different direction. If that's the mother ship, how did she get there? She is traveling only a little faster than we are. At her present course and speed we'll meet in about three hours. Of course, in two hours we hit the solar jet."

Dandy thought for a moment. "Okay, keep an eye on her. If she doesn't change speed or direction we'll ignore her. Maybe she'll think we don't see her. More likely, she'll figure there's nowhere for us to go."

Time started to drag. The crew members fiddled and fidgeted on their couches. Candie's image came on one of Dandy's monitors. "You know, that jet isn't very big."

"We have no choice."

"It's going in the wrong direction."

"We still don't have any choice."

"We have to turn toward the mother ship to enter the jet."

"No choice."

"We could be getting within firing range—yeah, I know. No choice." Candie's image clicked off.

Chapter 52

Dandy kept the same speed and direction. The alien ship maintained its course too. The only thing that could screw up the works now was if the mother ship accelerated enough to bring an intercept prior to their reaching the solar jet. He had no idea if they could fire on Taran from that angle or distance. Of course, the Bips didn't know the armament potential of the intruders.

Candie entered a course change so he could make an approach to the jet. Dandy had been debating with himself whether he should make an abrupt turn to enter the jet or if he should begin a longer, looping turn. He was afraid that if he made a quick move, the Bips might react violently at what might be viewed as an aggressive act. On the other hand, if he made a wide, slow turn it would take considerably longer to get into the jet. Once they were in the jet, he was going to have to accelerate almost at the alien.

No one was saying a thing. The crew was leaving him to do his job. He still was debating the question when he reached the point at which he would have to start his slow turn. The decision and the turn came at the same time. He was committed. The jet was slightly lower than the level of the mother ship. He started to dip early, too. He wanted to just meld into the jet without being obvious.

"Is the mother ship reacting at all?" Dandy said.

Candie didn't reply immediately. "With their propulsion system, they don't have a tail I can measure. If they powered down, it would take time to tell, but I think they've backed off a bit. We're getting closer faster."

"Tom," Dandy said. "Set your timer for 3 minutes. This jet is going in the wrong direction. We really don't want to get much further from home, but we want to get out of range of that ship."

Taran entered the jet faster than ever before. They were already close to three Gs and their speed began increasing immediately.

"The charge is building rapidly. Hang on," yelled Tom.

Things got mushy for a moment, before settling down to normal. Dandy cut back on the speed.

As soon as they exited the jet, Candie was scanning for the alien ship. She knew where it should have been, but her instruments weren't picking it up. She fine-tuned the long range sensitivity. "There she is. She's changed course, but she is not following us. Maybe the Bips have given up."

"Let's hope so," said Dandy. "But keep an eye on her. Now, lets find our way home."

Candie found another solar jet heading in the right direction. She gave the coordinates to Dandy, who changed course. Also he slowed the speed so the crew could move about and to save fuel. He didn't want to have to burrow through glaciers to find more.

They were still in the Tau Ceti system, so they had to maintain a watch because the chances were good that there was more than one spaceship. They weren't interested in testing the friendliness of the locals.

Dandy set up duty schedules. It was going to be a couple of days before they could pick up the new jet. Tom and Corky spent their time fiddling with the probe. Beatrice was back into her dictionary and her recording of the Bip message. Candie was catching up with her mapping of the system. When he wasn't on watch, Dandy spent most of his time on his couch with his ankles crossed and a heel against the control panel. No one bothered him until he came up for air. He was plugging into his mental scenarios all of the new information they had accumulated. He wanted to be prepared.

A call came from Corky below decks. "I think we have company." In the background, the probe was squalling.

Candie was on duty. "Ship to our port. The mother ship isn't in its former location. Here's a demonstration of that light speed the Bip was talking about."

Dandy immediately whipped Taran about to head away from the mother ship. He lined up the solar jet, but at a more distant point. "Corky, get up here. Strap in, everyone."

When all were secure, he accelerated. Taran was in full flight. Pressure increased to the highest point any of them had experienced. Initially the mother ship fell behind, but gradually it gained speed and it was holding its own. Ever so slowly, the speed increased until it was closing the gap.

Candie was doing calculations. "If this is top speed for them, they'll catch up with us about an hour short of the jet. If they can go faster--" She gasped for breath. Conversation came at a high price.

"Any idea how they got here from there?" said Dandy.

"They didn't ride a jet like we do," said Candie.

"But they must have ridden something."

"Gravitational strands," said Tom.

"What are gravitational strands?" asked Corky.

"For some time there's been a theory that gravitational forces coalesce into strands that drift about like our solar jets. I'm pretty sure that gravitational force is the basis for much of their technology, like communication and propulsion."

Hours passed. Everyone was exhausted from the constant G forces. Beatrice was have a particularly hard time. Candie managed a comment. "I hope the Bips are as uncomfortable as I am."

"Probably not," whispered Beatrice. "They are used to heavy gravity."

The mother ship came gradually closer. They were just short of the solar jet. Taran wasn't going to make it before the aliens reached them.

Both ships were hurtling through space at incredible speeds. Dandy mentally reviewed the various scenarios he had been visualizing. He decided to put their eggs in a Rimlick maneuver.

"We're not going to make it this way," Dandy said, "so I am going to try a wrinkle to gain some time. Hang on."

Dandy checked all the read-outs and then shut down the engine. Without sustained thrust, Taran began to slow slightly. By maneuvering jets, he began changing the attitude until he had performed a 180-degree flip. He refired the engine, causing retrofire. Though Taran was still going in the same direction at an incredible speed, it was at a gradually reducing rate. The intervening distance between the two ships began to close rapidly The rate of decrease in the interval got scary.

"Are we playing chicken?" said Corky.

"They don't dare shoot now, Dandy replied. "They would run into our debris."

The two ships were like freight trains on collision course.

The mother ship tried to back off on its speed, but it wasn't going to help. They were too close.

Someone was going to have to maneuver. Taran was minuscule compared to the mother ship, but the alien vessel would still never survive a collision at those speeds.

"Andy--" Candie cried.

The alien ship filled the view screen. The crew felt the A/G generator kick in, followed by a change in the pressure from the restraining straps on their couches. The mother ship rose to the top of the view screen as Taran's attitude changed. Dandy increased the engine thrust. They were still going in reverse, but the new angle caused a lateral push, dropping Taran slightly lower in the alien trajectory.

The mother ship streaked toward them. Dandy held his breath. He was worried he had waited too long. Suddenly the blackness of space showed on the monitors. A shudder ran through Taran. Then they were tumbling. With all of the various pressures exerted on his body, Dandy had problems manipulating the maneuvering jets to bring the ship under control. Finally, Taran regained stability.

"What was that?" gasp Tom.

"I think our propulsion systems mingled," said Dandy.

A substantial interval had opened up between the two ships. Dandy shut down the engine and the A/Gs so he could flip Taran again. The alien vessel was in front of them, slamming through space. Their engines did not seem to be working.

"Candie, give me the closest jet."

Dandy fiddled with the new course. He still had to contend with the stored momentum they had gained. Eventually he was able to head in the direction he wanted. The speed had reduced sufficiently and the crew was more comfortable.

The alien ship was racing through space, its engines still not working.

Taran approached the solar jet. "Tom," Dandy said. "Set your timer on twenty minutes. I'm getting tired of this. Let's get far enough away so we can take a breather."

Chapter 53

As soon as the crew got themselves together after exiting the jet, Candie scanned the area. "I don't find anything at all in our immediate area."

"Can you find out where we are?" said Dandy.

Using Beatrice's method Candie located the CETI signals. It took a little while, but she pinpointed their location.

"We're no longer in the Tau Ceti system. We moved sideways out of the system. We aren't closer or further from home than we were when we found Nacho."

Dandy put the scanners on auto alarm. "We should be well out of range of the mother ship. Let's meet in the Fish House in twenty minutes for a leisurely meal."

The crew used the time to clean up and change clothes. As they met in the Fish House, there was an easing of the tension that had built over the last several days, but they were still light years away from home. There was no telling what lay ahead.

Over coffee Dandy broached the topic everyone knew was

coming. "We have to make our way back home. We have to figure out how we're going to do that. I think we'd better start by taking an inventory. "Tom, how are we doing on fuel?"

"We have enough on hand that we could get home if we have direct routes. If we had to slog too long between solar jets we may find ourselves short. Our run from the mother ship put a good dent in our water supply because of the speeds we were traveling. If we find another supply, I wouldn't pass it up."

Dandy turned to Corky. "How about food?"

"We are in great shape. Do you realize it's less than a month since we got our Christmas package from home?"

"That's impossible," said Candie.

Everyone stared at Corky as they mentally reviewed the recent events in that time frame.

"Who worries about time when we're having so much fun?" said Corky, with a little flip of his hand. The crew laughed.

The meeting continued in a more jovial mood.

"How are we doing with computer capacity, Beatrice?" Dandy said.

"We have tons of space since they brought the rest of the system on line. My only concern is that we can't download any of this. If something happens to us, everything's gone."

Dandy made the rounds of the various crew members to find any known areas of difficulty. Everything was in good shape. They were well provisioned. No problems of any significant consequence had arisen between crew members. Everyone was relieved to escape further contact with the Bips. They had been lucky. Taran was not equipped to handle that kind of contact. She couldn't defend herself.

The question and answer session slowed. "Boy," said Tom. "Do I have a long list of suggestions for those armchair engineers back home."

Candie laughed. "Me too, but we're going to have to cut them a little slack because they never dreamed we'd be where we are at this moment. They may have done things a little differently if they had known there were real two-headed aliens out here. I can visualize a lot of priorities that might change."

Dandy terminated the session. "Let's go back on our watch schedule. After everyone has had a chance to sleep under normal gravity, we'll get underway. We still don't know the physics involved in what got us here, but we know how to use it. Let's head for home."

"Right. Back to Colonel Tokla," added Corky.

Candie shuddered. "Thanks a lot."

Chapter 54

Taran was currently slogging between jets. It had been a week since they had played chicken with the Bips. They had made up over a light year, but that rate of progress was much too slow and none of their routes had taken them near any system where there were any chances of getting water.

Dandy was spending much of his time tilted back in his seat with his ankles crossed on the console. He had reviewed all the available scientific data concerning water. Now he was shifting to anecdotal information. He had even gotten far enough afield to try recalling the science fiction on the subject.

Although nothing had been said, it was coming down to the point that they needed more fuel than they had to get back, unless they were incredibly lucky. Dandy knew everyone was aware of that fact. They weren't putting pressure on him to come up with a solution, but the pressure was there nonetheless.

Dandy unlocked his ankles and made the drinking motion to Candie who nodded agreement. With the beverages he settled down on the edge of her map table. As Dandy passed her a cup of tea he asked, "Have you come across any comets in any of your scanning?"

"I'm really not sure. I've spotted any number of objects that I have suspected were comets, but it is rather difficult to distinguish between them and asteroids. It would take a lot of time and observations to be sure. Why?"

"The closest thing to water we may find out here is the muddy sludge that usually makes up comets. There are all sorts of theories on mining asteroids or moons for water trapped in the rock, but we don't have the equipment to do that. If we can find a big snow ball maybe we can melt enough to gas us up."

Candie looked skeptical. "How would you go about that?"

"Oh, I really don't know. I imagine it will depend on the size of the comet and its composition. Out here between galaxies there isn't much choice. I'm looking for some alternative to pure luck that a solar jet will take us to a filling stations. Don't worry about it now, because in a few hours we'll be hitting that jet, but when we come out, keep an eye open for one."

The intercom came alive. It was Corky calling for Tom to come down to the workshop. Ten minutes later Corky was calling for Dandy.

When Dandy stepped off the elevator the two men were closely inspecting the innards of a computer terminal.

Corky said, "Take a look at this."

He was using a fine pointer to indicate a tiny white spot. Tom handed Dandy a magnifying glass. A closer look showed a minute quantity of powder.

Handing the glass back, Dandy said, "What? Your terminal has termites?"

"I hadn't check inventories since we got away from the Bips. When I turned on the machine nothing happened,so I popped the top and noticed that. That is what remains of the silicone chip. It has apparently disintegrated into practically microscopic crystals."

"You're telling me that the microprocessor, the thing that makes that machine run, has been destroyed?" said Dandy.

"You've got it."

Dandy was aghast. "There are chips all over this ship performing involuntary functions we don't even know about. Have you found any other problems?"

Corky shook his head. "We haven't really looked yet. We called you as soon as we knew what we were looking at."

"No one has used this terminal since we left P-5?"

"Tom replied, "Neither of us have touched it. I don't know about the rest of the crew, but I would suspect not."

"I'll check to make sure. But the most important thing now is to find out whether there are any similar problems elsewhere. Corky, take this level. Tom, you start working your way down. We will need a ship-wide systems check. I'll start them from top side. Don't depend on any automated system that could malfunction because of a faulty chip."

As Dandy stepped into the elevator, he had a momentary second thought but decided that since everyone had been using the conveyance, danger would be negligible. On the command, deck he went to his station. He roused Beatrice, who was in her rest period.

Beatrice was rather bleary-eyed when she appeared. "Bea, get yourself some coffee. We have a lot of work to do before we get to that jet." After she had made her way to her station, Dandy told her, "Corky has found a micro processing chip in his parts terminal that has disintegrated. I have never hear of such a thing before." Horror spread over the librarian's face as she contemplated the possibilities. "The first thing I want you to do is run a full computer check to see if we have any other problems. Check all your hardware and then make sure everything is backed up. Also, check to make sure that the problem in Corky's terminal didn't spread into other systems."

Candie had been listening to Bea's instructions. "What do you want me to do?"

"Check out all of the systems you use. See if there are any problems whatsoever. Then go back into the original training tapes to find the tutorials involving ship-wide functions like the toilets, alarm systems, fire suppression, food handling, all those automatic functions we don't usually mess with."

Dandy returned to his station. Keying the intercom, he asked Tom check out both shuttles. Then he instructed the two technical men to start trying to find out the source of the problem.

Dandy cut power so that Taran was moving only under momentum. He did not want to hit the solar jet before finding out if there was a further problem that had not surfaced yet. As he worked his mind kept reviewing the time frame. The last time Corky said he had used that particular terminal was just before the Bip mother ship had found their tunnel in the ice. Since then they had that hide-and-seek encounter with the mother ship. Other than those two incidents, everything had been pretty much routine. They had jumped aboard three different jets, plus plowing through the space in between.

One niggly little notion persisted. It must have had something to do with their encounter with the mother ship. But he couldn't figure out why only that system had been affected. He was still pondering that when Tom and Corky came back up for something to eat. It had been hours since the checking process had begun.

The whole crew assembled in the Fish House. In between bites, Beatrice reported that all of her files were secure and backed up. She had found no problems outside of being unable to access that one terminal. She also said that all Corky's parts records were preserved. Nothing had been lost.

All reported they had found absolutely nothing wrong. Everyone was vastly relieved that there appeared to be no spread of the problem. However, Dandy wanted Corky and Tom to continue their search for the source.

Corky suggested that he replace the chip to find out whether the machine had in some way been responsible for the chip failure. Beatrice warned him to sever the connection to the system before toying with the machine.

Ten minutes later Corky called in, "Dandy, can you come down to the shop?"

When Dandy got off the elevator for the second time that day, he found both Corky and Tom staring at the alien probe lying on the work bench.

"Come take a look at this," said Corky. He moved off into the storage area. Several of the bins stood open. All component parts were wrapped in a type of clear bubble wrap to prevent damage while floating around while there was no gravity. Corky reached into one of the bins and handed Dandy a package. Besides all the code and parts numbers, there was a printed title, "Micro Processor."

"All the chips in these three bins are in the same shape as the one in the terminal. However, There are chips in surrounding bins that are perfectly all right. As I figure it, we have an area of destruction about two or two and a half feet across. Now look at this."

Corky led the way back to the shop. "Those bins are right behind this durathane wall. The terminal is right in front of it. Line up the two and they point to that alien probe lying on the work bench. Tom was still inspecting the device. He had removed the cover so he could examine the innards.

Tom straightened up. "Remember that little tube that was creating the vibrations that activated the bi-metal strip? Then we put the casing back on. It then became the speaker through we could hear the Bip's transmission. That tube must put out some sort of energy flow to activate the strips. That tube is pointed right at the terminal and subsequently the storage bins beyond. My working theory is that when we activated the A/G generators to get out of the hole, it in turn sent some sort of charge through that tube, which destroyed the silicone.

Remember that agonizing scream and a big puff of smoke from the probe when A/G came on line? I think we burned something out. Later, when the mother ship caught up with us, we got a whimper out of it, which told us of the mother ship's presence."

"I activated the A/G again when we played chicken with the mother ship." objected Dandy.

"That was after the burnout. If there was a whine, we weren't here to hear it. We were all in the control room. It wasn't very loud when the mother ship reappeared."

Dandy sighed. "It looks like we have another of those mysteries. We know what happens, but not how it happens. Try to find all of the properties of the thing. Figure out what burned out and if you can fix it in case it becomes important. I'm going to head for the jet again and see where we come out."

Chapter 55

Dandy put Taran into the jet for a moderate time. Candie quickly found their location on exiting. The jet was going in the right direction so they pulled back into the flow for double the time. They made some good progress but the jet petered out as it meandered in another direction. They hitched a ride on another tiny jet to move them toward a more promising larger one.

Most of their motion was lateral instead of on a straight line home. They were logging phenomenal numbers of miles, AUs, or what ever. It was slow going and hard on the crew, but they were making progress. Dandy had been in hopes that they would pass through the Epsilon Eridani system, where he would have looked for planetary water, but the jets had taken them in another direction.

Candie called up her star charts on the crew screens. She located Taran on the map. Giving the crew the latest positions, she said, "We are about eight and a half light years from home. We're complete about a quarter of the trip. We are about the same distance from earth as the Lalande system although it is off to the side a fair bit. It is thought to have some M2 planets."

"How far?" asked Dandy.

"Too far for a direct flight. We'd have to hook onto some local solar jets and then we'd probably have to do a lot of flying under our own power to get into the system."

"Are there any jets generally going in that direction?" asked Dandy.

"I'll have to check again, but the last time I looked there were a few little ones. No major jets."

Very slowly Dandy said, "Maybe we are going about this all wrong."

"How so?" asked Tom.

"Remember, the original principle that we were going to check out was to see what kind of speed enhancement we could get by entering a solar jet. That first time, we increased our speed by fifty percent, and we hadn't even reached three Gs. I hadn't really taken the engine far beyond idle when we started building that positive charge. Everyone knows what happened then. On our trip back we have been trying to duplicate the accident which got us suddenly 11.8 light years away.

"Maybe we should go back to basics. Hop a jet and gradually build power to just under where we produce that heavy charge. If it does build, we can slide out of the stream and take care of it without ending up in another galaxy. We can keep track of where we are and in which direction we are going. If the jet looks promising we can go for the big jump. If not, we can move at greater speed with less fuel consumption looking for a better one."

"It sounds reasonable to me," said Tom.

Candie and Corky nodded their agreement. Beatrice had already moved on to some other consideration.

For the next four days, they made pretty good time. Dandy kept popping in and out of jets and occasionally taking a wild ride. If a choice arose, he opted for the one that would take them the closest to Bernard's Star, hoping that around a star system they would run into a planet with water. If there was water, it would probably be in the form of ice, but that was all right, providing he could figure out a way of thawing it.

Candie was taking a shift at the controls so they could continue to travel in their new mode. But after four days of four hours on and four hours off, there was going to have to be a break.

Dandy came out of his room to relieve Candie. He stopped at the food dispensers, but he had trouble trying to remember which meal he should be eating. He settled on beans and franks, which was normally the case when there was no clear cut path. Candie wrinkled her nose again at his selection.

"Boy, do I need some fresh veggies and fruits," said Candy. "My diet is shot and I can't get down to my exercise machine."

"I think it is time to take a little break. We either have to do that or bring Tom and Corky into the routine."

"I think a break would be better," said Candie. "I can't sleep very well while we are in a jet. Then if we jump, that really fouls up my rest period. A new, jerky driver would make it even worse. Besides I may have a reason to break up the routine."

"What's that?" asked Dandy around a bite of wiener.

"I have been watching something that might be a small comet. We would have to make a side trip to find out. It could be an asteroid. If it is a comet, it is so far from a star there is no visible tail or coma. Of course, if it is a comet, there is no guarantee that there is water."

"How long would it take to catch up with it?" asked Dandy.

"We're talking three or four days of trying to cut it off if we are under our own power. If we can work the jets, we should be able to cut that down considerably."

"We need to cut it down as much as possible. Give me a jet and then take your break. We'll discuss it when you get up."

Dandy grabbed the jet that Candie indicated. Now that he had an immediate goal, he rode it like a jockey in the Kentucky Derby. In the four hours before Candie reappeared, he had made good time. He found he could ride even smaller jets than they had ever suspected. They weren't as fast, but they were better than slogging through space.

Dandy shuddered as Candie ate her fruit cocktail over rice.

"You've made good time. We need to be a little closer before I can tell very much about it. If we had those analytical machines on board, we could tell now if it is what we want."

"Can you make a guess as to the size?" asked Dandy. "I have no way of knowing how big it has to be before we could land on it. It may be tumbling too fast to make an approach. Right now I'm just shooting in the dark."

"No, we're just going to have to get closer. There is no sense in making plans on just wild speculations."

By taking double shifts, Dandy caught up with the comet in two days. They could have looked out the window to see it if there had been a window. The comet was tumbling end over end, but at a slow rate. As far as Tom and Candie could determine, it was something like half a mile long and about half as wide. The indications were that there was a lot of ice there, although it wasn't readily visible. It looked like a big potato with a very rough skin.

Fortunately, they came out of a jet in the near vicinity. Their velocity was quite similar to that of the comet, so Dandy didn't have to expend much fuel to come into a parallel course.

Candie was going over the data. "It is not big enough to have any gravity of its own. It is spinning end over end, but not very fast. It is making less than half a revolution per minute. To have the equivalent of 1 G. the spin would have to be much faster. Our A/Gs won't be of any used. I'm sure that our main engine would just push us apart in a virtually weightless environment."

Beatrice did some more calculations. She estimated there

would be about one tenth of a standard G out on the end of the comet.

Dandy put Taran into a parallel path far enough away to insure safety. His accumulated speed was enough to match the comet. Then everyone sat down to a group meeting and meal. Tom finally put out the question. "It looks like we've found water. At least rock and ice. How are we going to get it?"

Now was the time for Dandy to produce. They had made him pilot and given him command. Everyone knew they didn't have fuel enough to get back. They had not badgered him yet about water. Candie found the water, now it was his responsibility to figure out how to get it.

The comet was on the screens so all could see. Dandy started out in a slow, almost Texas kind of drawl. "Oh, I suppose we'll just have to do like we did on Nacho." Everyone looked surprised. I think it would be kind of hard to land Taran on the spinning ice cube. The ship has to come straight down keeping its legs underneath. It is not like landing on P-5. We can't use our engines in weightlessness and the A/Gs are no good as Candie pointed out. But the shuttle can come in for a landing like an airplane. With its maneuvering jets, it can compensate for the spin.

"The shuttle engine puts out a lot of flame. More than enough to melt ice. I think we can anchor the shuttle to the surface in ice and then use the winch to pull Taran down. I think the best place to do this is on the end with the big knob. If we tried to set down in the middle, the mass of the comet would be continually rotating at us and could well smack us if things didn't work out quite right."

Dandy went on to explain his thoughts. He picked up numerous suggestions and some objections. Gradually, a plan was formulated and a schedule set for the attempt twelve hours later. Before then, the crew rested and did what preparations when necessary.

Dandy felt jumpier on this operation than on any of the others.

The main difference was that this action was not being done as a response to an immediate hazard. He dreamed this one up on his own. Tom and Corky would handle the first phase. The artificial gravity was turned off in the shuttle bay, but the atmosphere was preserved. The two of them were able to maneuver the pickup into an attitude where they could strap the nose cone from the supply rocket onto the rear compartment. They also loaded considerable lengths of their strongest cable. It was slower going than they had anticipated. A break was ordered so that Corky could rest since he and Dandy were slated for the next phase.

Corky was at the controls as the shuttle slipped out into space. After a sufficient fall to clear Taran, he fired the main engine. The next hour was used practicing coordinating his speed with the velocity of the comet and its tumbling motion. Corky was still nervous, but he figured he was as good as he could get without an actual try.

He matched the comet's course while sideslipping until he was actually over the comet. The target was the smoothest looking spot on the knob, which turned out, upon much closer observation, to be terribly cracked and irregular. It was hard on the stomach as Corky powered down close to the surface which kept moving away from him. Alternately, it looked like that irregular surface would come up and squash the shuttle or they were flying off into space. It was a classic case of oversteering with the maneuvering jets.

With some encouraging comments from Dandy, they finally made contact. It was a pretty hard jolt as Corky goosed the jets just before he touched the surface. However, following the bounce, the jets kept the craft on the surface. After the jitters had calmed down, Corky was able to moved the shuttle more toward the center of the area. They were also looking for a crevasse or some similar structure. It really wasn't hard to find an acceptable one.

It was Dandy's turn. Letting himself out of the airlock with his pack, he tethered himself to the shuttle so he wouldn't float away. Gradually he pulled himself along the shuttle to the crevasse. Using a bar with a hook on one end, he pulled himself down into the split in the surface. It was only about twelve feet to the bottom. Dandy would have liked it a little deeper, but this would do. He wedged himself against the walls while he ripped rocks and ice out of one side. Into the hole he place the pack of explosives that had protected the food shuttle. The remote detonator was then attached.

Using the tether Dandy pulled himself out of the hole. Before long he was safely aboard the shuttle. Corky moved them beyond a line of sight.

Dandy called the ship. "Can you see the explosive site?"

"Yes," Candie answered.

"Tell us when you see it blow." Dandy threw the detonation switch. They had no indication anything had happened.

Candie came on the radio. "That was quite an explosion. I'm glad we're this far away. You're clear. Without much gravity, you won't have anything falling back on you."

Corky moved them into position again. The explosion had done a magnificent job of removing material. There was a hole fifteen feet across and about as deep. It was a clean cavity. All loose material had been blown away.

"I hope that's big enough," said Dandy. "We don't have any more explosives and I'd hate to try digging that out by hand."

"Let's go see," said Corky. He closed his face plate and waited until Dandy did the same. Then he depressurized the cabin so that they could come and go without having to cycle the airlock. He set the maneuvering jets to keep a downforce on the shuttle while they worked.

Dandy went back into the hole where he drove in an oversized piton, to which he hooked a pulley and cable. Then the two men detached the nose cone and slowly moved it into position over the hole. With the cable they were able to winch the cone down into the hole. The base of the pyramid didn't go all the way to the bottom, but they decided it would do. They tied off the lines, securing the rocket part upright in the hole.

As they retired back to the shuttle, Candie came on the radio. "It is time you guys came back up."

Dandy objected. "There isn't that much more to do."

"No more. You've been out too long. Your oxygen is running short and you vital signs are reaching their limit. You don't have enough of a reserve in case something were to go wrong. Besides, the shuttle needs to be recharged too. We're not in that big of a hurry. Come up."

Dandy didn't argue much. It had been a long day with more exertion than one would think working with no weight to worry about. Corky didn't volunteer any comment. He just pressurized the cabin and waited for an order.

Twelve hours later, they were at it again. Corky brought the shuttle down with a great deal more ease than the first time. He smiled as he said, "See, even old dogs can learn new tricks." With the maneuvering jets holding the shuttle in place, Dandy and Corky unloaded foot square boxes which they anchored in a circle about ten feet back from the edge of their hole. The packets contained a Thermite compound which burns with intense heat. It was a special concoction Corky had put together with chemicals for the searing heat, plus an oxygenizer to sustain ignition.

The problem was to raise the temperature from close to absolute zero to a point where the ice would melt without becoming vapor. They had to produce a liquid that could be forced down into the hole to freeze the cone into position, becoming their anchor. There was enough spin gravity to move any liquid water into at least one side of the hole.

Once the packets were in place, the duo returned to the shuttle. They took a short break before the next phase. Corky sighed, "I don't like working out there. You have to think too much."

"What do you mean?" asked Dandy.

"You can't do anything automatically. I'm programed to live in gravity. Without it, nothing works right. You can't even walk from one point to another. You can't shove something away without you floatin' away unless you're anchored. You have to keep thinking about little things instead of important things."

Dandy considered the comments before answering. "I know what you mean. Aren't we lucky we don't spend much time that way?"

Corky snorted and moved the shuttle about a hundred feet above the surface, but keeping up with the rotation. Dandy touched off the first of the boxes as an experiment.

The detonation was spectacular. "It looks like the Fourth of July," cried Corky. The expanding gases produced a brilliant flare of light in the darkness of space, expelling up great plumes of vapor as the ice turned to gas. The Thermite compounds hit the boiling of water point in a vacuum almost instantaneously and proceeded on to produce a super heated vapor, which quickly lost its heat in the absolute coldness of space. Crystals formed. The expansion of the gasses pushed the material out in all directions. Great plumes of ice crystals covered the area. Rocks began exploding with the drastic temperature changes, throwing shrapnel-like projectiles into space.

The shuttle hovered only a hundred feet above the site. Rock fragments raked the underside of the shuttle sounding like machine gun fire. The cabin was breached by some of the larger chunks. Air pressure started dropped, setting off alarms. Simultaneously, Corky lost attitude control. The shuttle began to spin out of control. Corky's hands were flying over the controls. Dandy snapped his face plate shut, which turned on his oxygen supply. Corky was too occupied with the controls to take cognitive notice of the hazard. Dandy shook off his safety restraints and launched himself toward Corky yelling, "Your face plate!" Being weightless in a tumbling craft and being strapped to a bulky backpack greatly impeded his movements. As Dandy shot by Corky's hunched figure, he was just able to snag one of the seat safety straps. His flight was jerked up short.

Corky was still frantically fighting the controls. The monitors showed the rotating radius of the comet getting closer and closer. Corky was holding his breath and appeared to be coming to the end of his capacity. His eyes were getting buggy. Dandy reached around to trip the lever closing his face plate. Air rushed into Corky's suit.

With renewed vigor, Corky manipulated the thrusters until he got the nose pointed toward open space. Then he punched the main engine. Dandy was slammed into the rear wall. It was fortunate that the escape velocity kept Dandy pinned there, because he was only vaguely aware of his surroundings. Once away from the comet, Corky eased off. He slipped his straps to get back to Dandy, who groaned loudly through the intercom.

"Are you hurt?" demanded Corky.

Another little groan came before Dandy said, "I think I'm all right. It is hard to tell in weightlessness."

"You stay here until we get back to the ship." Corky grabbed a couple of bunji cords to anchor Dandy in place. He slipped back into his pilot's seat. To the ship he said, "Get the shuttle bay doors open. As soon as I get in, close the door, repressurize, and turn on the gravity."

Candie was in the command chair. "Roger."

Corky found out why he had been having trouble stabalizing the shuttle. One maneuvering jet was not functioning and another was pushing at a strange angle. But it didn't take long to get things righted and return to the ship.

By the time Corky got everything shut down, Candie had the air flowing into the bay. Corky opened the shuttle hatches to pressurize the interior.

Dandy was struggling to get himself upright, but he couldn't reach the bunji cords. "Corky, get these things off me."

"Oh, hold your horses. You don't have any pressing appointment. I want to make sure you're all right before you go jumping around." Corky snapped his face plate open to sniff the air. He decided it was sufficient, so he unhooked Dandy and opened his helmet. Peering in he said, "Now we have gravity. Wiggle everything and find out if things are still working."

While Dandy was taking an inventory, Candy popped into the cabin. "I wish you guys would take better care of one another. If you get hurt, guess who is going to be your doctor? Me."

Dandy groaned.

"What?" demanded Candie.

"It's just the thought of you being my doctor," said Dandy.

Corky pleaded, "Come on you guys, knock it off. Do you have anything wrong?" Corky was feeling responsible.

"Nothing seems to be broken. I think I may have a stiff neck where I hit the helmet mounting ring, and when I get this thing off I think I'll find a goose egg on the back of the head. Help me up."

A couple of hours later, the crew settled down for a group meal and review of events.

Dandy had been right about the neck and back of his head. He had taken a pain killer, so he was not suffering greatly. Tom and Corky had taken a look at the damage to the shuttle.

Tom started out by giving a damage report. "The underside of the pickup was hit any number of time by splintered rock Two pieces were big enough and had enough velocity to penetrate the durathane. One went through the bed of the pickup and the other through the floor of the main cabin. The one in the cabin was the big one. It made a 4-inch hole in the outer skin and ripped a seam loose in the floor. Fortunately, neither hit disrupted any vital function. I can patch the holes easily. Another piece killed one of the thrusters. It will have to be replaced. A second one was knocked askew. It should be replaced too. There are all sorts of little dents. One chunk hit the cowl surrounding the engine and glanced off. It that had gone through we'd had come out and tow you home. Repairs and recharging can be done by tomorrow."

Dandy started to shake his head, but thought better of it. "It didn't even occur to me that the rock would explode like that. I figured a 100 feet was probably overdoing the safety factor. I wanted to stay close to get a good look."

Corky nodded agreement and then added, "It does't look like we got what we wanted. Everything went to vapor and it was blown away. Nothing got down in the hole to anchor the nose cone.

"We really don't know that until we take a look," said Beatrice. "The site rotated out of view before the emergency was over and we really can't see anything from this distance in the dark. It never occurred to me either that the thermal shock would had that dramatic a reaction. But, none of us have ever really worked in a vacuum before." She smiled a little wanly at Dandy. She was supposed to be the brain and think of such things.

Candie watched Dandy gingerly testing his neck. Candie changed the subject. "My grandad used to say I shouldn't joke with the truth. When I pointed out that if one of you guys got hurt, I'd be your doctor I was being funny. Really, it's not funny. Back when we were in the simulation, if something happened, like Dandy breaking his neck, the program would have been shut down and the medical people would be called in. That's a real long distance call now. I've gone through all the medical programs, such as there were. I also know the computer is full of medical information that I can call up, but that doesn't make me or any of us a doctor. I think we'd better reevaluate our actions to err on the side of caution where injury could result. I don't want to be paranoid about the whole thing, but I think we had better be more careful."

Everyone nodded agreement. Candie pressed on. "After Tom gets the repairs done, Corky and I will go down to see what happened." When Dandy started to object, she said, "We don't want you traipsing around down there when you could have a concussion or something else wrong we can't see. Corky can fly and I can look."

Chapter 56

Practice was making landings easier. Corky put the shuttle down a few feet from the hole. Actually there were two connecting holes, the one Dandy and Corky had blasted out and the other left from the force of the Thermite package. Candie made her way to the edge of the holes. The lights from the shuttle didn't illuminate the bottom, so she carried a powerful lamp. She slowly viewed the area, with Beatrice continually warning her to slow even more. After the first scanning, Candie began a commentary on what she was seeing.

"It looks like we had only partial success. Much material is missing. It has been blown far away. Probably, the first material to go was the methane ice. That is probably what made that immediate cloud so we couldn't see anything. A lot of rock has disappeared, blown away by the instantaneous heat contrasts. However, we did get some ice, of some kind, but it on the wall of the hole on the spin gravity side. It didn't go down to the nose cone."

Candie slowly moved around the site trying to understand what she was seeing. "It looks like three of our charges have been blown away. They didn't go off. There are no holes. You know. what I think happened, was that the charge heated the rocks and the residual heat melted the ice, and then that water or snow or whatever form it took, was pulled aside by the rotation gravity until it froze again. The heavier rock stayed in place, so we got a separation.

"I want to try something. If I put one of the charges on the up side of the cone, the gravity pull should carry material to the cone."

"That sounds reasonable," said Dandy, "but get clear out of sight before you set it off."

"You bet," said Corky. "I don't want the go through that again."

When it came time, Corky moved the shuttle clear around to the other side of the comet. Beatrice watched the blast and reported its detonation. Corky landed again.

"We did some good," reported Candie. We got a much better return on our effort. Spin gravity took the material right down to the cone, but we aren't getting enough yield from a charge. We're losing too much. Corky, can you reduce the intensity of the charge?"

"Sure. I can change the recipe to make the charge cooler and longer burning."

"Let's give it a try. This isn't working well enough. I think maybe a large electric blanket would do better."

It took the better part of a week to accomplish their task. Corky made lighter charges and changed the composition several times before a serviceable formula emerged. Finally, they got the nose cone firmly anchored in the comet. Then the roles shifted. Corky remained shuttle pilot. Tom became the outside man. Dandy stayed aboard Taran to handle the landing. It fell to Candie to suit up and operate a newly installed winch in one of the legs. Beatrice became everyones eyes and ears. She was to coordinate the efforts.

Finally, they were ready for the landing. Candie played out considerable cable through the clean-out hatch. Outside, Corky and Tom snagged the line and descended to the comet. Beatrice kept Dandy advised on the amount of slack, the rotation of the comet and all other data so he could maintain his speed relative to the comet. He kept changed attitude to keep the legs pointed at the rotating ice cube. Tom anchored the line to the cone. Candie started reeling in the cable while Dandy nudged Taran toward the surface. The cable kept Taran in sequence to the rotation. Gradually, the two bodies came together. Taran settled onto the comet. The winch and Taran's thrusters held them down.

The leg with the winch was tied off to the nose cone anchor. In a natural weightless environment and with a nominal spin gravity, it didn't take much to keep such a huge ship tethered. The leg directly opposite the tether was down gravity. It had become the pumping station.

Corky brought the personnel shuttle to the surface. It was lashed to the anchor leg with its engine pointed toward the pump. The shuttle exhaust flame was angled to just barely brushed the surface. When Tom touched off the engine at its lowest setting, great plumes of vapor were generated, but almost immediately they condensed in the ambient temperature into snow or ice crystals. The force of the engine pushed the water products in the desired direction. Since the heat was not as intense there was minimal rock shattering. Quickly, a trench was dug. The residual heat absorbed by the rocks thawed the ice at a more gradual rate. Some water was formed but most of the product came in the form of ice crystals.

Corky fabricated a large impeller pump that could supply a six inch line. He had to install a filter to keep the courser rock out. By changing the angle of the shuttle, Tom was able to move the puddle or drift to the pump.

It was back breaking, slow work. Once everything was in place, Dandy called a halt for a rest period. Everyone was beat. Outside of someone on general watch, the crew relaxed for two days. Dandy had been prepared to take even more time off to regenerate, but after a couple of idle days, tension started to build, so he restarted the operation. Once engaged, the crew pressed on with determination despite repeated setbacks and failures.

Gradually, their water supply built up. At a meal period, Tom announced he had approximately 60% of capacity. He had found that by moving the recovered material up into Taran where he had artificial gravity, he could separate the rock from the liquid. He had taken numerous pickup loads of rock well out of the mining area so they would not have to deal with it again or get clunked by a piece drifting by. He chuckled, saying he was creating his own little Oort cloud.

Another week and they were at full capacity. There was a discussion about recovering the nose cone and the rocket cylinder. The two girls didn't want to spend the time. They wanted to blast off and head for home. They were tired of mining.

Tom wouldn't hear of it. "We can't do that. There is no telling when we may need it again. What would we do if we had to get water from another comet?"

Corky was appalled. "Those are the biggest pieces of metal we have. They are too valuable to lose. No, we must salvage them as well as all the lines we used. We can't replace them out here."

Candie glanced at Dandy. She knew she was beaten so she graciously acknowledged defeat, with a shrug of the shoulder and a parting salvo, "Packrats."

It really didn't take much time to clear out. Using the shuttle, they unfroze the two pieces of equipment, which were lashed to Taran. The shuttles were docked and Dandy gently lifted Taran clear of the comet. The pieces were reeled in and secured.

Candie had been scanning for a promising solar jet.

"We've got a small one very close by that is running in generally to right direction," she said. "Now might be a good time to try our new technique. Another thing has occurred to me. Whenever we come out of a jet I have to go through the same routine of locating the CETI signal to find out where we are. I'm going to establish a constant monitor and have Tom set it up with its own direction finder so we can tell at a glance which way is home."

"That's a great idea. Have it set up so I can see it on a monitor. That way I can make more educated choices when we come to a split. Why didn't you think of that earlier?"

Dandy's question was answered with a dark sideways glance and a little snarl. It was worth it, because by keeping an eye on the direction finder, he could maintain a more direct route. They were making good time running the jet currents even without their period jumps. They were using only a fraction of the fuel that would have been needed to slog from one major jet to another. Their jumps ate up large chunks of space, but not all the time were they going in the right direction.

Then during a meal, Candie announced that they were nearing the Alpha Centauri system, which meant they were just a little over four light years from home.

Beatrice immediately came up out of some deep consideration. "Are we going to be going through the system?"

"No. It is quite a ways off to the side. It would be a sizable detour." said Candie.

"What an opportunity. We should detour through that system. This is a binary system with G and K stars. It has long been considered that there could be planets, and maybe those planets could contain life. We already know there is other life in the universe. Alpha Centauri life would be our closest neighbors." Beatrice was talking herself into an intellectual frenzy.

The rest of TC stared at each other in wonderment. This was the one who was petrified at the prospect of lifting off the New Mexico desert. Now, she wanted to go traipsing off across the galaxy to check on scientific hypotheses. Beatrice wasn't looking at the rest of the crew as she speculated. Dandy could see at a glance that her suggestion was getting a frigid reception.

Dandy stepped in. "Well, that's not quite as easy as it sounds. I'm hoping to have enough fuel to get us into our own system. I really don't want to go through that water extraction routine with a comet again. On the next voyage, I hope the engineers can come up with a better recovery system than we cobbled together."

"The next voyage," said Candie slowly.

"Sure," said Dandy. "Why not? Didn't Malvane say we're the crew? Who else knows what we know? If there isn't another flight, what do you suppose would be a fulfilling job? Can you think of another post in Gal X that could hold your interest more than five minutes? At one time I would have found any number of jobs challenging, but they no longer hold any sort of fascination for me. We've been to the mountain top, so sitting in the foothills would not be acceptable to me, and I certainly can't retire before I reach 25."

Beatrice didn't argue about Alpha Centauri. Instead, she gave one of the few personal admissions she had ever made. "As a little girl I found out I had a phenomenal memory. I dreamed about learning everything in the world. I've been stuffing my head full of facts ever since. I really didn't want to come on board Taran, but I knew that it was the greatest source of information on certain subjects in the world, and that I would probably not have another opportunity. Up until we took off, I was dealing with information collected by others. I was a file clerk. But now I know...." She stopped and looked around the table before continuing. "We know things that no one else in our world knows. We are information collectors, not just processors and filers. With my memory to back me up, I am beginning to see patterns, correlations and theses. I am becoming an active thinker, instead of a passive sponge. Oh, the hazards frighten me badly, but they seem to be the price of first hand information. I'd go on another voyage." Realizing she had let quite a bit hang out, Beatrice ducked back into her shell by dropping her head and hunching her shoulders.

Beatrice reemerged from her shell long enough to state emphatically. "That is, providing we are provided with some way of getting all this information back so it is not lost if something happens to us."

"I'd go on another trip," said Corky, "if they'd put nachos and cheese in that tin cafe."

Candie flashed her dangly earrings. "I'm with Corky. Only if they get some decent food in that machine."

Tom shrugged. "This duty isn't bad. At least you don't have to drive through Houston traffic to get to a cribbage game."

"Great," said Dandy. "I think we make a whale of a team, but before we leave on a second voyage, we need to take care of a few more pressing things. First, we have to get home. We seem well on our way to doing that. Next, we have to decide what to do when we get there. We are carrying information that will cause a sensation, if not social upheavals. It has long been my opinion that governments have made every effort to hide anything that could indicate the existence of any other life forms. There are all sorts of conspiracy theories about coverups. I'm afraid that when we get back and our government learns about the Bips, we will find ourselves labelled "crazies" and be put away for our own safety. All evidence will be confiscated and will disappear for ever. I don't want to see that happen for several reasons.

"I propose that we prepare a broadcast to be made soon after we enter communication range. At that time, we tell our story including the alien contact complete with photos and what audio we might have. We shouldn't give away any information of value to Gal X, like the gravitational strands and communication. We can see if Malvane can set up a broadcast the way he did for our Christmas party. With a little publicity, most of the world's TVs should be tuned in. All the news channels should carry the important features. That way, no one can bury us and our information so the world won't know.

"We're still a ways off, but I hope you guys will be thinking about it so, when the time comes, we can get it together," concluded Dandy.

The crew was heartened by the progress they were making through space. The pilot and navigator took turns pushing Taran along the solar jets. They were getting close to their own system. During a duty change Dandy brought the ceremonial tea and coffee, which they normally drank together. With their four-hours-on, four-off routine, this was the only time they really got to talk any more.

"How close do we have to get before someone is going to pick up up on some telescope or radar screen?" asked Dandy.

"Oh, I imagine they could pick us up now if we stayed on any course long enough, but with us bopping in and out of the jets, going at all angles and directions and then suddenly disappearing when we hop a quick ride, they aren't believing anything they see. No one knows we have such capabilities, so we are being shrugged off as some anomaly. Besides, in the scheme of things, we're pretty small."

"How close do we have to be before we can start broadcasting?"

Candie smiled, "We could start broadcasting now, but we will probably beat the signal there. There is one thing, though. Bea is so afraid something will happen to all of her information, she would like to send it on its way now. The problem is that anyone could intercept it, even Centurion. We have no secure channel."

"Maybe we should have her record what she thinks is so vital to humankind and have it ready to send at an instant's notice," said Dandy.

"It would take some time to send that much data. If we get into trouble, we may not have time."

Dandy shrugged. "Then have Tom and Corky make a pod that we can eject if we see a problem developing. It can broadcast independently of us." Dandy finished his coffee and exchanged seats with Candie. She headed off to her room.

Dandy kept Taran in the small jet they had been following. He was cruising at a fair speed in the general direction of home. On the scanner, he could see a much larger jet coming into view. They had long since determined that the dendritic pattern of the jets was like that of a river with the small jets flowing into the larger ones. The only problem had been concerning their direction. The very large jets tended to wander less. Dandy kept an eye on the new jet as well as the directional finder showing home.

Dandy keyed the intercom. "Everyone to your couches in ten minutes. We are going to make a major jump." Tom came up from down below. Corky had been asleep as had Candie. Beatrice was at her station as she was most of the time. When the crew got to their stations, he filled them in. "We are coming up on a major jet that looks as if it's going in the right direction. We are in a small branch, but we should be able to mesh right into the larger without slogging through space. Tom, set your time for an hour. Candie, when we pop out we'll need a quick location to see where we are. If we are going anywhere near the direction we want to go, I'm going to dive back in for a two hour stint. Then we'll see where we are. This is a big jet that should take us quite a ways."

The crew went through what was now a familiar routine. It took Dandy a little longer to build up the speed because the jet was so small, but finally Tom threw the switch and everything went mushy again. When the timer cut off, the charge and the surroundings regained their substantiality, Dandy pulled out of the stream. Candie went to work. It didn't take her long to calculate their position.

"We're in a good one. It looks like it is still going in our direction. Let's try it again," she said with enthusiasm.

Dandy put the ship into the big jet where speed was gained rapidly. After the two hour jaunt he popped out again. Candie plotted their position again. "We're heading down below the ecliptic, but that's okay. We're really making time. I'd say go for an even longer shot, provided you give me ten minutes first."

"Okay. Ten minute break and we go again," said Dandy, who put Taran on autopilot as everyone scrambled to get ready for the next stint.

When the crew was ready, Dandy said, " I think I'll go for a longer jump."

Candie came right back. "I don't know if that's a good idea. This jet is getting larger and larger. It is straightening out considerably. We are traveling much faster. I'd hate to come out of jet in the corona of the sun. We're headed in that general direction."

"You've got a point there. How about a series of three hour jumps?"

"That sounds prudent," said Candie.

Three jumps later, Dandy pulled out. Candie advised, "I wouldn't try another jump like that. We could get into the sun's gravity well. This jet is just too strong and it seems to be veering in the wrong direction. I'd suggest hooking up with a small one to get clear."

"What's our relative location to home?" asked Corky.

"We're at right angles to the plane of the planets and what you might figure as below, in most of the illustrations we normally use. We've made some good time. We could start broadcasting. Our signal should get home in a month."

Dandy considered that for a bit. Beatrice and Tom were on the bridge. They didn't say anything. They were obviously awaiting his decision. "I think I would rather get closer before announcing our presence. I don't want to give Centurion all that much time to come up with a surprise. Let's get a little closer."

"Bea, have you finished recording the information you want in the pod?"

"Yes," she said. While I was going through the files, I also pulled out the information that might be good to use on the little TV program you suggested."

Chapter 57

As earth neared, anxiety mounted. Dandy and Candie stayed with their four-on and four-off, which gave neither of them time for much other thought. But Dandy made sure the other three members of the crew were well occupied. He had Tom and Corky testing the Bips' probe. Then he gave them a construction project to make the time pass faster. Beatrice was deeply involved in the broadcast taping. Dandy kept making suggestions that did more to irritate Beatrice than further the project, but it kept her from thinking about home.

About an hour into his shift, Dandy spotted a substantial jet going in the direction he wanted. He moved into it and accelerated only enough to increase speed, but not enough to trigger a jump. After another hour he had everyone strap in. He jumped three times in quick succession without pausing to get a location. He was headed in the right direction.

When he popped out of the jet and everyone had regained their equilibrium, he asked Candie for a location.

"Wow!" screamed Candie. "Were only about two astral units

from earth."

"How long would a radio message take?" asked Dandy.

"About sixteen minutes."

"Tom, set up the radio for Walter's ham frequency. I want to record a two-word message to be repeated every five minutes. We have no idea the time on earth, so I want to have a monitor set up for a return message. As soon as we get it, we will send the response, Then they can compute how far away we are."

When Tom was set up, Dandy recorded a voice message, "Rimlick returns." Then he recorded responses, "Rimlick time one" and Rimlick time two.

Dandy couldn't return to the jet because they did not know if messages could be sent or received from inside a jet, and they didn't have time to experiment.

It was a tedious wait because not much could be done until the messages were exchanged. After seven hours, doubts started creeping in. Maybe Wayne wasn't home. Maybe something had gone wrong. Anything could have happened in the eight months they had been plowing around through space.

Corky was on the monitor when a faint "Welcome back," came through. Corky immediately keyed the next recording. A cheer went up form TC, which woke Dandy, who was sleeping.

With Taran two AUs away, Walter placed a call to Artis Malvane's home. No one normally answered the phone, but when Walter's name showed as the originator, the CEO took the call himself.

"Sir, Taran is back. They are 16 light minutes away."

Malvane caught his breath. "How do you know?"

"Andy is apparently playing it safe. He sent the message to my ham set, "Rimlick returns." As soon as I could get from the bathroom to the transmitter I sent, "Welcome back." I set my clock and it took 33 minutes for the response, "Rimlick time one." I answered immediately and 32 minutes later "Rimlick time two" came through. They didn't transmit anything further. They are still a good distance away. I suspect they are putting us on notice to give them instructions when they get closer."

"Don't even hint at this to anyone. Meet me in my office in an hour. We have some planning to do."

With all of Taran's maneuvering and variant speeds, none of the earth observatories picked Taran up until they moved out into clear space about twice the distance from earth as the moon. Dandy had been riding smaller and smaller jets to control speed and direction. Finally, he ran out of them and eased into view of ground instrumentation.

Before they caused a world-wide panic Dandy broadcast on the old channel to Gal X. "Taran reporting for duty. Sorry for the slight detour."

Almost immediately, Artis Malvane appeared on the screen, seated before his impressive desk in his private office. With a vast smile he said, "Taran, Galaxy Enterprises extends a hearty welcome back. We look forward to your reports. Is there any service necessary at this moment?"

Dandy smiled and flipped a switch so all work stations and the crew members showed on the screen. "The entire crew is well and the ship is in good conditions. We need only two things. The first is that we wish to make a statement the earth population before we land, such as we did for the Christmas show. Secondly, we need to know where to park this thing."

"The second item is easy. Since you cleared most loose debris away on your takeoff, you won't cause too much of storm to land at the old site. It has been prepared for your return. It will be properly secured. We will advise all necessary agencies not to interfere.

"The first item will take a little doing. What will be the subject matter?"

Dandy chose his words carefully. "We bring information to be shared with mankind. We will not be buried with our story. This will also save the company untold problems. We will broadcast from Taran on frequencies that all TV stations and radio receivers can pick up. That way we cannot be blocked. We just need the date, time, and frequencies made public. We will do the rest. Following the broadcast we have one little Rimlick maneuver to perform, and then we will land if the coast is clear."

*****

Hacker was alerted to Taran's radio communication with Gal X just in time to hear the part about the Rimlick maneuver, which fueled a gigantic rage. His nemesis had returned. Orders went flying over the computer network. Tokla was summoned. All stations were ordered to find Taran. Around the clock monitoring of Taran and Gal X were ordered. Word went out to all spies to redouble information gathering efforts.

When Tokla finally arrived, Hacker was still fuming. "Taran is back."

"Yes, I heard that on the radio on the way over here. All stations are carrying the news, but no one knows any more than that. Somehow it appeared right on top of us without any of or early warning systems sounding the alert. The military is up in arms. The so-called experts are asking why the government how it got so close without being spotted. Everyone is asking questions. No one seems to have any answers." Tokla was just barely able to keep a smirk off his face, because Hacker was as much in the dark as anyone else.

Hacker sensed Tokla's feelings, although nothing showed. He vowed to even the score later, but right now he needed that disfigured bastard. "One thing we do know is that the ship is going to land at the New Mexico site. We still don't know when, but I want you to be ready to shoot it out of the sky. Use those four very expensive jet fighters, on which you have been lavishing my money. When Taran comes in for a landing in New Mexico, I want you to shoot it down. Put Air Force markings on the planes and use Air Force transponder signals. We can point a finger if anyone complains."

Tokla acknowledged his orders without comment. Hacker was in no mood for any thing, but immediate compliance.

It took three days more for Taran to get into a synchronous orbit over New Mexico. The crew put the final touches on their TV broadcast. Gal X was a little hesitant because Dandy wouldn't elaborate on the reasons. Over a frequency that Centurion and probably the rest of the interested world could monitor, TC wouldn't go into detail other than to guarantee that no company secrets or competitive information would be revealed.

At the appointed hour, TC were dressing in their uniform coveralls and seated at their work stations. Dandy gave an introduction, identifying and showing each member who made a brief statement about how glad they were to be back. Corky asked for nachos and a Corona. Then Dandy filled the screen. He gave the bare facts about what had happened from the lock-in exercise to the assault by Centurion and their subsequent takeoff. To escape various self-seeking governments and civil adversaries, they had attempted to go to Mars, but were accidentally flung into the Tau Ceti system. Without explanation, he concluded with the comments that they had been spending most of their time getting back home.

Then he turned the commentary over to Candie who showed various star charts depicting their journey through space. She did not indicate how they had made such a journey, but confined herself to the journey itself. She did point out numerous unknown items concerning the galaxy.

Dandy returned to the screen. Nothing that had been said was astounding. It was what was not said that had everyone's interest. Taran's voyage had defied all known propulsion systems. Dandy said, "By now you have guessed that we have made some interesting discoveries. Of course, these technological discoveries belong to our employer, Galaxy Enterprises, to use as they see fit. However, there is one interesting discovery that we wish to share with the world. We do not believe that it would be in our best interests to remain silent and thus risk having this information buried along with us. For this part of the presentation I turn you over to Beatrice Bell, our librarian. Load your recorders because you are about to see an amazing episode in human history.

The view changed to Beatrice seated on her couch in front of her work station. Now Dandy saw the result of a lot of buzzing around by the girls in the last couple of days. Bea's hair had been cut and done into a current style. She was wearing a smidgen of makeup that Dandy had never seen before. Candie was beaming like a proud mother. Dandy gave both of them a thumbs up, which pleased the pair.

Initially, Bea look pretty scared, but as soon as she started getting into her material she leveled out and became a real pro.

She started out, "One of the time-worn questions of mankind is, 'Are we alone'? The short answer is 'No'. Taran encountered a sentient, space-going species in the Tau Ceti system. We had direct, face-to-face contact with them over a several day period. I am going to give you a chronological account of our encounter."

Bea started with Candie's first suspicion that there was an unnatural object orbiting the moon of the fifth planet of Tau Ceti. She showed videos of the approach to the object which Corky had dubbed "Nacho" because of its triangular shape. The narrative continued through the discussion of what to do once it was discovered that Nacho was going to crash. Bea show telephoto views of the Nacho. Then she switched to views from the shuttle as it circumnavigated the ship. Dandy's and Corky's commentaries were included. Bea included all the landing procedures and conversation of Dandy doing a space walk on the hull of the ship. Then came Corky's call, "You better look behind you." Dandy's camera swung around to show the opening of the panel and gradually an alien life-form took shape. Bea showed the whole contact, including all the TC conversations of the moment. Vital to the commentary were the photographic proof and the verbal descriptions of the crew members concerning the physiology of the alien after their separation demonstration.

Corky's nickname "Bip" was introduced.

Of course, there were great chunks of conversation between the crew on board Taran that were not recorded. Bea gave a summary of the speculations and then followed up with the subsequent rescue mission and the "thank you" meeting, including the warning concerning the mother ship. She mentioned the encounter with the mother ship, but didn't go into any great detail, because there were too many things involved that should be left for Gal X to ponder. Nor did she get into any discussion of the return voyage.

TC was on the clock with an hour on the frequencies that Gal X had set up. Bea ran a little long, so Dandy's summary was rather brief, but he drove home the message that humans were not alone. He didn't philosophize, just reported.

After the report TC had no idea what was happening. Candie was tuning around to various radios and TV stations, but apparently their announcements had come as such a surprise that no one had a talking head ready to respond. The reports were just paraphrases of what Bea had said and replays of the visuals.

Twenty minutes after the broadcast, Artis Malvane called back. "That was quite a bomb you lobbed in our direction. Our switchboard is jammed. So are all other forms of communication. Various government bureaus are absolutely furious. Some are claiming we have jeopardized national security and world tranquility. Others are demanding we hand over all technology to them. They want not only any technology you discovered on your journey, but that technology that got you to Tau Ceti. We aren't even taking calls from sundry religious leaders. Every news agency in the world is trying to get interviews with anyone who will stand in front of a camera, whether or not he knows anything. You guys will be raw meat in a pond full of sharks. But, at least, we have a little time to prepare. Keep in mind we are not secure in any of our transmissions."

Dandy replied, "We figured as much. Apparently our broadcast was picked up by enough stations that it couldn't be blacked out."

"From what we can tell, the whole world was tuned in. It is early evening here. By midnight everyone with a TV or radio set will have heard. Apparently you really have fuzzed up the Vatican."

"How secure is our landing site?"

Malvane chuckled. "We figured we had it covered, but now we will have to bolster everything. The whole world will want a piece.

The military and some governmental agencies may create a problem. But we should be able to handle the situation."

"We will stay put for the night unless someone tries something stupid. We come down around noon tomorrow, if that is all right."

"We'll be waiting for you. Happy Landing."

Chapter   58

At the appointed time, Dandy started his decent. A few minutes before Taran started down, four jet fighters took off from a strip east of Denver. They were headed for the New Mexico site. However, Taran suddenly altered course generally to the north. A call from Centurion caused the jets to make a fast turn to head back home.

Taran had been watching for any air activity. The military had been warned off, so any pursuit would be civilian and probably unfriendly. Candie picked the jets up early. When they made the U-turn, she had a pretty good idea of their identity. As Taran approached Denver the jets came screaming on an intercept course. Dandy brought Taran to a point right over the Red Rocks just west of Denver. Below was the world headquarters of Centurion nestled back in the rock. The building was huge by any standards, but in the towering rocks, it looked diminutive.

Bea announced the jets were coming into firing range for their missiles. With sadistic delight, Candie keyed her mike. "Oh, Colonel Tokla, so nice of you to be welcoming us back. I hope you have manual ejection on those toys of yours."

Dandy flipped Taran over on its side and opened a shuttle bay. He fingered the switch that sent a current to the Bip probe, which Tom and Corky had mounted so as to point down between the legs of the ship. The cone shaped beam generated by the probe instantaneously fried all the computer chips in the four approaching jets. All power was lost. Nothing worked. The jets started falling like rocks into the foothills of the Rockies. One after another, parachutes appeared. All pilots got out safely.

Dandy righted the ship, slipping into a hover over Centurion International Headquarters. It was Dandy's turn to talk to the opposition. "Hacker. As it turns out, I'd like to thank you for all your meddling in our affairs. It resulted in wondrous discoveries, which never would have been possible without you. I would like to share with you one of those discoveries." Dandy sent power to the probe.

As Colonel Tokla drifted toward earth, Hacker was thrown into total darkness. All his computers crashed. The computer-regulated lighting system and air conditioner units shut down as silicone flour sifted out of their innards. None of the phones worked, and the doors to Hacker's offices were frozen shut. Since he couldn't even order Chinese, he had to vent his rage by kicking the soundproof door of his office with his sneakers,

Over the monitors, TC watched all the complex lights vanish. All cars stopped. A prolonged cheer went up as Dandy turned Taran on a course for New Mexico.

ISBN 978-0-9847524-1-6

www.ingramcontent.com/pod-product-compliance
Lightning Source LLC
Chambersburg PA
CBHW050600260626
47157CB00002B/638